DEATH OF AN HEIRESS

Death of an Heiress

Anne Louise Bannon

HH
Healcroft House, Publishers
Altadena, California

Copyright

ISBN 978-1-948616-21-8

Library of Congress Control Number: 2022903474

Healcroft House, Publishers, Altadena, California, United States of America

Contents

Dedication

To Cornelia Ann Klarner. Let's both keep fighting

Acknowledgments

It's a little crazy-making every time I try to pull together a list of people to thank. There are so many, and I inevitably forget somebody. So, if I have, pray forgive me.

As for the people that I have remembered to write down, Paula Bernstein, MD, again acted as my medical consultant. I can't say which I appreciate more, the accurate details or her friendship. I'm glad I have both. Author J.R. Sanders helped with some gun issues, and very generously, too.

Then there are the librarians at the History Desk of the Los Angeles Public Library, Central Branch. I cannot function without you.

My beta readers, Beth Camp, Elizabeth Cornwell, and Mac Daly all had excellent insights and really helped. And my editor and dear friend Carol Louise Wilde – you made this so much better.

I have to thank all the friends and other writers who have provided so much support. This book was written during the Pandemic, and thanks to G.P. Gottlieb, and the rest of the Lady Sings the Clues Author Pod; and Tracey Phillips, and the rest of the Blackbird Writers, the isolation seemed so much less onerous. I also have to thank the Sisters in Crime/ Los Angeles Chapter for their support, too.

Finally, there is my in-house historian and wonderful husband, Michael Holland, who kept me fully supplied with facts on demand, the occasional snack, and plenty of his good angelica.

Dramatis Personnae

Some of the characters in this story have the real names of people who were living in Los Angeles in 1872. However, since this is a work of fiction, they are technically fictional characters who may, in varying degrees, bear some resemblance to the real people they are named after. Those with real names I have noted. As for anyone else, the reader may assume that he or she is fully the product of my fevered imagination.

RANCHO DE LAS FLORES

Maddie Wilcox, owner, winemaker, physician

Sebastiano Ortiz, winery manager, husband of Olivia, brother to Enrique

Olivia Ortiz, cook, and wife of Sebastiano

Elena Ortiz, assistant to Maddie, daughter to Sebastiano and Olivia

Damiano Ortiz, son to Sebastiano and Olivia

Enrique Ortiz, vineyard manager, husband of Magdalena, brother to Sebastiano

Magdalena Ortiz, housekeeper, and wife of Enrique

Hernan Mendoza, field hand, husband of Maria, cousin to Emilio and Pascual

Maria Mendoza, maid, wife of Hernan

Rodolfo Sanchez, field hand, husband of Anita

Anita Sanchez, nanny, wife of Rodolfo

Emilio Mendoza, field hand, brother to Pascual, cousin to Hernan

Pascual Mendoza, field hand, brother to Emilio, cousin to Hernan

Juanita Alvarez, personal maid to Maddie

MADDIE'S FRIENDS

Angelina Sutton, undertaker's wife who prepares the bodies for burial

Walter Lomax, a deputy on the city police force

Mrs. Ruth Lomax, wife to Walter Lomax

Mrs. Sabrina Lomax, second wife to Walter Lomax

Ernesto Navarro, a deputy on the city police force

Regina Medina, madam, sister to Thomas Mahoney

LADIES OF LOS ANGELES SOCIETY (and their husbands)

Mrs. Carson, she and her husband Mr. Carson are presumed to have existed. Mr. Carson owns a stationery store

Mrs. Glassell, she is presumed to have existed, as her husband, Andrew Glassell, was a prominent attorney in town at the time, he also founded the Glassell Park neighborhood and helped found the City of Orange, California

Mrs. Hewitt and her husband Mr. Hewitt may have existed. They own and run the buggy manufactory

OTHER ANGELENOS

Lavina Gaines, sister to Timothy Gaines

Timothy Gaines, land agent, brother to Lavina

Mabel Gaines, wife to Timothy

Efrem Smith, ranch hand for Mrs. Costa

Cipriano Alverno, a court clerk

Judge Phineas Gresham, a court judge and coroner

Biddie Mason, a real woman who lived in Los Angeles

Mr. Larson, a grocer

Mr. Wiley, agent for Maddie

Mr. Samples, a shepherd

Mr. Lyons, manufacturers agent

Mrs. Davies, landlady to Mr. Lyons

Chapter One

There was no sound more final than the crack of Judge Widney's gavel as he struck the bench that morning of May 27, in the year of Our Lord 1872, to end the probate on the estate of one Robert Gaines. I had attended Mr. Gaines as he slipped away to his final reward a month before. His last words were a promise to his loving daughter, Lavina, that she was well-provided for. Indeed, when the will was read, Lavina was to inherit half of her father's estate, with the other half going to her older brother, Timothy. Alas, the elder Mr. Gaines had no idea that the brother's greed would hold sway, and in a move so duplicitous that even Judge Widney questioned it, Timothy Gaines robbed his sister of her inheritance.

The robbery was completely legal, which is why Judge Widney was forced to approve it. For all that His Honor might have questioned the younger Mr. Gaines' motives, it was not entirely unreasonable for Mr. Timothy to request that he hold Lavina's bequest in trust until such time as he saw fit to give it to her. Most men left inheritances to their unmarried daughters in such trusts. However, most such trusts were generally only to be held until the time of the marriages of said young women, or until they had achieved some age or other. The younger Mr. Gaines had insisted, however, that giving him full discretion over when the inheritance was to be handed over would better protect his sister from fortune hunters, not to mention affording him the opportunity to build up his sister's fortune on her behalf. Had Lavina been less sensible and more easily swayed by the attentions of men, I might have been forced to assign some limited merit to his argument.

My testimony to Lavina's temperament and sensibility was not allowed to be heard, nor was Lavina's. We women were seldom allowed to testify in court. My colleague, Dr. Skillen, did testify in Lavina's behalf, but could not testify as to whether the elder and late Mr. Gaines had been of sound mind in the weeks before his death, as I had been the physician caring for the old man. Mr. Timothy, or rather, his attorney, had argued that, while the senior Mr. Gaines' affection for his daughter was commendable, the fact that he had left half of his estate to an eighteen-year-old, unmarried girl did not speak to being of sound mind. In addition, the attorney argued that I had unduly influenced the dying man, and my sympathies toward letting women take on mannish roles were well-known. Sadly, the will had been made in those same final weeks, which made it hard for Lavina's attorney, Mr. Melvin, to counter the arguments.

As Judge Widney approved the trust and made the probate final, I could not help but be proud of Lavina. Instead of giving in to tears, however much they were warranted, she held her head up as we walked out of the courtroom. Mr. Melvin later told us that His Honor seemed somewhat surprised, and perhaps chagrined, to see such dignified behavior rather than the tears of a weak woman. As I have noted in my earlier memoirs, Lavina Gaines was, indeed, eminently sensible and intelligent, nor was she easily swayed by a man's attentions.

Men frequently paid their attentions to her. She was a comely lass, with a round face, a perfect nose, and soft brown hair that she generally wore in ringlets, although that day, she'd pinned her hair back from her face into an upswept arrangement. Her small bonnet was fitted with black lace and had a short veil off the back of it. She, of course, still wore her mourning dress of coal black, although the tucks and gathers on the skirt were pulled back into a modern, and very tasteful, bustle, decorated with silk lace dotted with jet beads.

As we left the courtroom and passed by the clerks' office, one of the clerks came out from behind the counter between the door and the clerks' desks and bowed to Lavina.

"Miss Gaines, if there is anything I can do to help, it would be an honor," he said.

It was a courtesy that I was surprised to see. Mr. Cipriano Alverno's nature was such that most people in the pueblo believed he had not the least understanding of courtesy, let alone the ability to extend such to another. Many of us had cause to rue any intercourse with him, even though it was sometimes necessary, he being a clerk in the county court. He was singularly unhelpful most of the time and generally behaved as if he were suffering the worst of impositions any time someone requested his aid.

He was a small man with black hair scraped in strands over his bare scalp. Like almost every man of the day, he wore a full beard, his being equally black as his hair and trailing into wisps at the bottom. His clothes were dingy. I supposed they were clean, as he did not smell as he would have had they not been. One of his front teeth was missing and it was his habit to suck on the other when annoyed, which he generally was.

"You are most kind, Mr. Alverno." Lavina smiled politely at him, then held her head up again. "I would like to leave now."

Poor Lavina. Her behavior was quite noble given the circumstances. However, she was not made of stone, and so I took her at once to my home on the Rancho de las Flores, where I held several acres of vineyards and had a winery, that being the primary source of my living in those days. We doctors were not very well-paid at the time, even those of us who had full medical degrees, which I did.

Once in the parlor of my adobe, Lavina finally broke down, sinking onto my sofa and weeping for all she was worth.

"Oh, Maddie, I am so ashamed of myself," she cried after some minutes. "To present you with such a display."

I sat down next to her. "There, there. Your tears are utterly warranted. Imagine such perfidy."

"I am trying to be charitable and believe that my brother truly intended my well-being."

I sighed. "As am I. I suppose if we are going to call ourselves Christians, we should assume the best intent in his motives."

I forbore to mention, however, that it was again curious how often it happened that a man's good intentions for the welfare of a woman in his care seemed to coincide more with his own interests than with hers.

Lavina pulled a handkerchief trimmed in black satin ribbon from her reticule.

"I was so looking forward to managing my own affairs." She dabbed at her blue eyes. "I could have lived quite nicely on what I was to receive, perhaps have bought some land and a house. And if I passed the exam for my teacher's certificate, I would have been comfortable enough even without a husband. That was Father's greatest worry. He was so pleased that I planned to undertake the exam, and even let Schoolmaster Lawrence tutor me and Julia Carson at home." She sniffed. "Now, if I am to leave my brother's house, I must take the exam and hope that I can live on a teacher's salary."

"Or you might marry."

Lavina blinked. "Not for a while yet. My darling Efrem insists he has further work to do to build his fortune sufficiently to take me on as his wife. He promised Father, you know."

The unhappy circumstances under which I had met Mr. Efrem Smith the previous fall would not have led me to see him as a worthy suitor for any young woman. However, in early January, he and Lavina had met at a croquet game, the sport having become quite fashionable in our tiny pueblo of Los Angeles. He became enamored of her and thus underwent such a transformation in resolve and kindness that I had come to rather like him.

Lavina's father, at first, had been less than impressed. After all, Mr. Smith was a mere ranch hand. But Mr. Smith accepted the challenge with great vigor and even though his means were small, he sought to better them with careful investment. Indeed, by the time the senior Mr. Gaines entered into his final illness in early April, Mr. Smith had shown considerable industry and had even consoled the old man in his final days.

When Lavina learned that her father had left her half of his estate in cash and real estate, she'd been overjoyed. Mr. Smith, however, told her in no uncertain terms that she was to keep good care of her new wealth, as he would not marry her until he could support her in comfort without it. This, too, spoke well of the young man and I was glad to hear of it.

"Well," I said. "Given the turn of events, if Mr. Smith is still determined to eventually support you, at least you will have further proof that his heart is, indeed, true."

"I will endeavor to see that as a blessing." Lavina gasped and blinked furiously against the tears but failed to stop them.

I put my hand on her shoulder and let her cry. She had been truly grieved when her father had passed, in spite of the fact that she had deserved considerably more kindness from him than she'd gotten. We had been friendly for some time, but over the course of the spring as her father's health had failed, our intimacy grew to that of true friends, and we had begun using each other's Christian names.

Outside, I could hear the two rancho dogs barking as a buggy and team of horses pulled into the yard. A minute later, there was a knock on the door. I opened it to find Mr. and Mrs. Timothy Gaines on the other side.

Mr. Gaines had the same soft brown hair as his sister and a portly figure. He did keep his beard long, but neatly trimmed to a point at the bottom. His wife almost towered over her husband. She had a sharp face and looked at everyone with some deep suspicion, of what, I had no idea. They were newly married as of that winter.

I abhor the idea of a woman being ruled over by her husband as lord and master, especially having been so ill-used myself by my late and unlamented husband. Dragging me away from home and family in Boston out here to the lonely, miserable place that was Los Angeles in those days was but one of many miseries Mr. Albert Wilcox visited upon me. The only graces were that he'd written me a letter before we married, promising me all of his property should I outlive him, and that he'd died soon after we'd arrived.

That being said, I see no reason why a woman should rule her husband, either. It seems to me that the happiest marriages are those in which both husband and wife live together in respect, if not equity, each supporting the other in their daily tasks and work. Although it could not have been easy to be married to Mr. Timothy Gaines, as he was just as bombastic, ill-tempered, and miserly as his father had been, I must say that the young Mrs. Gaines had determined to not only avoid being mastered by her husband, but to rule him, as well.

"We've come for Lavina," Mrs. Gaines announced, looking down at me.

"I was not aware that she had asked you to do so." I smiled in spite of my pique. "She is here as my guest and I can see to bringing her home, should she wish it."

Mrs. Gaines huffed. "Mrs. Wilcox, as you well know because you were there, the judge has given the care of our sister over to my husband. We would be utterly derelict in our duty to her if we were to allow her to form inappropriate attachments. I'm sure you understand."

"No, I do not, Mrs. Gaines." I remained standing in the doorway. "In what way am I an inappropriate attachment for your sister? I would like you to tell me."

Mr. Gaines cleared his throat. "Mrs. Wilcox, we mean you no disrespect. However, Mrs. Gaines is right. If my sister is to marry well, we must think of her position in the city, and you do have a reputation."

"As what? A caring and effective physician? A woman of means who manages her business in a tidy and profitable manner? I do not see how either of those attributes, for which I am well-known, make me an inappropriate attachment." I smiled. "However, I suppose my reputation for thinking for myself does present some difficulty in terms of you being able to manage your sister."

"We are only concerned for her care!" Mr. Gaines stammered.

"Of course, Mr. Gaines."

Mrs. Gaines snorted. "And she is in mourning."

"Indeed." I glared at her, wishing to imply that Lavina's grief over her father's death was certainly more sincere than Mrs. Gaines'. "Still, it is not improper for a young woman in mourning to spend time in the company of good friends. Therefore, if your sister wishes to remain here, she shall."

"No, Maddie, dearest." Lavina came up behind me. "I'll go with my brother and his wife. However, I hope to see you soon."

She kissed my cheek and I quickly kissed hers.

"I shall make a point of calling on you in the next few days." I grasped her hands, then glared at her brother and his wife. "And I will take it very much amiss if I find that you have not been given every consideration and kindness, as due a loved member of the family."

As Lavina left the adobe with her head down to go to the buggy in the yard, I pressed my lips together. My one greatest failing has always been my temper. I'd been made angry enough by the judge's ruling. To see Lavina going off with her brother and his wife worried and infuriated me.

However, I did not have much time to contain myself. There was work to be done in the winery and on the rancho, and while most of the physical labor was undertaken by my partners in the venture, Sebastiano and Enrique Ortiz, there was a significant amount of business that I had to oversee or tend to, as well.

In addition to that, there was my medical practice, which was fully occupying me at that time as there was an outbreak of measles in the pueblo. Admittedly, there is not a lot that can be done once a patient is afflicted with the miserable disease, except watch for fever and other complications. But there were enough fevers and complications among the children, who were the majority of the victims, to keep me and the five other physicians in the pueblo quite busy, not to mention the usual host of other diseases including, but hardly limited to, pulmonaria, scarlet fever, croup, whooping cough, diphtheria, dysentery, and tetanus. Then there were the accidents and the broken bones that often went with them, burns, wounds from various fights, and the occasional gunshot wound. There were also the complaints of old age, which meant cardiac disease, rheumatisms, and so on, and babies to be born, with the complications that often arose from that.

I had worn my new visiting dress to the court hearing. It was a silk bombazine of dark ochre. The overskirt was swept back, creating a deep bustle. The basque was closely fitted about my midsection with pretty black silk lace trim that was also on the skirt. It was a lovely dress, but not one suited for riding all over the pueblo to tend to patients, who frequently left unsightly messes on my clothing.

I called my maid and confidante, Juanita Alvarez, and asked her to get out my oldest riding habit, a brown dress of linen and wool. The right shoulder of the dress was getting rather worn from the strap of the over-large leather bag that I carry with me everywhere. Never knowing what illness or injury I might be sought out for, I kept the instruments and cures that I used the most with me almost all of the time.

Juanita helped me out of the visiting dress, insisted on tightening my stays, then helped me into the riding habit.

"Juanita, are you still thinking about getting married?" I asked as she finished buttoning me up.

"All the time." She laughed as she turned to my visiting dress and shook it out.

"And to the same young man we've already discussed?" I adjusted the basque of my dress.

"Oh, I see." She picked up the clothing brush and attacked the hem of the bombazine. "You are still unhappy with Mr. Navarro."

"He is a rogue of the worst sort."

Juanita shook her head. "And there is no possible chance

that he could reform himself? You wouldn't have thought it of Mr. Smith, and yet you believe he has."

She had considerable justice on her part. It was my duty as a Christian to believe that the sinner could turn from his sins and become a new man, and Mr. Smith had proven that it was, indeed, possible to do so. However, Mr. Navarro was quite a dashing young police officer in the pueblo who was exceptionally charming and knew how to use such charm to considerable effect, not only on miscreants, but on vulnerable young women. I also had good cause to know that he was not very temperate in his habits, either. That he had cast his eye on my darling Juanita did not make me the least bit happy.

"Mr. Navarro has yet to display any evidence of such reform," I grumbled.

"He has to me." Juanita's eyes glittered with mischief. "Maddie, I know very well why you do not like him." She shrugged. "And I must say you have some reason for your worries. But he has shown me nothing but kindness and courtesy." She looked up from the bombazine with a smile utterly filled with guile. "And I assure you, Maddie, that I will accept nothing less from him."

I smiled softly. "There is some hope, then."

Juanita laughed and shook her head. It is possible that I was not being entirely sincere in my statement. Nonetheless, there was little more to be said, nor did I have any time to say it.

As I made my way to the parlor, where my bag waited by the front door to the adobe, I could hear loud complaints in rapid-fire Spanish from outside in the courtyard kitchen. Maria Mendoza, the house maid, was decidedly angry. Her husband, Hernan, was one of the ranch hands, and they and their three young children lived on the rancho, as did all of my workers and partners.

"What is going on?" I asked, going into the courtyard where Olivia, the cook, and wife of my partner Sebastian Ortiz, was listening with a disapproving frown to Maria's tirade. I spoke in Spanish, as I had come to be as fluent in that language as most of my household had become in English.

"The grocer, Mr. Larson," Olivia said. She was a stout woman with dark hair laced with gray, and a sour face that belied her normally cheerful nature.

"He took liberties again!" Maria snapped, still in Spanish. For all she was on the short side and well-rounded, thanks to a coming child, she could be exceptionally fiery. "I was forced to slap him." She stopped and swallowed. "I hope there will be no complaint."

I sighed and shook my head. "It will do him no good if he complains. Your word is far better than his, to my mind. But why do you go to his store if he is prone to such despicable behavior? There are other grocers in the pueblo."

"But he is the only one who carries those French sugared violets you like," Maria said.

"Oh, for goodness sakes," I groaned. "I have but to send a telegram to my sister and I will have plenty of them within a month or two. We no longer have to wait for them to go around the Cape and pray the ship doesn't sink. There's an intercontinental railroad to San Francisco. Something small like sugared violets are no trouble to ship."

Maria sniffed. "Thank you, Maddie. I will no longer give that man our custom."

I returned to my front parlor wishing that all troubles were so easily resolved, but, alas, no. As I gathered up my bag, I could hear the sound of running feet outside. Yet another boy had been sent to request my presence at the sick bed of some family member.

The family member in question was a little girl of barely three years, Marielena Reposena. She had the measles, as so many children in the pueblo did, and her forehead burned with fever. There was little comfort I could offer beyond a soothing salve for the rash and cool compresses. Neither helped her. Her soft, dark curls framed her face as she breathed her last.

I spent what time I could with the mother, who was deeply saddened. But I also had other patients to see, most of whom were doing well enough. Still, I felt utterly helpless.

As I pen my memoirs, it is perhaps tempting to pretend that I was (or am) a paragon in the art of healing. I most certainly was not. Nor I am so foolish as to believe that I can heal everything, even in these enlightened days of the Twentieth Century, when we know so much more than we did back in 1872. Nonetheless, one cannot help but feel overwhelmed at times, and watching a perfectly charming young babe succumb to a disease that most other children manage quite well was quite distressing.

That night, as I lay in my bed, commending my mind and my soul to the tender mercy of our Most Loving Savior, I could not help but think that the day had been lacking in the least satisfaction. Had I but known that a greater tragedy awaited me.

Chapter Two

The next morning, I once again put on my brown riding habit. While breaking my fast, Sebastiano, Enrique, and I discussed the chores that needed doing about the rancho. That time of year, the vast majority of the work centered on the care of the vineyard, although there were always items in need of repair, not to mention the vegetable and herb gardens that needed tending, and the barrels of wine to be sent to our various customers, as well as barrels to be put in the care of Mr. Wiley, our agent, who would see to selling said barrels in San Francisco and elsewhere.

We decided that the vineyards needed weeding again, and that Hernan and Pascual Mendoza, a pair of cousins, should see to getting barrels to Mr. Sedonez and Mr. Mahoney, who were saloonkeepers in the pueblo. There was not much that I, personally, could or would do, and so, shortly after eating, I was left to visit those of my patients who were ailing. Alas, one of those was Sebastiano's youngest child, Sofia, who was eleven years old.

By rather odd happenstance, everyone on the rancho addressed each other by their Christian names. Part of that stemmed from the excellent example of my beloved, but late and lamented mother, who had taught me that all people were Children of God, and deserved respect as such. The other part was sheer practicality, as both my partners and a good many of the people we employed were related and shared the same family names. Sebastiano and Enrique, for example, were brothers, and in the early days of our association when I would call for Mr. Ortiz, inevitably, the brother I did not require was the one who responded to my call.

Those of my partners and employees who were married had their families on the rancho, and the wives also contributed to our general well-being. Sebastiano's wife, Olivia, was our cook. Enrique's wife, Magdalena, was the housekeeper. One of the hands, Rodolfo Sanchez was married to Anita, who served as schoolmistress to the several children on the rancho.

That day, not all of the young ones were getting lessons. Sofia had the measles and remained in the care of Elena, her older sister. Elena, who would turn eighteen later that summer, had quite the healing touch and I'd been training her.

"She is getting restless," Elena said, sighing. The older girl looked a great deal like her mother, Olivia, although Elena's hair was still coal black. Elena even had Olivia's perpetual scowl. "It's been five days since she got sick."

I nodded. "Then we should start seeing some improvement in her. At least, we've been able to keep her away from the babes."

"Of course. But that doesn't always help."

I sighed. "I'm afraid it doesn't."

Most of the children on the rancho, including those too old to be considered children anymore, had already had the measles. Our concern was for the youngest among them. Ignacio, Hernan and Maria Mendoza's eldest child, had been the first to succumb, but being a strapping, solid boy of eight years, had managed quite well. Likewise, Lupe Ortiz, who at seven years was Enrique and Magdalena's youngest, was almost well, herself. However, Hernan and Maria's youngest two, namely, Adriana, who was four years old, and Elias, a little over a year-and-a-half, were, by virtue of their young ages, the most vulnerable to complications. We did not want to see them contract the disease until they were older. Alas, the nature of the contagion was such that even our best efforts to protect the babes from contracting the measles when they were most vulnerable could still come to nothing.

So far, Adriana and Elias had been spared, but both Elena and I had relentlessly seen to keeping the babes as far as possible from the sick children. The moment Ignacio had coughed, I brought him to the sick room in my adobe, one of three adobes on the property. Sebastiano and his family lived in one of the two remaining adobes, with Enrique and his family in the other. All the other hands lived in the large barracks, including those who had wives and children. The babes had been restricted to the barracks, and Maria, who normally helped Magdalena keep our houses, was kept out of my adobe lest she bring the contagion to her younger two.

Maria was also expecting at the time. Elias had been born under the most trying of circumstances and I could but hope that this next child would be delivered safely and easily.

However, that was not likely to happen for a good month or more.

After leaving the sick room, I washed my hands. Sanitation was of the utmost importance in an outbreak such as we were seeing, and I normally insisted on it, anyway. The concept of germs was still very poorly understood, although we physicians were learning more and more about them. I was having considerable success using Mr. Lister's methods of sterile surgery and had even convinced the good sisters at the Los Angeles Infirmary to let me create a sterile room for such use.

One blessing of the measles is that I was finally able to convince the men of my household that I did not need to be followed around by one of them at all times. True, Los Angeles was a violent place in those years, and it was also true that I had made myself a target for such violence by seeking after justice for certain individuals. Nonetheless, when Ignacio came home with the measles, I convinced Sebastiano and Enrique that they did not need to send their sons with me everywhere. Indeed, it was safer for the boys that they didn't. The measles was hardly the only infectious disease I came across in my work.

Rodolfo, a large man with a stooped back and drooping mustache, had Daisy, my roan mare, saddled and ready for me in the yard when I finally left my adobe. As I rode off, I couldn't help thinking about the grave injustice that had been done to Lavina Gaines the day before. After checking on two measles cases, a ranch hand with dysentery, and another expectant mother, I decided to call on Lavina. However, I was turned away by Mrs. Gaines, who insisted that Lavina was not at home. I'd heard Lavina's voice before the door had opened, so I knew that Lavina was, in fact, at home. Still, I resolved not to question it until a week had gone by and I'd still been denied a visit.

There was one other call that I decided to make, to Mr. Larson's grocery store. I was not concerned about him accosting Maria again but did want him to know why he was losing my custom.

Given that Maria generally saw to the stocking of those groceries we purchased, I did not know him well. However, the few times I'd had opportunity to speak with him had left me feeling considerable dislike for the man and questioning his honesty. Indeed, while his advertisement in the daily paper claimed that he offered San Francisco quality at Los Angeles prices, there were many in the pueblo who complained that the reverse was true.

"Good day, Mr. Larson," I said in my sternest voice.

"Hello, Mrs. Wilcox." He was a small man with dark hair and a roughly trimmed beard and his smile was disingenuous at best. "Have you come to buy some more sugared violets?"

"You have accosted my housemaid one time too many," I said, pulling myself up to my full height. "Therefore, I will no longer buy sugared violets nor anything else from you, and I shall be happy to let the rest of the pueblo know why."

Mr. Larson chuckled. "I do not accost housemaids. I may tease a little, but accost? No. I am a decent man, and you will find few in this pueblo who will not say so."

"Then why did she complain yesterday that she had to slap you?"

"You're taking her word against mine?" He shook his head. "I have no idea why your housemaid would make up such a ridiculous tale, but I assure you, it did not happen."

"And I am assured that it did, Mr. Larson. You can protest all you like, but I do take Mrs. Mendoza's word over yours. Good day!"

I turned and strode from the store.

I returned to the rancho just as the bell in the Clocktower Courthouse struck noon for luncheon. It was quite warm, so we ate under the oak tree in the middle of the yard. The tree and the space around it were surrounded by six buildings. On one side was the winery, closest to the gate, then the barn, where the animals and other tools were housed, and finally the wooden barracks building that had two floors and room for everyone but the two Ortiz families. On the other side of the circle were the three adobes. I and Juanita lived in the middle one, Sebastiano and his family lived in the one closest to the barracks, and Enrique and his family in the adobe closest to the gate.

I had just sat down at the outside table when Pascual jumped up and ran to the yard gate. On the other side, Mr. Alverno stood. Pascual brought him over to the table in the shade.

"Judge Gresham needs to see you," Mr. Alverno announced, his forehead beaded with perspiration under his dusty hat.

"Is he ill?" I asked.

Mr. Alverno rolled his eyes. "If he were ill, he would summon someone else. He said I was to bring you to the courthouse immediately."

"I am having my luncheon right now. Would you like to join us?"

"No, thank you." Mr. Alverno sucked on his tooth and rocked back and forth on his heels. "I'll just wait here."

I sighed. "Why don't you walk ahead? Tell His Honor that I will be there as soon as I am able."

Mr. Alverno made a huffing sound but did as I asked.

Sebastiano looked at me, suspicion glowing in his dark eyes. He was a tall man with full shoulders and a square face. His dark hair and beard were just starting to be sprinkled with gray at that point.

"Maddie, what have you been doing that would cause Judge Gresham to summon you?" he asked, alas, not entirely without reason.

"For once, I am blameless," I said, turning my attention to the lovely cold chicken that Olivia had set out. "I have no idea why His Honor would require my presence, unless he were ill or injured, and Mr. Alverno made it clear that was not the case."

If I waited until I'd finished eating to go back into the main part of the pueblo, it was because I did not want Mr. Alverno as a walking companion. I also wanted to ride Daisy, as I suspected I would have further visits to make after conferring with the judge, who was also the county coroner.

As it was, I arrived at the courthouse in time to see Mr. Alverno go inside. I tied up Daisy and entered after him, going to the second floor, where the offices and courtrooms were. We had three judges hearing cases at the time, including Judge Widney, who mostly heard probate and other civil cases.

I could hear Judge Gresham from the stairwell, berating Mr. Alverno. Shaking my head, I went to his chambers at the back of the block.

"You imbecile! I told you to bring her directly here. Why can't you follow directions? You are useless!"

"Excuse me, Your Honor," I said, coming into the office doorway. "I had just begun my lunch, and, given that Mr. Alverno was kind enough to assure me that you were neither ill nor injured, I sent him on ahead to let you know that I would be here at my earliest convenience."

Mr. Alverno looked at me with the tragic face of a dog that has been beaten by its master, implying at the same time that it was my fault that he'd been beaten.

Judge Gresham was well-rounded in figure and somewhat tall in stature, with a red cauliflower ear. His full beard was shot through with gray, as was what remained of his hair. He snorted when he saw me.

"Mrs. Wilcox, a body has been found near one of the farms on the southern edge of the city. Dr. Skillen thinks that it would be best if you examined it, as it is that of a woman."

"Do we know who it is that died?" I asked.

"Some Indian. She was found near the Oliver's farm. Mrs. Oliver has seen to keeping the body. We'll have an inquest tomorrow at ten. I'll need you there about an hour beforehand to examine the body."

"I suppose I can make time." I smiled as if he'd asked me to be there rather than ordered. "Is there anything else, Your Honor?"

"That will be all." He rocked forward onto his toes as he clasped his hands behind him.

I left the office feeling considerable pique at His Honor's presumption. The judge's demand now necessitated an additional visit for me. However, it was one that I was happy to make, as it was to my dear friend, Angelina Sutton.

Angelina, the undertaker's wife who prepared the bodies for burial, was quite happy to see me. She brought me into the small sitting room next to the workroom. The little salon was a cheerful space with two armchairs, a large desk, a sofa, and a little writing desk on wheels that Angelina pushed to wherever she happened to need it. I settled myself on the sofa while she fetched some tea and biscuits from the kitchen. After serving me, she settled herself into her favorite armchair and smiled.

"So, have you come to vent your spleen over the Gaines probate judgment?" she asked, her tone merry, albeit sympathetic.

She was a small woman, which belied her steely strength. Her hair was dark black, and her deep brown eyes frequently sparkled with mischief.

I couldn't help groaning. "It is, alas, only one of several events to trouble that organ."

I did not, in fact, believe that the spleen was the body's vessel for anger, as many of my brethren had even up until a few decades before. There were still a few of my colleagues who held that humors where what governed the functioning of the human body, but fortunately, not many. I was profoundly grateful to Our Loving Savior that good, solid science was finally gaining ground over such ridiculous ideas. Nonetheless, Angelina's metaphor was apt, which was why I chose to continue it.

As for the venting of said organ, I had learned through the harsh lecture of experience that I was better off doing so rather than simply trying to banish the anger from my heart.

"However, let me begin by reciting the latest of my aggravations," I said, after nibbling on a biscuit. "After all, it does mean we have some business to consider and settle."

I explained to her about the body of the Indian woman found near the farm belonging to Mr. and Mrs. Oliver, and Judge Gresham's demand that I show up before the inquest to examine the body.

"It was bad enough that he insisted that I go to the courthouse to be given the information when he could have simply written a note," I said. "However, when I got there, he demanded that I show up a full hour before the inquest."

"Will he let you testify?"

I couldn't help it. My eyes rolled Heavenward. "One can but hope, and it is a faint gleam at that. Nonetheless, would you be willing to come with me? I will pay for the funeral. It seems the least I could do for the poor creature."

"Your charity is noted." Angelina smiled. "Are we about to go on another adventure?"

"I have no idea. But your studies on rigor mortis will be most useful, whether we are allowed to testify or not." I shuddered. "It is exceedingly unjust. You are possibly one of the most intelligent people in the pueblo, man or woman, and yet neither of us has any say on anything."

"It is extremely vexing, Maddie, dearest." Angelina shrugged. "Sadly, it is the way of the world. At least, you and I have the work that we do and that we enjoy. How many women do we know who are as intelligent as we are but who only care for their men and their children?"

Regrettably, I knew several, and Angelina was right, it was extremely vexing. However, she was also right in that the two of us were uniquely blessed in our respective situations.

The next morning, Sebastiano hitched Daisy to my buggy. I wore my indigo walking dress, which I'd recently had re-made to add a more stylish bustle, rather than the full hoop skirt with swept-back trim. The bustle did make sitting somewhat uncomfortable, but it was a great deal easier to walk modestly in the ridiculous contrivance than in a hoop skirt. It is entirely possible that a great deal of my problem centered on the rather mannish gait that I confess that I had. I preferred to call it an aversion to shilly-shallying, but there were those, my grandmother among them, who were convinced that I could have walked with greater daintiness.

We went first to Angelina's home to find her waiting for us on the front porch. Sebastiano helped her into the buggy next to me. As she settled herself on the seat, she told me that she'd arranged for two of the men employed by her husband for such tasks to bring the body back to her establishment.

It was not a long drive to the farm owned by Mr. Oliver. We actually arrived closer to eight-thirty in the morning, rather than nine, and Judge Gresham was not yet there.

Sebastiano chose to remain with the buggy and pleasantly chatted with Mr. Oliver. Mrs. Oliver, a round woman with a kind and pleasant demeanor, showed Angelina and me to the shed where the body had been laid. It was that of a woman, with long, dark gray hair. Her cheeks were sunken in, as might be expected, but it wasn't just the ravages of death.

From what I could see of the body, her entire form was emaciated.

"Mama Jane," Angelina whispered.

I looked again at the body. "Indeed, it is. I thought she'd left the pueblo when Father Gallar began preaching against her."

Mama Jane was a bruja, or witch, in the pueblo. In many cases, that actually meant a woman with some skill in the healing arts. Indeed, before I had revealed myself as a trained medical doctor, I was known as a bruja. Mama Jane had considerable skill with poultices and unguents. However, she was just as likely to be sought after for her various love potions and other charms.

Father Gallar, on the other hand, was newly arrived in the pueblo as of a month or so before. Father Jimenez had been re-assigned to the Mission San Gabriel, and Father Gallar sent out as pastor to the Catholic Church in the pueblo. He'd barely been in his new pulpit a week when he began fulminating against the superstitions prevalent among the local populace, and in particular, against the several brujas, including me.

The good father did not believe women had any place healing people, beyond the basic cures most women knew. Anything else reeked of superstition, never mind that, in my case, I had better schooling and skill than most of the other doctors in the pueblo. I had lost a few patients among the Catholics as a result of his sermons. Mama Jane had lost a great deal more, since much of her living came from peddling the very charms that had Father Gallar so distressed.

"I heard that she'd gone to San Buenaventura," Angelina said sadly. "But she couldn't sell enough of her charms to feed herself. The people there didn't know her, and so didn't trust her. So, she came back here about a week ago."

I coughed lightly. The smell was getting rather overwhelming. Angelina lifted the corpse's hand.

"Rigor mortis is completely gone," she said.

"And look at this," I said. "Bruises on her neck."

Angelina's eyes opened wide. "Someone strangled her."

"I am inclined to believe so."

At that moment, Judge Gresham arrived, full of bombast, with Mr. Alverno just behind him.

"The jury should be arriving shortly," the judge said. He glared at me and dismissed Angelina. "Well? What do we have?"

"An older Indian woman known as Mama Jane," I said. "The body is quite emaciated—"

"Ah. A sure sign of dissipation." The judge rocked on his feet.

Making a face, Mr. Alverno got out a notebook and a pencil.

"Or starvation," I said, aghast. "To the best of my knowledge, Mama Jane did not imbibe spirits or wine."

"To the best of your knowledge." Judge Gresham's smile was unctuous at best. "However, I have seen many of these cases, and I assure you, she died of dissipation and exposure."

"And what do you make of the bruising on her neck?" I managed to keep my temper in check, but only just.

Judge Gresham stopped rocking. "Oh. I wonder what accident could have caused that."

"No accident, Your Honor." I pulled myself further upright. One of the greater difficulties in dealing with men of

Judge Gresham's ilk was that, while they could often be quite sensible, they also tended to take great umbrage at the least thing, and it was nigh on impossible to tell which reaction one would get. "It appears that someone strangled her."

"Well, that's odd." The judge smiled again. "Why would someone strangle her when it would be easier to simply shoot her?"

It was, in truth, a much better question than it sounded, His Honor's complacency notwithstanding. At that time, most men in Los Angeles carried some sort of firearm, as did many of the women, myself, included.

Mr. Alverno gagged.

Judge Gresham turned on him. "Oh, for goodness sakes, you spineless dog. Yes, it smells awful in here. But if Mrs. Wilcox can manage it, I should think you could, too."

Mr. Alverno remained silent, sucked his front tooth and looked balefully at me. I forbore to say anything, although I dearly wished to do so. His Honor was being patently unfair. As a physician, my sense of smell has been assaulted by all manner of foul things. The smell of a corpse is not pleasant, by any means. However, it was not the worst stench I'd come across.

Furthermore, most women I knew were assaulted by smells just as bad, if not worse, in the course of caring for their families. It still befuddles me to this day that men insist on seeing women as dainty and delicate creatures, when the vast majority of the women that I have known deal routinely with all manner of things that would, and do, bring the strongest of men to their knees in horror.

"Be that as it may," I said. "There are the marks of physical violence on this poor woman's corpse."

"Potential violence, my dear Mrs. Wilcox." Judge Gresham again graced me with his most unctuous grin. "It is, indeed, worth remarking upon, and I will when the jury gets here. I appreciate your opinion."

I sighed. "Then may I deduce that my presence here is no longer necessary?"

"You may, indeed, madam. I am most grateful for your examination."

He turned and left the shed, Mr. Alverno on his heels. I looked over at Angelina.

"My men will be here shortly," she said. "We will examine her further when we get her back to my workroom."

As it turned out, Angelina's men had already arrived, but they would be forced to wait until the jurors for the inquest had observed the body, and only then would they be able to bring the body to Angelina's workroom. Angelina and I made our farewells to Mr. and Mrs. Oliver. Sebastiano helped us into the buggy, then mounted the driver's seat. He had just gotten Daisy started, when he pulled up.

Approaching us from the road were two men, one leading a horse. Both were dressed in dark, but dusty suits, with dark hats. The one leading the horse was considerably shorter than his horseless companion and his name was Mr. Ernesto Navarro, the swain who had captured my Juanita's heart. His hair and beard were black and as shiny as coal, and his dark eyes often gleamed with merriment. Mr. Navarro's companion, however, was as solemn as Mr. Navarro was merry. Mr.

Walter Lomax was tall, and brown-haired, with a square face lengthened by his beard. Both were policeman in the pueblo.

"Good day, Señor Ortiz," Mr. Navarro exclaimed, then doffed his hat in salute. "And Mrs. Wilcox and Mrs. Sutton. It's good to see you ladies."

Angelina smiled. "It's good to see you, Mr. Navarro, and Mr. Lomax."

"How do," said Mr. Lomax as he tipped his hat. Mr. Lomax tended toward the laconic.

"Are you here as witnesses for the inquest?" Angelina asked.

"Jury," said Mr. Lomax.

It seemed odd that two policemen would be serving as part of the jury, however, I was grateful that Mr. Lomax was. He was entirely honest and quite shrewd. Mr. Navarro, if I am to be truthful, was honest, as well, no matter how fickle his heart may have been in regard to the young ladies of the pueblo.

"Are you ladies here for the inquest?" Mr. Navarro asked.

"We were asked to give an opinion prior," I said, my voice cool.

"And that opinion was?"

Mr. Lomax shook his head. "Mr. Navarro, we are supposed to listen to the proceedings without bias."

"I suppose." Mr. Navarro shrugged. "However, what are the odds we are going to hear anything but Judge Gresham's bias?"

Mr. Lomax sighed, then looked at me with his eyebrow lifted.

"There are bruises on the woman's neck that suggest she died at the hands of another," I said. "Mrs. Sutton and I will examine her more thoroughly when we get back to the pueblo."

"And who was the woman?" Mr. Navarro asked.

"It was Mama Jane," I said. "Are you familiar with her?"

From the nervous look on Mr. Navarro's face, I deduced that he was.

Chapter Three

When we arrived at the Sutton home, I let Sebastiano go back to the rancho. Angelina and I returned to the little parlor next to her workroom, then Angelina went to her kitchen to get our usual refreshments.

"How many people knew that Mama Jane had returned?" I asked, settling onto the small couch as Angelina returned.

"I don't think it was well known." Angelina thought it over, then placed the tea tray on the table next to her favorite chair. "I'd only heard that she had from Mr. Navarro's cousin Constanza Delgado, and that was yesterday morning. And Miss Delgado only said that it was rumored that Mama Jane had come back, not that it was certain."

I pondered that as Angelina poured. We'd barely had time to take a sip when the men returned with the body, and we went into the workroom.

Angelina removed the clothing from the corpse in preparation for washing, and I was shocked to see that the emaciation was even worse than what I'd supposed based on her arm.

"It would almost appear as though she'd starved to death, but for those bruises," I said.

Angelina sighed. "Which quite probably means that whoever strangled her did not get much of a fight from her."

"The poor woman."

Both Angelina and I looked her over very carefully, but the bruises on her neck were the only sign of violence.

"I'd best make some record of this," I said.

I suppose we could have found a photographer. There were several in the pueblo, but it seemed an unnecessary delay, not to mention the expense. I got my notebook from my leather bag and a pencil and went to work drawing the corpse from the shoulders up, making sure to catch the bruises from three different angles.

"Who could have done such a thing?" Angelina asked as she sorted through Mama Jane's garments.

"I have no idea." I thought about it. "Given that His Honor insisted on jumping to a base conclusion, I find it unpleasant to give any credence to his observation regarding it being easier to shoot someone rather than strangle that person. However, he did have a point." I frowned as I finished my second drawing and began the third. "I find it hard to imagine wanting to kill anyone, therefore why anyone would do so makes little sense to me."

"And yet we see it all the time." Angelina said. "Tempers rise, people start fighting, then get out knives or guns."

"But with an old woman? Admittedly, Mama Jane could be quite acerbic." I stopped drawing for a moment. "Perhaps that is why she was strangled. The killer became enraged, and not expecting her to be armed, attacked her physically."

I finished drawing and held out my work for Angelina to see.

She peered at the pages, then nodded. "That is nicely done."

"Do you know if Mama Jane has any relatives in the pueblo?" I frowned as I looked at the corpse again.

"None that I know of. Why do you ask?"

"I think I should like to do an autopsy. We can verify why and how she died."

"You probably should." Angelina shuddered a little. "It just seems a little drastic and disrespectful."

"I know." I sighed. "But if I don't, we will not know for sure, and there may be other things to learn from the body."

Angelina agreed and while I set to work on my unhappy task, she began mending and folding the various garments she'd removed from the body, carefully going over each piece. The autopsy showed me exactly what I'd suspected, that Mama Jane had, indeed, been strangled. However, there was one hopeful sign. She'd eaten before she'd died. Indeed, I was able to ascertain that she'd had food for at least a couple days.

I sighed as I stitched the body back together.

"It would seem to indicate that she'd been able to sell some charm or cure," I said.

"I agree." Angelina looked at the pile of clothing thoughtfully. "I think she may have been moved from where she was killed."

"I certainly saw signs of it," I said.

Angelina frowned. "That's why I went through her clothes. Perhaps there was some weed or something that might show where she'd been. The only problem is that the only bits I found are from weeds that are all around here."

"That is unfortunate." I went to the basin that Angelina had set up next to the back wall of the workroom and washed my hands and my instruments. "We shall have to find out. It may have some bearing on who killed her."

"So, we are having another adventure." Angelina smiled.

I shuddered. "Given how badly the last one ended up, I should think you would have had enough of them."

Alas, Angelina had been shot and wounded the previous autumn and had barely regained her full strength by that point.

Angelina laughed. "Maddie, we live in Los Angeles. There's a murder a day here. Surely you must expect that we would find ourselves looking for another killer."

"A murder a day is a gross exaggeration," I grumbled. "This place is miserable enough. Let's not make it any worse than it is."

It was quite true that I had no affection for the pueblo. It was a violent, backward place. As for how often murder truly happened in the pueblo, it could be hard to say. Fights in the various saloons were quite common and would occasionally result in the death of one or more of the combatants, either directly or from wounds that became infected and festered. Such fights did not necessarily result in the charge of murder, especially if the victim was Chinese, Negro, or Indian.

Angelina shrugged. "I know I exaggerated, but we do get at least one murder a month, it seems."

"I fear I must agree." I shook my head, then looked at the poor woman's body again. "As for Mama Jane, let us see that she has a nice funeral."

"I will take care of everything." Angelina smiled softly at me. "You are so kind-hearted, Maddie."

"We shall see."

Angelina was prone to sentimentality, while I found such expressions quite embarrassing. Fortunately, I had instruments to return to my bag, and it was time to head back to my rancho for the mid-day meal, which I did after thanking Angelina.

I arrived home somewhat tardy, but still in good time to settle down with the rest of the household to a pleasant lunch of cold rabbit. Alas, I'd barely begun to eat when a messenger boy came running up along the road to the main part of the pueblo.

"Mrs. Wilcox!" the dark-haired waif cried. "It's Mr. Gaines. Miss Gaines says it's urgent."

Lavina had sent the boy, which probably meant that her brother was in serious need of my services. I sighed as Rodolfo hurried to get Daisy saddled. Juanita scrambled into the adobe to get my riding habit ready.

"Please tell Miss Gaines that I will be there as fast as I am able," I told the boy, then stuffed a few more bites into my mouth.

It was not a terribly ladylike way to eat, but I was quite hungry. There was also the need to appease Olivia, our cook. She was annoyed enough that I'd been late to the meal. She felt it her duty to see to it that I ate sufficiently and felt quite put upon when I had to forgo a meal in order to attend to a person in need.

I was changed in short order and trotted Daisy into the

pueblo to the Gaines house. It was of white-washed clapboard, with a tidy yard in front. I hitched Daisy to the post provided at the end of the front walk and hurried to the door. Lavina had it open for me, apparently having seen me arrive.

"He's upstairs in Father's bedroom," Lavina said. "I sent you for right away."

"What's going on?"

"I'm not sure. He says it's as though his chest is on fire, and he finds it hard to breathe."

"Oh, dear." I took the steps quite quickly.

The young Mr. Gaines was in his bed, his wife in a chair nearby, holding a handkerchief to her face, which was filled with fear. Mr. Gaines' face was, fortunately, neither flushed nor ashen, although that was not a conclusive sign, by any means.

"So, when did you start feeling this pain in your chest?" I asked, moving the strap of my bag over my head.

"Right after lunch," he gasped.

I set the bag on the edge of the bed and began rummaging through it.

"I see." I found my stethoscope and put it on.

His heart beat quite soundly. I took his pulse and it, too, was perfectly normal. I bent him forward and listened to his lungs, and while he did gasp, it didn't sound as though he was having that much trouble breathing.

"After lunch, you say." I looked at him. "What did you eat?"

"Nothing different. A steak, some stewed carrots and cabbage,"

Mrs. Gaines began to wail.

I gave Mr. Gaines a good solid thump on the back. I had tried it before, although I had never read anything in my journals about it. That being said, it worked with infants.

"What did you do that for?" Mrs. Gaines cried.

The problem I have had all along in this process of writing my memoirs is that human beings do all sorts of things that are not to be spoken of in polite company. I have always striven to be a lady in all that I do. Yet I always strive for complete honesty, which does make it awkward when the truthful retelling involves some effluvia or other impolite sound. Specifically, in this case, Mr. Gaines' malady was relieved when a loud and grossly impolite noise erupted from him. Then he slowly began to smile.

"It's gone." He made another indiscreet noise, though a far softer one. "The pain in my chest. It's gone."

"You have dyspepsia," I told him. "A couple grains of bicarbonate of soda mixed in warm water before and after meals should help prevent another such attack."

"Is that all?" Mrs. Gaines looked utterly affronted.

"Better he should have that than heart disease," I replied, putting my stethoscope back into my bag.

Mrs. Gaines glared at Lavina, who remained in the doorway to the room.

"Our sister insisted that we send for a doctor." Mrs. Gaines sniffed angrily.

"And Miss Gaines was right to do so," I said calmly, picking up my bag by its strap. "The symptoms of heart disease and dyspepsia can be remarkably similar. Better to find that your husband is suffering little more than an upset stomach than to have him die for want of care. Now, I'm sure you wish to see to his care right now, offering him the soothing of a loving wife. I can see myself out."

"Dear sister, I will see Mrs. Wilcox to the door," Lavina said firmly.

I had a strong suspicion that I knew why she wanted to see me out.

"Are you being treated well?" I asked her once I got downstairs.

She shrugged her shoulders. "Well, enough, I suppose."

I couldn't help it. My eyebrow quirked up in inquiry.

"They do keep me at home," she said, finally. "I am not even allowed to visit with Julia Carson, let alone you."

"Why, pray tell, not?"

"I am in mourning. Although, they allowed me to seek out my friends before the will was probated." Lavina sighed. "I do believe that it's because they do not want me to marry. Well, my dear sister surely doesn't."

"And how does that benefit your brother and sister-in-law?"

"It's quite simple. Once I marry, it will be hard for my brother not to hand over my share of Father's bequest. After all, he only put it in trust so that I might be protected, as I have no husband."

"Hmph!" It was not the most lady-like response, but fully justified. "I would think that your sister would want you out of the house."

"Except that she wants my money more. She and my brother are true kindred spirits in that respect."

"Oh, dear. I do believe that we shall have to petition

the court on your behalf. Alas, I'm afraid it will take some months of keeping you mewed up before we can with some legitimacy."

"All the more galling, as I do have a suitor that Father approved of before he died."

I heard creaking on the stairs above me and lifted my voice a little. "Your brother is quite fortunate. Your father's disease began in much the same way. But do not forget yourself. You cannot stay inside all the time. It's not healthy, and we do not want your brother and sister-in-law to be accused of not seeing to your care."

Lavina hid her laughter behind her hand. "Indeed, Maddie. It would not at all be fair to them."

Mrs. Gaines made her way slowly down the stairs.

"Are you finished, Mrs. Wilcox?" she asked severely.

"Yes, I am." I smiled at her, my lips feeling rather tight.

I had no sooner left the house when Enrique Ortiz rode up on one of our mules. Somewhat larger than Sebastiano, Enrique was the younger of the two brothers. He and Sebastiano looked much alike, otherwise, although Enrique was given to shaving his chin, unlike most of the men in the pueblo.

"Maddie, a wagon overturned on the Basenio ranch. One of the hands is injured."

I sighed, but mounted Daisy quickly and we trotted to the northern edge of the pueblo. The Basenio family owned a small rancho just under the steep hills that rose up from the edge of the Porciuncula River. They mostly raised sheep and cattle but had two small orchards of citrus and olive trees, as well.

As Enrique and I rode up, a group of ranch hands were

gathered around the poor man who had met with the misadventure. Sadly, there was little I could do. I had him moved to the ranch house, hoping to set his leg. But there was too much bleeding and he expired even before I could clean my instruments in preparation for the surgery.

Mrs. Basenio had four of the ranch hands bring their comrade to the Suttons' funeral parlor. I followed the little cortège, walking Daisy, having sent Enrique back home to the rancho.

I was surprised to see Angelina in a completely foul mood.

"Oh, dear, what can the matter be?" I asked.

"Father Gallar." Angelina almost bit the name off as if she were trying to bite off his head. "He will not let Mama Jane be buried in the Catholic cemetery."

"He won't? Good Heavens, why not?"

"Because she was a bruja. She was evil and apostate."

"He has no right to decide that!" I must confess, my mouth hung open in my rage.

"He thinks he does." Angelina trembled, equally as angry as me.

"What if she came to see the evil of her ways right before she died? How could he assume that she hadn't?"

Angelina's groan was eloquent. "He can because he's a priest, which, as far as I understand, means he can converse with Our Lord directly. I'm just a woman. I know nothing of the ways of God."

"That is utter nonsense." I tried to bite back the angry words, but knew that it would not only be futile, it might make things worse when I finally became so filled with ire that I could no longer contain it. "I do not understand it, when the dictates of Our Loving Savior counsel in favor or love and kindness, and against bitterness and judgment, why so many so-called men of God instead insist on judging in the meanest fashion!" I looked at Angelina. "Have you any idea where we can bury Mama Jane?"

"Reverend Stokes, of St. Athanasius, agreed to let us use a plot in their cemetery." Angelina sighed. "It is possible that I neglected to tell him exactly which Indian woman needed burying. He'll do the service tomorrow morning at nine."

St. Athanasius was the recently founded Episcopalian church in the pueblo.

I sighed deeply. "I shall be there."

But, first, I had another errand. I mounted Daisy and rode to the Catholic Church, which was off the plaza. There were rumors they were going to build a fountain in the middle of that plaza, but they had yet to.

Having hitched Daisy, I found Father Gallar outside the church, itself, resting in the shade of the building. It was rather hot that day, so I could hardly blame him for that.

He was short and somewhat gaunt, with white hair at his temples and a full head of coal black hair, otherwise. He was clean-shaven, too.

"You will be happy to know that Mama Jane will be buried as a Christian," I told him.

"She is no Christian." He glared at me as if I were no Christian, either. "I thought I had driven her from the pueblo, only to have her return again to that little hut by the Negro shepherd's farm."

I knew well which shepherd the priest meant. He was Ted Samples and he owned several acres on the northeastern edge of the pueblo, right next to the farm owned by Mr. Lomax. As I thought about it, there was indeed a small hut on the other side of the road from where the two pieces of property met.

"She was a harmless old woman," I said. "She even had some skill in healing, which few enough do around here. Even if she hadn't, as I understand the gospels, mercy is to be our byword, not judgment."

"We are to be perfect, as our Father in Heaven is perfect." He shook his head. "Perhaps you find that difficult to understand because of your sinful nature."

"For which I have been forgiven, or did Our Lord die in vain?"

"He only died in vain if He did not rise from the dead." He moved away from me. "You do not know what you are talking about. How could you?"

"I know my Scriptures better than most Catholics I know, and I strive to follow them."

He shook his head and not only moved away but slid into the church. I suppose I could have followed the priest inside, as I had attended many a funeral and the occasional wedding in that edifice before. However, I thought there was little to gain by it. It was perhaps unworthy of me, but I couldn't stop a passing thought that perhaps Father Gallar had killed Mama Jane. There seemed little likelihood of it, however. After all, he'd already consigned her soul to perdition. Why would he send her there sooner rather than later?

Nonetheless, he had, unwittingly, helped my cause by telling me where Mama Jane had lived. I unhitched my horse and rode out to the place mentioned by Father Gallar.

It was easy to see why the structure had escaped my notice. The thatch of the roof and the brown bricks of the walls blended so completely with the surrounding countryside, that the tiny hut looked more like a small hill rather that a dwelling, what one could see of it among the scrub and the drooping branches of a very old oak tree. I tied Daisy up to one of the tree's branches, and went to find the door.

I was forced to stoop as I entered the hut, and I am not an overly tall woman. Small chinks of light shone through the cracks in the packed clay bricks that made up the back wall.

A pile of rags lay next to one wall. On the opposite side of the room, a shelf had been carefully built, and it was filled with small pots and bundles containing Mama Jane's various herbs and other ingredients for her cures and charms. There was nothing I could discern from the pots and bundles, but as I went through the rags, it became obvious that not only were the rags her only blankets and coverings, they were in disarray, as if someone had pushed them aside overly quickly.

I returned to the outside of the hut and, upon circling it, found the source of the chinks in the back wall. There had clearly been some sort of struggle there, and there was a small indentation in the bricks.

Daisy nickered and I heard the branches rustle as she tossed her head. I desperately hoped that didn't mean a rattlesnake was nearby. As I came around the front, I saw immediately that it wasn't a snake or anything remotely like one.

He was a tall man, with pitch dark skin broken up by the scars of that most hateful institution of slavery. Ted Samples, as he often did, had his rifle in his hand, but had lowered the barrel.

"I thought I saw Daisy here," he said. "Couldn't figure what you was doing, though."

"Good day, Mr. Samples." I smiled. "I hope I haven't alarmed you. I'm given to understand that Mama Jane made her home here."

Mr. Samples nodded.

"Have you heard the sad news?" I asked.

"About Mama Jane dying? I sure did." Mr. Samples shrugged, then looked down the road toward the pueblo proper. "Not surprised, though. That old priest came out a couple times and finally run her out of there. He didn't have no call to do that. She were a harmless old woman, and had some good cures, too." He smiled briefly at me. "Not meaning any disrespect, ma'am. I do prefer using yours, and Mrs. Samples does, too. But lots of folk liked Mama Jane."

"I'm afraid there was at least one person who didn't." I looked back at the hut. "Besides Father Gallar, I believe. I'm afraid Mama Jane was murdered."

Mr. Samples' eyebrows shot up. "That be true?"

"I'm afraid so."

He frowned. "That do account for her landing all the way over on that south farm. I was wondering what she was doing over there. She didn't like to move around much."

The sound of footsteps on the road caused Mr. Samples to withdraw into the drooping leaves of the oak tree and raise his rifle. It was naught but Mr. Lomax. He came from the direction of the pueblo and, as he had overshot the path to the front door of his house, appeared to be headed our way.

"Mrs. Wilcox?" he called, his voice filled with caution.

"I'm right here and quite well," I replied, my voice

slightly lifted that he might hear me. "I'm speaking with Mr. Samples."

Mr. Lomax walked up and tipped his hat at me, then at Mr. Samples. Mr. Samples tipped his hat in return, lowering the barrel of his rifle slightly.

Mr. Lomax looked curiously at me. "You looking for Mama Jane's killer?"

"Who else will?" I replied. "It appears she was killed behind her hut."

I pointed and Mr. Lomax saw the hut, his eyebrows raising in surprise.

"This her place?" he asked.

"I have reason to believe so," I replied and told him what I'd already found.

Mr. Lomax nodded. "I'd heard she had a bed or something around here but didn't know this was the place. It would explain why I saw Mr. Navarro out here a few days ago. I thought I'd seen him talking to her, but he said he hadn't seen her since before last week."

I swallowed my fear back. "Oh, dear. You think he lied."

Chapter Four

There was little to be done. Mr. Lomax was quite certain he'd seen Mr. Navarro speaking with Mama Jane late Monday afternoon, but it had been at a distance, as Mr. Lomax had been returning from his fields. He hadn't thought much about it at the time, then thought he might have been mistaken when Mr. Navarro had told him he hadn't seen Mama Jane, until now when I pointed out that Mama Jane had lived, and presumably died in that place.

It was only a suspicion. If Mr. Navarro had committed the foul deed, then we would have to find other evidence. I returned to my rancho and ate the evening meal with my household. I forbore to mention my suspicions regarding Mr. Navarro, however, and hoped desperately that I should not regret it.

That night, however, as I wrote in my journal, but before getting dressed for bed, I was summoned by a young colored woman that I realized worked for Mr. and Mrs. Carson.

Mr. Carson, a stout man prone to bombast, owned a very successful stationery store in the pueblo. The equally stout Mrs. Carson and her bosom friend, Mrs. Glassell, were two of the worst gossips in the pueblo. Mr. and Mrs. Carson were the least favorite of my patients. That was an unkind thought, especially in light of what happened that evening, but they were both very demanding and often forgot that I expected to be paid for my services.

Nonetheless, I got my bag from the front of the house and hurried after the maid to the center of the pueblo.

"It's Miss Julia, ma'am," the maid told me as we walked. "She bleeding really bad."

Julia was the second of the Carsons' five children, and the only daughter. She was seventeen years old, quite comely, with golden curls, and she was very popular among the young people of the pueblo. I could not understand why Lavina Gaines was so fond of the lass, as Miss Julia could be decidedly vapid and Lavina was anything but.

"Was there an accident?" I asked the maid.

The young woman shrugged as if to say she did not know.

When we got to the house, the situation inside was dire. Not only was Miss Julia hemorrhaging, her face was also flush with quite a high fever.

"At first, I thought that her monthly courses were simply over-heavy," Mrs. Carson said, weeping. "But then the fever started."

There was a basin and ewer on the bureau across from the small bed where Julia moaned.

"I need clean cloths," I said, pouring water into the basin. "As many as you can bring. And we'll need more water."

I washed my hands, then went to the side of the bed to examine Miss Julia. As I did, I stepped on something. I bent and picked up a knitting needle, crusted with blood. It was then that I knew what had happened, and my heart sank.

As I have noted earlier in this account, the practice of medicine often involves events that are not to be mentioned in polite company. Nor do I wish to descend into the sensationalism that is so fashionable in these days of the early Twentieth Century. But however shocking Miss Julia's situation was, unfortunately, it also became quite important later, and therefore I must make mention of it.

Miss Julia had conceived, and apparently had tried to rid herself of the problem. At the time, most people were not terribly worried about such things, as long as the baby had not quickened. I, however, deplored the practice, mostly because Miss Julia's condition was the all too likely result of such an attempt. That night there was also the additional complication of Mrs. Carson. I do not approve of keeping things from patients, and in the case of young people, from their parents. So I was quite torn about whether to mention the knitting needle to Mrs. Carson, especially when I so greatly feared for Miss Julia's life. With her condition so perilous, there seemed little to be gained by telling her mother what had probably happened and telling would only add to the woman's grief. That is why I quickly wrapped the needle in one of the cloths in my bag and pushed it to the bottom of that noble sack.

Then I forced my focus to trying to bring down the fever and stop the bleeding. Alas, I was not successful in either case, and Miss Julia breathed her last barely two hours later. I held Mrs. Carson as she sobbed, then went to break the news to Mr. Carson and his sons.

"What happened?" Mr. Carson's face was ashen and the beard on his jowls quivered in his grief.

"There was an infection," I said simply. "Her fever got too high, and nothing I did could bring it down. I was able to staunch the bleeding, but it clearly did not help and with the infection raging within her..."

I looked away, blinking back tears. I again decided not to say anything about what had caused the infection. After all, it would not ease their grief any to know that their daughter had been less than modest in her dealings.

Although, as I walked back to my rancho, it struck me that Miss Julia, however vapid she may have been, had also been perfectly modest and circumspect in every way imaginable. I wondered if some man had forced himself on her. It was not one of the more common crimes in the pueblo, but it happened far too often for my liking. I was glad that I had chosen not to say anything about the knitting needle. Even if Miss Julia had been breached unwillingly, there would always be those who would doubt that she had been unwilling.

I took a few breaths of the cool night air to try and calm my ire and gazed up at the vast cavern of the sky, which was liberally strewn with stars. The waning half-moon lit the clouds to the west as they began their nightly spread over the pueblo and environs. It was a beautiful sight, and however grieved I was feeling at that moment, the twinkling display did soothe me.

As I left Alameda Street to head toward my rancho, I heard a scuffling sound to some paces away to my right and behind me in the small copse of trees next to where the two roads met. I had my hand inside my bag in less than an instant and whirled around. At first, I saw nothing and turned back from the sound toward the rancho, all my senses tingling. I also looked over my shoulder as I walked. Father Gallar's head slowly emerged from behind an oak tree, then he scuttled away toward Alameda Street and the Plaza. I wondered that he felt it necessary to hide his presence. After all, as a priest, he certainly had cause to be abroad even at that late hour, coming and going as needed to minister to the sick and dying.

Breathing heavily and trying to calm the racing of my heart, I pulled my gun from my bag. I should have had it at the ready before leaving the Carson's house, but once again, I had neglected to. The gun was part of the concession that I had made to Sebastiano and Enrique when they agreed to let me move about the pueblo unaccompanied. They had trained me in the gun's use the winter before and continued to insist that I practice shooting. I was to carry the large revolver with me at all times, and after dark I was to keep it in my hand. I had yet to shoot anyone. I was hoping not to, having seen more than plenty of what guns could do to the human form.

I took another soothing breath and gazed briefly at the starry sky above me, then hurried home.

The next morning, the sky had once again clouded over. No rain portended. It was merely that time of year when the shore, some fifteen miles away, became enfogged, and the clouds were blown inland overnight by the ocean breezes.

I broke my fast with my household, then took on a few chores, including checking on the ailing children, but soon Juanita called me in to help me get dressed for Mama Jane's funeral. I wore my ochre visiting dress, and my mien was certainly somber enough after the night before.

It was a nice little service at the graveside, with the common prayers. I will give Reverend Stokes a great deal of credit for choosing kindness and mercy when he realized just who he was burying. He even spoke highly of Mama Jane's skill at healing and said nothing about the charms that she sold. Angelina stood with me as we commended Mama Jane's soul to the loving Mercy of God.

Later, as we walked from the cemetery, I sighed.

"Is it safe to assume that you are aware of the other sad event last night?" I asked Angelina.

"Do you mean Miss Julia?" Angelina cocked her head. "You are unquiet about it."

"Have you seen the body?"

"Of course. It's in my workroom. I wasn't sure if what I saw was a hemorrhage or heavy courses. I'm told she died of a fever."

"She did, but there was also a hemorrhage."

Angelina's sigh was profound. She'd seen such an instance often enough to know what it meant.

"Poor Miss Julia," Angelina said, making the Sign of the Cross on herself. "She certainly did not seem like the type that would get into that kind of trouble."

"And I am uneasy in spirit because I do not think she was."

Angelina's eyes opened wide and the word that fell from her lips was anything but ladylike.

"But who could have done such a thing?"

"I fear we must ask," I said. "It is strange, but I almost hope we do not learn who the monster was. After all, it is a sad truth that the only way we will find him is if he preys on other young women, which will mean more such deaths."

"It is a sad truth, indeed." Angelina's head shook in dismay. "But that is exactly why we must try to find him and stop him as soon as possible."

"Of course." I sighed. "I did not mean to suggest otherwise. We will have to be very careful in how we go about such an inquiry. We do not know for certain that Miss Julia was the object of such an attack, nor do we wish to impugn her character, even if she were a willing participant in her disgrace."

"To be certain, indeed. Perhaps we should make a list of all the young men with whom she had contact." Angelina loved making lists.

"And probably some of the older men, as well," I added, suddenly shivering as a truly evil thought crossed my mind. "I must say that it is utterly demoralizing to look at one's neighbors and make the worst of suppositions."

"It is." Angelina made a face. "Well, I must be off home to prepare Mr. Sutton's luncheon."

"And I should think about going home to mine. We will confer later."

We parted ways, Angelina to her home and I to mine. Lunch was not quite ready when I arrived back at the rancho, so I changed to my indigo walking dress, lest I be summoned to a patient, then went to my study to write up my notes from the night before. However, I became engrossed in reading the morning's paper, only to become immensely annoyed when I read the outcome of the previous day's inquest.

"Oh, for goodness sakes!" I threw the paper onto my desk with considerably more force than necessary.

"Maddie!" Olivia bustled in from the kitchen across the hall from the study.

Because both Ortiz families are each fairly large and because I and Juanita are the sole occupants of my adobe, mine is also where the small indoor kitchen is. The outdoor kitchen is on the patio surrounded by the three adobes.

"What is going on?" Olivia demanded.

While normally a cheerful soul, Olivia did have a temper and did not scruple to hide it when someone crossed her. Alas, I frequently did, usually by coming home late to a meal, or forgetting to eat altogether.

I picked up the newspaper and carefully folded it. "I am vexed. I made it quite clear to Judge Gresham before the inquest into Mama Jane's death yesterday that Mama Jane was most probably murdered by strangulation. And it says here in the newspaper that it was ruled that she died of dissipation and exposure to the elements. What rot!"

"I do not know why you let such things bother you. We both know that as far as His Honor is concerned, all Indians are drunks, and as such, when they die, it is from dissipation." Olivia snorted. "At least, you had the kindness and grace to see that she was buried as properly as possible."

"I suppose. It seems so little, and grossly unjust."

"Then you will find her killer and see to it that he is brought to justice." She shook her finger at me. "But you best be careful and try not to make that man want to kill you, or anyone else want to kill you for that matter!"

She returned to the kitchen, muttering to herself in Spanish that I had no more sense than an infant playing with a nest of rattlesnakes. She did, sadly, have some cause for her annoyance.

At luncheon, it was determined that I should pay a call on Mr. Mahoney at his saloon, as he owed us some money. It was not likely to be an unpleasant encounter. After all, Mr. Mahoney was a frequent customer for our wines and angelica. He had merely not been in the saloon when Hernan and Pascual had delivered his latest order. Mr. Mahoney did not allow anyone but himself to pay me or my men, so if he was not there when my men brought the barrels, then I would need to go after the money at a later time.

I decided to walk that day, and being already attired in my indigo walking dress, a lovely dress of heavy cotton, with a bustle and fine black lace for the trims, I felt quite ready to undertake a bit of business.

"I think I shall also pay a visit to Mr. Wiley," I told Juanita and I readied my bag about my shoulders. "He, too, owes me some money."

It did not take long to walk to Mr. Mahoney's saloon. It was not far from the Courthouse Clocktower, and, not surprisingly, was the preferred saloon of the Common Council members and a good portion of the pueblo's most powerful men. I was barred from the saloon, itself, by virtue of my sex. To the best of my knowledge, Mr. Mahoney did not allow women of fallen character inside, either. There were saloons in the pueblo that did.

I went through the back of the building, where Mr.

Mahoney's two daughters were preparing soup and stew, and baking bread for that evening's customers. Alice sent me to her father's office behind the main part of the saloon.

The tiny room in front of the storeroom barely had room for Mr. Mahoney's desk, a battered chair, and two wooden crates of whiskey that Mr. Mahoney used to seat himself at the desk, which was littered with papers and bottles and other ephemera. Mr. Mahoney held out the chair for me and I adjusted my bustle to perch on the edge of the rickety thing.

"You've come to collect for your barrels," he said.

He was a tall, rangy fellow, with a thin gray beard that he often shaved off, dark gray hair, and green eyes.

"Indeed, I have," I said, smiling.

He sighed as he pulled his money box from one of the bottom drawers in the desk, however not because of needing to pay me.

"Have you heard about Miss Julia Carson?" he asked, sadly.

I couldn't help it. My eyebrows lifted.

"Have I heard about what in regard to Miss Julia?" I asked cautiously.

Mr. Mahoney looked at me oddly. "Her death last night. There was talk of little else during the lunch hour in the saloon."

"Do you mind if I ask what the talk concerned?"

"I don't understand."

I sighed, then pressed my lips together. "I cannot say entirely. That is why I asked what the men were talking about."

Mr. Mahoney scratched his chin. "Mostly that it was so puzzling. She was abroad in the pueblo yesterday. In fact, she came by the back of the saloon to visit with Alice and Annie. I was much obliged. Not many of the young women of the pueblo will be so friendly to my girls."

"That was a kindness indeed." I smiled softly at him.

It was hardly just. Mr. Mahoney's daughters were just as well brought up as any young women in the pueblo, and even better than some.

"Can you tell me what happened?" he asked.

My eyes filled in spite myself. "She had a fever. There was no help for it."

He shook his head. "A sad affair, indeed. Mr. Carson is greatly grieved."

I frowned. "Mr. Mahoney, were there any fellows who seemed to have their eye on Miss Julia?"

Mr. Mahoney opened his eyes wide. "It seemed as though most men did, as she was quite charming. But there was no impropriety. Of that, I am certain. She was a good lass."

"She was," I replied, holding my tongue against saying more.

There had obviously been some impropriety, although I was becoming certain that it was not on her part.

"It's the second time a woman has died under sad circumstances this week," I continued. "I can't help but wonder what the men have been saying about Mama Jane."

Mr. Mahoney looked puzzled. "About who?"

"An Indian woman whose body was found near the Oliver's farm, southeast of here."

Mr. Mahoney frowned, then let out a musing grunt.

"Was that the body in the newspapers these past two days?" he asked.

"She was."

"Haven't heard anything about that, really." Mr. Mahoney mused again. "I read in the newspaper that the coroner ruled the death as being due to dissipation and exposure."

"To be sure, I read the same article," I said, my voice far more annoyed than I'd intended. "However, she clearly did not die of dissipation, but from being strangled."

"Are you searching for another killer, Mrs. Wilcox?"

"I am afraid so," I said, forbearing to add that I was also looking for an additional miscreant who was at least as evil as Mama Jane's killer.

Mr. Mahoney sighed but nodded. I took my leave shortly after. I made my way onto the Calle Primavera to visit with Mr. Wiley, who also wanted to know about Miss Julia. Again, I asked why.

"She seemed like such a nice young lady," he said, blinking his blue eyes. He was small and gaunt, with sand-colored hair. "I saw her in her father's store just the other day. She said hello quite pleasantly. Her death seems quite sudden."

"It was," I sighed. "But fevers can do that. You're the second man today to ask about her. It seems she was quite popular."

"She had a pretty face and was quite charming." Mr. Wiley smiled sadly. "Not much of that in the pueblo, I'm afraid."

I tried not to roll my eyes. There were quite a few lovely young women in the pueblo, but the larger majority of them were Mexican, which meant they were beneath Mr. Wiley's notice. As he counted out my money, I asked him about Mama Jane, and he did not seem to know her or care that she had been strangled.

I left shortly after, feeling some distress, as I did not know in which direction I should go. I decided to visit a few of my patients, but there wasn't much to be done on that account. So, I soon made my way back toward my rancho.

As I walked up to the gate of the rancho, I saw Juanita and Mr. Navarro standing outside on the road, some distance away from the gate, itself, but in plain sight from my vantage point. Because Juanita's back was to me, I could not see her face, but I could see Mr. Navarro's, and his smile was unmistakable.

I called out to Juanita. She turned, saw me, then waved and ducked under the fence to the rancho and ran toward our adobe. I approached Mr. Navarro feeling decidedly annoyed. He, however, smiled the smile of the utterly unrepentant.

"Mrs. Wilcox!" he called in greeting. "How good to see you."

"Mr. Navarro, you are presuming that I find it equally good to see you," I replied.

He was quite taken aback. "I did not think—"

"It is irrelevant what you thought," I said, possibly more angry than I should have been. "You are paying your attentions to a young woman who deserves your complete fidelity, and I know well just how fickle you are."

"Not anymore!" he gasped. "I am true to Señorita Alvarez and will remain so. How could I not?"

"That is easily said."

"Perhaps. But the señorita is less than convinced that I am true." He sighed deeply. "I have even tried the best of love charms and she remains unconvinced of my devotion."

"Love charms?" I asked.

He flushed. "Yes. I bought a charm from Mama Jane a few days ago."

"Where did you find her?"

"At her hut near the Lomax farm. Where else?"

I looked at him severely. "Indeed. Mr. Lomax told me just yesterday that he'd seen you speaking with her, but that you said you hadn't. Would you care to explain that?"

"Well… I…" Mr. Navarro gulped and looked around. "Honestly, Mrs. Wilcox, I didn't want to say why I visited her. It's really rather foolish, don't you think? It was easier to say that I hadn't spoken to her. I didn't mean anything else. Honestly, I didn't."

I snorted. "Honestly, indeed. Why, in Heaven's name, would you purchase a love charm? If you can't convince Miss Alvarez on your own merit, what good will it do to attempt fooling her with magic? It would be a false affection, at best."

"But if it tips the scales in my favor, it wouldn't necessarily be false."

If only I didn't already know that Juanita was already well disposed toward his suit. I bit my lip.

"It is of no consequence," I said. "Until you can convince me of your change of heart, I will not support your suit. More importantly, you must convince Miss Alvarez, and I assure you that will take some doing."

The statement was not at all true, and I suspect Mr. Navarro knew it. However, I did not trust Mr. Navarro and had good reason not to. There were many young ladies in the pueblo whose hearts he had broken.

"Now, I wish you good day." I moved toward the gate to the rancho.

He moved away up the road as I opened the gate and slid inside. I looked back at him walking away. Alas, he was far too charming for his own good, and especially for Juanita's.

Chapter Five

Shortly before dinner, a messenger arrived with an invitation that I fully expected, but not with any happy feeling. There would be a viewing of Miss Julia's body at her parents' home at seven o'clock that evening. Almost at the same time, another message arrived from my good friend Regina Medina. She wanted me to visit as soon as possible, as one of the young women in her employ had the measles and was ailing.

I returned both messages in the affirmative, then ate my dinner in some apprehension.

The viewing was quite dismal, which was not unexpected. I offered condolences to Mr. and Mrs. Carson. There was little more to be done.

"It's simply terrible," said Mrs. Hewitt.

She was a small woman with the temper of an annoyed rattlesnake. We had become friendly by virtue of the fact that I knew her secret. In truth, it was no great secret that her husband was prone to drunkenness. But while most of the men of the pueblo congratulated him on his ability to manage his buggy manufactory in spite of his tendencies, almost none of them knew that the reason he was able to do so was that Mrs. Hewitt actually did the managing.

"It is, indeed, terrible," I said.

"She was such a sweet young girl," Mrs. Hewitt continued.

I looked around the front parlor. Mrs. Glassell, a round woman of average height, was holding court next to Mrs. Carson, whose full mourning garb consisted of a black silk gown trimmed in black lace with jet beads, heavy veiling, and lovely black kid gloves. Mrs. Glassell wore a dark blue walking dress that was apparently made of wool, as her face was somewhat flushed, and a tiny rivulet of perspiration ran down her full cheeks.

It was rather warm in the crowded parlor, filled with many of the Pueblo's elite citizens. Not surprisingly, everyone had something kind to say about Miss Julia, who lay in her coffin next to the back wall of the room. Nonetheless...

How do I write this? It is usual that people say good things about the deceased at the viewing and funeral. That does not necessarily mean that the people saying those good things believe them. One does not intend to be so insincere. One simply does not wish to cause the bereaved any more grief, not to mention the reality that we will all meet the same end, and presumably, wish to be remembered kindly.

However, that evening, it was my impression that the kind words were uncommonly sincere. Perhaps that was because Miss Julia was so young, not even eighteen. But I soon realized that it was also because Miss Julia had been particularly kind and well-behaved, alas, unlike her mother, who was an inveterate gossip and seldom had anything good to say about anyone.

I did not stay long. I needed to return to my rancho to change clothes, which I promptly did, then made my way to Regina's house, riding Daisy.

It was possibly the strangest friendship I have ever cultivated in my life, but it was uncommonly strong. I had lived in Los Angeles for just over ten years when it finally became known that I had a medical degree. Prior to that, I was known for my healing skills, and while most respectable people (mostly Americans) in the pueblo preferred the American doctors, who were naturally all men, there were many who could not avail themselves of those services and they had turned to me. Among those were the several women in Regina Medina's employ.

You see, Regina was a madam. She owned and ran the richest brothel in the pueblo, and the one that was preferred by the wealthiest men there. One would think that Regina's customers would want their female companions to be well taken care of. Sadly, if the men gave the women a second thought, it was only in regard to the potential for contracting the diseases that such places were notorious for. As for the other doctors, they would not lower themselves to care for such women. It was hard enough to get those men to care competently for the respectable women.

I, however, decided that it was my duty as a Christian woman to help the poor girls as I could, and as I did, I became friends with Regina. Regina was not only exceedingly grateful, she opened my eyes to a number of realities that I had previously been sheltered from.

So, when one of the young women quickened with child, or otherwise fell ill, I was the one Regina called. Her house was on the western side of the pueblo, just under a large hill. It was a large white clapboard building with two stories, and big bushes planted at various vantage points so that if one wished to enter without being seen, one could.

The entrance I preferred led to the house's kitchens and back rooms. The kitchen maid sent me directly to the sick room, a small space next to the kitchen and close to Regina's tiny office. The ailing young woman, Arabella, was blonde and petite, and flushed with fever. The other girls were taking turns placing cooling compresses on her forehead. Arabella's cough was getting a little on the nasty side, and once I listened to her lungs, she clearly had some pneumonia in one of them.

After applying a plaster to her chest, I requested some beef tea and also some warm milk, adding some of my own angelica to the milk, and insisted Arabella drink some of each as she could. There wasn't much more to be done.

"It's not terribly serious," I told Regina as I left the room. "At least, right now, it isn't. But I do believe she has some pneumonia."

"Oh, dear God," Regina sighed, the hint of an Irish accent in her low, breathy voice.

She was exceptionally tall and made herself appear even taller by the benefit of piling her glossy black hair on top of her head and wearing tall top hats. She also wore lacy jabots to the top of her jawbone, although the rest of her wardrobe featured dresses that were the most fashionable in the pueblo. Many a respectable matron had been humiliated to find that the dress she'd commissioned as the very latest in mode had already been modeled by Regina some months before.

"We can but hope," I replied, patting Regina's overly large hands.

She shook her head dismally. "Why is it that all the nice and sweet girls seem to die of diseases and child bed fever, and all the more vinegary sorts thrive?"

"Regina, you know that I cannot say for certain that Arabella will survive. However, I am feeling somewhat optimistic in her case. She was healthy before coming down with the measles, wasn't she?"

"As healthy as a horse." Regina snorted. "How is it that these tiny, tiny things called germs can kill us?"

"I'm not entirely sure I understand it, myself," I replied. "However, Mr. Pasteur's work has been quite conclusive, and to my mind, it makes more sense than simple bad air."

"Hmph!" Regina shook her head. "Germs? Bad air? Does it really make that much difference?"

"It does in terms of how we fight it." I sighed. "That is the next battle, you know."

"Fortunately for me, it is not one that I will be fighting. However, my darling Maddie, I have yet another problem." Regina bit her lip. She was the soul of discretion as her business required it. However, she frequently confided in me and Angelina. "You are aware of Mama Jane's passing?"

"Very much so, I'm afraid." I shivered a little. "Judge Gresham asked me to examine her body. Not that it did any good, according to the newspaper this morning."

Regina snorted and added a decidedly vile epithet in regard to the good judge's sensibility.

"That verdict was complete rot," Regina continued. "Mama

Jane certainly did not die of dissipation. She only used a few spirits in her concoctions and never drank any."

"I take it you knew her?"

"Given my business, of course I did. I needed Mama Jane's herbs regularly. They were the most effective with the fewest complications."

Regina went on to explain that the herbs were needed to rid the young women of the expected result of their activity.

I could not help sighing. "I wish Miss Julia Carson had consulted Mama Jane."

Regina was aghast. "Julia Carson? I had heard it was a fever."

"There was one, but what she did to herself was the cause of it. I found the knitting needle."

"That is amazing. Not that I knew her." Regina sighed deeply. "But I knew of her. In fact, many of my guests complained about her."

"What? You're the first person I've heard say the least disparaging thing about her. Everyone has said nothing but how kind and good she was."

Regina's low chuckle rumbled. "Why do you think the boys were complaining? She was a coy one, but it was all in innocence."

"It is possible someone forced himself on her." I looked at Regina thoughtfully. "Given her condition and her reputation, it seems more than likely."

"I suppose." Regina's face grew serious. "It's also possible that she was seduced. Or was tricked, not realizing what the cad was after. Given that these poor girls are told so little about the ways of men and women, I'm surprised it doesn't happen more often. Believe me, Maddie, that's how many of my ladies end up in my employ."

I sighed. "And the men are never held accountable. It is so unjust."

Regina's chuckle rumbled again. "It is, dearest, but that's what I love about you. You thirst for justice and will not rest until you see it done. Well, you will find the villain that soiled dear Miss Carson."

"And Mama Jane's killer, I hope."

Regina gaped. "What?"

"She was strangled, Regina."

"Could it have been that awful Father Gallar?" Regina's eyebrows rose, and she looked a touch hopeful. "When he ran Mama Jane out of town, I was in quite a difficult spot. I was so glad that she returned in time to help Katerina."

"I suppose it's possible. But I have no idea how I will find out." I got up. "Do you wish me to stay with Arabella?"

Regina listened for a minute. "Her cough sounds better, and if she does have pneumonia, I can't see what you can do that you haven't already done."

"Very well, then. Please see to it that she keeps drinking the beef tea. She also needs milk dosed with some spirits. Angelica or brandy would be best, but whiskey will be all right. And cooling compresses. I'll be by tomorrow with a fresh plaster for her."

Regina saw me to the back door, then went back to her business. I rode back to the rancho feeling quite out of sorts.

The next morning was the funeral for Julia Carson.

Reverend Elmwood gave the sermon at the Carson home, then we all made our way to the cemetery, where we all stood through the short service.

I was surprised, though pleased, to see Lavina Gaines there. Mrs. Gaines was nearby, but happily occupied gossiping with several of the other women in the pueblo. For someone in mourning, she seemed quite chatty. Lavina, however, was greatly grieved. Both wore their mourning dresses, but only had short veils on.

There were a great many men in attendance, as well. Miss Julia, it seemed, had been very well-liked. I looked over the men, wondering who among them might have been the source of Miss Julia's unfortunate condition.

Lavina Gaines sidled up next to me as soon as Reverend Elmwood was finished, and Mr. and Mrs. Carson had left the cemetery.

"Maddie, I need to take you into my confidence," she said so softly I almost didn't hear her.

"About what, dearest?"

She placed her hand on her arm. "About poor Julia. She had a problem." Lavina sighed. "It was most indiscrete."

"I fear I have already deduced that. Trying to rid herself of it was what caused her death."

Lavina let out a soft sob. "I was afraid something like that had happened. I had been warned that doing such a thing could be dangerous."

I patted her arm. "I'm so sorry for your grief." Then I paused as something else struck me. "Then Miss Julia took you into her confidence?"

"Yes. She was quite distraught and needed a confidant."

"Do you know how her problem came to be?"

"The problem she was trying to rid herself of was caused by her true problem." Lavina blushed most becomingly. "During her last illness, my mother told me about what happens between a man and his wife. Father would not have been able to. We have no relatives in the pueblo, and with so many rough men about, she did not want me caught unawares or worse."

"How eminently sensible," I said. "Was Miss Julia aware of such things?"

Lavina's eyes widened. "Oh, no! When she told me, well, what had happened to her, she described it quite faithfully. It was forced upon her. She was devastated." Lavina wept. "And I had to tell her what it would mean if her courses didn't come. They must not have, if what you deduced is true."

"Oh, dear. Did she name the man?"

"No." Lavina shook her head, her brown curls shaking under her hat. "Julia didn't say who. She said she didn't dare."

My eyebrows rose. "How do you mean?"

Lavina looked around at the other mourners, then moved even closer to my ear.

"I believe he was married, and so threatened to ruin her if she said anything about what he'd done to her." Lavina sighed. "Some weeks ago, not that many, Julia told me that there was a man in the pueblo whose behavior was most rude and forceful. She was afraid of him, but could not say so, lest he ruin her reputation. She wanted to warn me, though."

"That is encouraging in a very bleak way," I said. "If she was afraid of him, then it will be harder for others to say he tricked her into compromising her virtue."

Lavina looked beyond me and suddenly smiled. Standing nearby was a tall man with built out shoulders and dark blond hair. He wore a dark suit with a black cravat. He also smiled back at Lavina. However, Mrs. Gaines finally noticed that her sister-in-law was not obediently standing behind her.

"Lavina, darling," the woman snapped. "It is time we were off. We don't want your brother's luncheon to be late."

Mrs. Gaines glared at the man who approached, then she took Lavina's arm, and pulled her away. I pressed my lips together lest I say something unforgivable. The man stepped up to me and tipped his hat.

"Good day, Mrs. Wilcox," he said, somewhat sadly as he gazed after Lavina.

"Good day, Mr. Smith," I said to him, feeling quite put out, although not with him. "I see you are not an approved companion for Miss Lavina, either."

"Not at all," he said with quite the profound sigh. "It would seem that Mrs. Gaines truly expects to keep her sister-in-law as near to her as possible. The worst of it is, I couldn't care less about Lavina's inheritance. If Mr. Gaines wants to keep it, that's up to him. I will soon have enough business interests to keep his sister well enough, and expectations for more. It's pure greed is what it is."

"I'm afraid so." I turned to follow Lavina and Mrs. Gaines back into the pueblo. "Alas, there is little we can do about it right now."

"As soon as I buy my land and get the house built, then I'm coming for her, whether she's in mourning or not." Mr. Smith took my arm and walked with me. His eyes glinted angrily.

"Even in mourning, there's no reason she shouldn't be allowed your company occasionally. Her father gave his blessing on your courtship. The only concession to her period of mourning would be delaying the wedding." I sighed. "I wonder if they'll let Miss Lavina take the teacher's exam next week. It doesn't seem reasonable to deny her that, especially since she has no real means."

Mr. Smith snorted. "It's hard to say, ma'am. Allowing Lavina to earn some money will mean they don't have to give up the trust as easily. But they do not like Lavina's independent nature."

I raised an eyebrow. "And you do?"

"Of course, I do." Mr. Smith laughed. "That's what I love best about her. Oh, I suppose it can be difficult when I need to make a decision for the both of us. But I have found that she is very sensible, and I am right to listen to her more often than not." He sighed again. "It's just that I promised her father that I would work in land agency rather than farming. Lavina doesn't mind that I want to farm, but she agrees that it is a more difficult life than what her father wished for her." Mr. Smith shrugged. "And I am not bad at buying and selling land. Just not as good as her father was."

"That you are doing as well as you are is quite respectable enough," I said. "Well, Mr. Smith, unless you are going to walk with me all the way back to my rancho, then I must leave you here."

Mr. Smith tipped his hat again and stalked off toward the center of the pueblo.

I returned to the rancho and changed into my brown riding habit. After our lunch, I checked on Sofia, who was recovering quite nicely, then went through my bag, adding to those medicines and herbs that I was short on, making sure that my tools were clean, and re-filling my flasks of carbolic acid.

It was a good thing I did. As I finished, one of Mr. Lomax's boys came running up to tell me that Mrs. Lomax was ailing. After questioning him, it was clear that I wasn't urgently needed, so I sent him on ahead home and had Rodolfo saddle up Daisy. I went first to Regina's and applied a fresh plaster to Arabella's chest. Her fever seemed to be coming down and her cough was not as severe, although it was still rough.

In the tiny adobe on the Lomax farm, Mrs. Ruth was in the sole bed. Her sister wife, Mrs. Sabrina, had the several children on the place somewhere outside, presumably doing chores of some sort. They had all managed the measles quite nicely and were completely healed of the contagion.

I should explain that the Lomax family was from the Utah territory and were Mormons. Mr. Lomax had come to eschew the religion, but it was not generally known that both of the women of his household were his wives. They usually claimed that Mrs. Sabrina had been his brother's wife and was widowed, which would explain why the six children all had Mr. Lomax's square face, never mind that their mothers looked nothing alike.

Mrs. Ruth's fever wasn't terribly high, but her rash was clearly causing her considerable discomfort.

"It's the measles," I told her. "You're fortunate that you do not have any pneumonia."

"It doesn't matter," she said sadly, as she sat up against the scant pillow on the headboard. “It would probably be just as well if I did. I am nothing more than a burden, as it is.”

“You won’t be for long,” I said in my most reassuring voice. “That is the blessing of the measles.”

She let out a soft sob. “It doesn’t matter whether I am well or not. My very presence is the worst of burdens to my husband.”

I bit back the shocked words that sprang to my lips. After all, Mr. Lomax had never expressed anything but tender concern for both of his wives.

“I don’t understand,” I said, instead.

“As long as we live in California, he will not be a husband to either me or Sabrina. He will not put one of us aside for fear of abandoning us, but he will not favor one or the other. As long as our marriage is considered illegal and bigamous, my husband will not be a husband.” Tears trickled down her cheeks. “I know it does not do to want him so. I am not a wanton, but I do want more children.”

I was in a considerable quandary. It was hardly the first time a patient had divulged details regarding their more intimate relationships and had done so irrespective of the patient’s actual condition. It was one of the more awkward parts of my work. However, I considered Mr. Lomax my friend, which made Mrs. Ruth’s confession all the more awkward.

“I have told him that he should put me aside,” Mrs. Ruth continued. “But he will not.”

“If he does not want to abandon you, I would imagine not,” I said.

“And yet, he prefers Sabrina, as well he should. She is younger and more fair and can have more children.”

"Ruth!" Mr. Lomax's voice filled the room.

I jumped. I had not heard him entering the house. Mr. Lomax looked at me, then down at his feet.

"There, there, Mrs. Ruth," I said. "I'm sure things seem quite bleak right now, but you'll be feeling better in a few days." I rummaged through my bag. "I've got a salve that might help your rash feel less bothersome. But the rash, too, will be gone soon." I patted her hand, then got up. "I'll return in the next few days to see how you're getting on."

I looked at Mr. Lomax and nodded toward the front of the house. He slid his hat back on his head and followed me outside. Once there, he sighed deeply.

"I take it you heard your wife talking to me," I said softly.

He nodded. "I have to be honorable. My union with Sabrina is illegal and it is not fair to deny her and indulge Ruth." He sighed. "And I cannot tell her lest it hurt Sabrina, but Ruth is the one I favor." He looked at me, suddenly anxious. "I would not have you think ill of Ruth. She loves Sabrina, which is why Ruth wants me to release her, instead."

"Couldn't you release Sabrina?"

"I fear I must." He looked out over the road. "There are those in the pueblo who are beginning to wonder about us, especially since Sabrina shows no sign of re-marrying." He blinked his eyes and took a deep breath. "The only way I will release Sabrina is to a good husband, but then…" He swallowed. "I lose my children."

Sabrina had two little ones to Ruth's four. The children ranged in age from fourteen to eight, although I was hard-pressed to tell which child was whose. One would not think it, thanks to Mr. Lomax's laconic mien, but he was an exceptionally affectionate father and deeply loved his babes.

"Indeed." I sighed. "Yours is an incredibly difficult situation, I grant you. But I am confident that it is not an impossible one." I looked back at the adobe. "Give me some time. I am sure I can find some workable solution. Until then, best attend to Mrs. Ruth. She seems quite despondent, and I fear that she will languish rather than force you to put aside Mrs. Sabrina. Have her drink some beef tea as often as possible." I handed him the small pot of salve. "This is for the rash." I paused. There had to be a decent way to make my suggestion without embarrassing the poor man. "As her physician, it is my opinion that the salve will have the best effect if you apply it to her person yourself."

His eyes widened, then he coughed.

"Pray forgive me," I said softly. "But both you and Mrs. Ruth deserve your happiness, as does Mrs. Sabrina. There will be a way to manage this without bringing down condemnation and persecution on your heads."

He chuckled, clearly not believing me. "I am sure you will do everything you can, Mrs. Wilcox."

"I must. If not out of friendship to you, especially since your friendship has stood me in good stead numerous times, then out of concern for my patient."

Mr. Lomax helped me onto Daisy, and I rode off, convinced that there must be a simple solution to Mr. Lomax's problem. There was, but it was only revealed as a consequence of a most devastating loss.

Chapter Six

I slept little that night. There was so much to consider. I had heard the occasional rumor regarding the Lomax family, so I knew Mr. Lomax was right to be concerned about keeping Sabrina. But I could hardly fault him for not wanting to turn Sabrina's son and daughter over to another man.

Then there was Miss Julia Carson's death. If Lavina were correct in her assessment of the situation, and there was little reason to doubt it, then it was entirely probable that a man of exceptionally low character was preying upon the young women of the pueblo. He needed to be caught before any more young women sought Julia's solution to their problem and, consequently, met the same end.

Finally, there was the murder of Mama Jane. I was still quite put out with the official results of the inquest into her death. There had to have been a mistake made. Judge Gresham's prejudices may have made him blind to many things, yet he was not an imbecile, either. In addition, there was the testimony of Mr. Lomax and Mr. Navarro, who would have said something were His Honor to rule as had been recorded.

As I made my morning ablutions, I decided that after lunch, I would go visit the court to see what I could find, and perhaps, speak my mind to Judge Gresham. Alas, it was also Saturday, which would necessitate a costume in which I could appear in public with some decorum, but also not fear ruining with blood and other stains.

Saturdays in the pueblo were my most difficult day of the week. It was the day that wages were distributed, which meant that the saloons would be filled, which in turn meant that there would be fighting and other violence that I and my colleagues in the pueblo would be called upon to stitch up and otherwise care for the results of that violence. Knowing what was coming, I had come to take on lighter, more restful work on Saturday mornings, such as catching up on my notes from the week before and writing letters to my family in Boston.

I put on my brown riding habit and after the midday meal, made my way into the pueblo and into the Clocktower Courthouse. The clerks' office was a small room, filled with bookshelves and ledgers, and crammed with four wooden desks. A long counter ran from one side of the room to the other, with a small, gated gap nearest the room's door. Mr. Alverno worked busily at his desk, which was the closest to the counter. I would have waited until he noticed me to say something, but he seemed to make a point to utterly avoid noticing people, especially those who required his services.

"Good day, Mr. Alverno," I said, stepping up to the desk.

He held up his hand without looking up and continued writing.

"Mr. Alverno, you are obviously quite busy. However, I do need to speak to Judge Gresham as soon as possible."

"Next Monday," Mr. Alverno replied.

"Excuse me?"

He sighed and sucked on his front tooth. "Next Monday is as soon as it will be possible to speak with His Honor."

"I need to find out what happened at the inquest on Mama Jane," I said.

Mr. Alverno sucked on his tooth again. "I don't see why you're so concerned. You have nothing to do with her."

"She was a fellow human being. It is simple Christian charity."

"It was in the newspaper." He dipped his pen, then went back to his writing.

I left the courthouse feeling quite ill-used, indeed. Granted, Judge Gresham's treatment of the clerk was most cruel and decidedly un-Christian, and, as such, I should have had nothing but compassion for Mr. Alverno. However, I am afraid that in my pique, I couldn't help thinking that Mr. Alverno seemed to be determined to be as unlikeable as possible, and possibly deserved his rough treatment.

I spent the rest of the afternoon checking patients, bringing more salve for Mrs. Ruth, who still seemed quite unhappy, and another plaster for Arabella, whose condition continued to improve. Finally, as the clocktower struck five, I headed back to my rancho. I ate dinner quickly while Sebastiano got Daisy and the two mules saddled. Elena Ortiz would join me that night, as would Sebastiano.

However glad I was to have Elena's help, I knew that her aspirations to a medical profession greatly troubled her parents. I did not think that they were afraid that she would imitate my tendency to search out murderers, which usually resulted in said murderers trying to harm me. She didn't show the least inclination or interest in my investigations of such. Nor did I think they were that worried about her interests being less than womanly.

As it turned out, they were desperately afraid that she would never return to Los Angeles if she left to go to medical school. At the time, however, it seemed exceedingly unlikely that I would be able to arrange medical school. There was incredible prejudice against women who wished to become physicians (and, indeed, it has only gotten worse) that was only exacerbated when the woman in question was not an American. Or rather, not of English ancestry. Elena was as American as I was and had even been born well after California had become a state in the Union. But her name was Spanish, which meant she might as well have been a complete foreigner.

There were five other physicians in the pueblo at the time. One was Dr. Wang Fu, my former field hand. Being Chinese, he mostly served the remaining Chinese population in the pueblo and sold herbs to anyone who came to visit his shop on the Calle de los Negros, next to the plaza at the heart of the pueblo. Dr. Richardson and Dr. Hayward both had offices in various blocks of the pueblo and preferred that their patients visit them there. Dr. Hayward, in particular, devoted his time to the care of the sick, which usually meant he had less interest in the injured. Dr. Richardson also practiced surgery, as I did, but held no little disdain for me, especially as my favorable outcomes often outnumbered his.

The remaining three of us, Doc MacKenzie, Dr. Skillen, and me, were the most likely to be abroad on a Saturday night. With the help of the Sisters of Charity, who ran St. Vincent's Hospital, I had created a small room that could be easily sterilized. On Saturday nights, when it was more likely to be needed, I would stay at the hospital while Doc MacKenzie and Dr. Skillen ran about the pueblo as they were called, sending those who needed surgery to me. Elena either helped me or, accompanied by her father, went off to deliver any babies that required it.

It was a more chaotic Saturday night than usual. Elena and I hadn't even gotten to the hospital when I had to send her off to deliver Mrs. Lawrence's latest. When I arrived, there were two patients waiting for me who had been in a buggy accident. I would later operate on two bullet wounds, restore the nose (as best I could) of a fellow who'd been in a knife fight, and operate on an arm that had a compound fracture, the arm's owner having been struck by a chair in yet another fight. Fortunately, Elena returned in time to help me with the nose and the compound fracture.

We made it home very late. The clock in my parlor chimed three of the morning as I stumbled through the darkness to my chamber. Juanita was barely able to rouse me in time to dress me for church services that next morning. Elena overslept and missed hers. Both of us spent the day resting, although I did go out after lunch to check on my patients at the hospital. They were all doing as well as could be expected, with a minimum of infection and fever.

After supper, however, I got an urgent message from Mr. Gaines. I felt decidedly put out by the summons, but wearily gathered up my bag. I chose to walk, mostly because I could walk there in the same amount of time it would take to get Daisy saddled and myself changed into a riding dress. Mrs. Gaines was in the front parlor with a handkerchief to her eyes when I was admitted. Mr. Gaines paced nervously back and forth.

"Where are you hiding Lavina!" Mrs. Gaines snapped the second she saw me.

"Hiding?" I stepped back in shock. "I'm not hiding her. I haven't seen her since Friday morning."

"Lavina is missing," Mr. Gaines said. "She went for a walk before supper and never returned."

"Oh, dear."

"Then you must have arranged for her to meet that despicable Mr. Smith." Mrs. Gaines bounced to her feet.

"I did nothing of the sort." I frowned. "Have you tried speaking to him?"

The couple looked at each other, suddenly nervous.

"If it's any comfort, when I spoke with him on Friday, there seemed to be little indication that he planned on stealing Lavina away any time soon." I sighed. "Therefore, if you will trust me, I shall go find Mr. Smith and see if he knows anything."

"I'll come with you," Mr. Gaines said, and called for his hat and gloves.

We walked to the small house on the southern edge of the pueblo where Mr. Smith had a room. He was not in, but Mr. Gaines put up such a fuss that the landlady admitted us to Mr. Smith's room. It was neatly kept, and nothing appeared to be missing.

"It is as I thought," I said as Mr. Gaines and I left. "He wanted a house of his own to bring Lavina to, and he clearly does not have one yet."

"But where is she?" Mr. Gaines blustered.

I looked out at the street. The sun had begun its final descent toward the western horizon, and shadows gathered. Lavina's character was such that if she had made her escape, it was likely that she would have found a way to let her brother know. It worried me that there was no indication of such.

"It is possible that she met with some misadventure," I said slowly. "What time did she leave?"

Mr. Gaines gaped for a moment, trying to remember. "Right after four o'clock."

"Perhaps we should try to retrace her steps." I looked up and down the street. "Do you know where she liked to walk?"

It was hardly surprising, but Mr. Gaines had little notion of his sister's habits. So, we went back to their home, and I devised a plan that allowed us to search in an ordered fashion. Mrs. Gaines was no more help than her husband, which is why I asked her to remain at the house in case Lavina returned of her own accord.

As Mr. Gaines and I moved along the streets, the sky darkened, and the gas lamps came on. Mr. Navarro spotted us and approached us.

"Mrs. Wilcox, Mr. Gaines, why are you abroad?" the young policeman asked.

"We are looking for my sister," Mr. Gaines snapped. "She is missing."

"Miss Gaines went for a walk before supper and never

returned," I explained. "We want to be sure she hasn't come to some sort of grief."

"Of course," Mr. Navarro said. "Would you like some help? Let me see if I can get some of the other fellows to look, also."

"Do we need such a hue and cry?" Mr. Gaines asked, clearly troubled. "We do not know for certain that she's in trouble."

"It is possible that she's visiting Mr. Smith or someone else," I said. "However, he's not in his room."

"I'm right here," Mr. Smith said, coming up with an angry frown. "I was told that Mr. Gaines insisted on seeing my room because his sister is missing."

"Has anyone thought to check with Mr. and Mrs. Carson?" I asked. "Miss Gaines was quite friendly with Miss Julia. Perhaps she went to console the family and has been unable to leave or let anyone know."

Mr. Navarro took Mr. Smith to continue searching while Mr. Gaines and I went to the home of the Carsons. We were told quite firmly by their maid that no one in the house was receiving and that Miss Lavina was certainly not there.

Whether a hue and cry were appropriate or not, there shortly was one. Mr. Navarro had gotten two of his confederates on the police force to bring some lanterns, and the search went on. We'd covered almost every street of the pueblo, even Bath Street, which was infamous for its houses of ill-repute, and spread the search to some of the roads leading out of the pueblo. Out of breath, Mr. Gaines returned to his house to wait for news. Mr. Smith walked with me. Mr.

Navarro had found three other citizens to help him and the two policemen search.

Just after the clock tower had struck the hour of ten o'clock, we heard three gunshots echo. The sound of gunfire was all too common in the pueblo and seldom meant little besides potentially more work for me. Three shots in measured succession meant something else altogether. Mr. Smith and I looked back at the pueblo proper, sniffing the air.

"Smoke," I said softly, my heart skipping a beat.

A minute or so later, the clock tower bell pealed the alarm.

"I've got to go," Mr. Smith said. "I'm one of the volunteers."

We would not get a paid force for some years yet. But the twenty or so men that volunteered was remarkably proficient. Given the arid climate, fire was an especial danger, one that could destroy the entire pueblo, which I believe was the only reason why Mr. Smith abandoned our search.

I followed Mr. Smith back to the center of the pueblo. One of our medical dispensaries was on fire, with flames shooting through the roof. I knew the shop well, as I tended to procure as many of my supplies as I could from Mr. Cortez, the owner. He was a short, stout man, and I saw him gasping as he ran up from his house nearby.

The volunteers pulled the tank wagon up and went to work and put the fire out quite promptly. Numerous people in the pueblo had also turned out to see the excitement. As soon as the flames were extinguished, many of us helped get Mr. Cortez' stock from the ruined adobe and brought it to his house on the next street. I helped, and it was quite heartening that Mr. Cortez lost only one or two items. I sat with him and Mrs. Cortez for a time. After all, I had seen my own home demolished by a fire and knew well what they were going through.

Unfortunately, by the time I left, it was far too late to continue looking for Lavina. I did stop by the Gaines house to see if she had returned, and she had not. Mr. Smith, who had come with me after having been dismissed from his duty as a fireman, was beside himself.

"I am worried, too," I said. "But I simply cannot stay on my feet any longer. We both need to get some rest so that we can take up the search again at daybreak."

Mr. Smith had to concede the truth of my words but insisted on seeing me back to my rancho.

I slept, but poorly, so that it was no surprise that I overslept myself the next morning. I had barely gotten dressed and broken my fast when Mr. Lomax knocked on the door to my adobe.

He had the worst news possible. Lavina had been found.

Chapter Seven

Mr. Samples waited for us under the oak tree that hid Mama Jane's hut.

"Has she been disturbed?" I asked, forcing myself to keep my voice steady.

As much as I wanted to break down weeping, I knew I could not just then.

Mr. Samples shook his head. "Haven't touched her. I thought I saw something last night, but it weren't much. Then one of the childrens found her this morning. I saw Mr. Lomax coming from his place and asked him to stand witness."

It was a necessary precaution, given the appalling attitudes in the pueblo toward colored people.

"It was as he said," Mr. Lomax told me. "I went to see, and it's Miss Lavina. She's got marks on her throat."

I felt myself gasp for air, but immediately mastered myself again. If there were marks on Lavina's throat, then it was likely no accident.

I got out my pencil and notebook from my bag. Lavina lay

on her back, her hands crossed over her chest. It looked as though someone had tried to straighten her hair, as well, but bits of weed still clung to the soft brown curls. At that point, I could hold it no longer, and began to weep.

Still, it would not do to continue, so I stiffened my resolve yet again, and drew what I saw, even as the tears trickled down my cheeks.

"I must ask you gentlemen to forgive me for such an unseemly display." I swallowed down my grief as best I could.

Mr. Samples merely shrugged.

"It's understandable," Mr. Lomax said.

I looked at Mr. Samples. "You said you saw something last night. What did you see?"

"It were dark, so not much, but there was a fellow on a mule. He stayed there a while, and with Mama Jane gone, I had to wonder. When he rode off, I saw something white, looked like it was hanging off his saddle. I didn't think much about it, until one of the childrens found the girl and come running to get me."

"Sebastiano should be here shortly with the carretta. We'll take her to Mrs. Sutton's." I swallowed again. "I will see to informing Mr. Gaines."

I waited only long enough for Sebastiano to arrive, driving the cart we used to deliver barrels and bring back supplies and all manner of other chores. This was hardly the first time the carretta had been used to bring a corpse to the Suttons' funeral home.

My heart heavy, I rode back into the main part of the pueblo to the Gaines' home. I was admitted by the young Negro maid almost immediately and sent to the front parlor.

Mr. Gaines hurried into the room, with Mrs. Gaines on his heels.

"There is news?" Mr. Gaines asked, his face anxious and drawn.

"I'm afraid so, and it's not good," I said, swallowing back the grief that would not let me alone.

I explained about how Lavina had been found and that I had seen her. Mrs. Gaines burst into loud, dramatic sobbing as Mr. Gaines sank into a chair next to the room's fireplace.

"I'm afraid she came to a grave misadventure," I said softly. "There were the marks of an attack on her person."

"This is all your fault!" Mrs. Gaines shrieked. "You're the one who insisted that we let her walk about the pueblo. We wanted to keep her inside and safe. We were taking care of her!"

"You were keeping her prisoner!" I snapped back. "I assure you, Mrs. Gaines, no one was fooled by your determination to keep her mewed up and unmarried. Even in her period of mourning, she should have been allowed to keep some company. You denied her even that, even though you did not mind her visiting me or her friends while the will was being probated. As for Mr. Smith, your father gave his blessing to the courtship, and there was no reason to believe the old man was not of sound mind when he did. Perhaps if you had not been so insistent that she stay inside and away from people, she would have not felt the need to walk alone."

I heard Mr. Gaines gasp and checked him. He was breathing easily, even if his face was somewhat ash-colored. While that sometimes can be a sign of heart disease, in this case, it was likely grief. I took a deep breath, my ire spent for the moment. It was time to be more compassionate.

"Mrs. Gaines," I said slowly and quietly. "Pray forgive my harsh words. We are both shocked and angered by this terrible event. It will not do for us to blame each other. Whoever murdered Lavina is the one responsible for her death, not either of us."

"She is right, Mabel," Mr. Gaines said softly. He looked sadly at me. "Are you sure she died at the hands of another?"

"I'm afraid so." I blinked back the tears that came to my eyes. This was no time for such a display. "But I assure you, Mr. Gaines, I will find out who did the terrible deed and see that justice is done."

He nodded. "Of course."

Mrs. Gaines let out another wail, and I got up from the sofa where I had landed.

"I can see myself out," I said softly. "Please accept my deepest condolences on your loss."

Mrs. Gaines ignored me and continued wailing. Mr. Gaines nodded. The maid showed me to the door.

I went straight to the Suttons' home and funeral parlor. Angelina was waiting for me and took me to her little parlor in the back, next to the workroom. There, she held me as I sobbed. We had spent many an hour in the little room in pleasant discourse, in conference while searching out some villain, or occasionally, holding each other in our respective grieving, although it seemed like Angelina was more likely to be holding me in mine.

Nonetheless, the opportunity to shed my tears did me no

end of good. It took some minutes, but I was eventually able to come to a more sensible mien and apply myself to the more immediate concern, namely the state of Lavina's body.

"Have you been able to deduce anything?" I asked Angelina as I dried my tears.

"Not much." Angelina shrugged. "Her dress is mostly whole, although there is one spot where some lace was torn off."

"That lovely one with the black jet beads." I swallowed at the memory.

"Yes." Angelina showed me her notebook. "If we find it, depending on where, it might help us. As for the body, she is still in full rigor mortis, so she died sometime within the past twenty-four hours, at least."

"We know she left her home around three o'clock yesterday to go on a walk," I said.

Angelina sighed. "That should help. When her body relaxes, that might give us a better idea of when she died." She paused. "There is one other issue. She was not wearing any pantaloons."

"What?" I frowned, thinking back to every instance in which I'd seen Lavina.

"It is possible that she didn't wear them as a matter of course."

"No. I'm fairly certain that she did." I shook my head. "In fact, I know she did. We had an extended conversation last spring about what to do when her courses ran heavy and stained them. She was worried because her new sister-in-law took issue with the situation and berated her rather soundly because of it."

Angelina's snort was less than lady-like. "What a miserable woman! How did she come to be here?"

The young Mrs. Gaines had earned Angelina's ire when the senior Mr. Gaines had died. Not only had the woman insisted on directing all of the arrangements for the funeral, but when Mr. Sutton presented the bill, she questioned every item on it.

"As I understand it, she is from San Francisco, was presented to Mr. Gaines through his cousins, and he wooed her through the mails and a few visits." I let out a sniff. "Well, I suppose I should examine..." I could not help but choke. "Lavina now."

I got out my handkerchief, finished drying my eyes, and followed Angelina to the workroom. Alas, seeing the cold, still form almost brought on still more tears. Angelina had covered the body with a sheet.

I took a deep breath. "Her pantaloons are missing?"

"It seems odd." Angelina frowned as if trying to remember something. "And I do believe there is a significance to it, as well."

I couldn't help shuddering. "We have reason to believe that there is a most evil man here in the pueblo who has forced himself on at least one young woman. I cannot help but wonder if Lavina came to grief at his hands."

Steeling myself, I pulled back the sheet and examined the body. It did not take long, and I found little amiss that I hadn't already seen.

"There is some good news." I sighed as I replaced the sheet over Lavina's form. "She was not breached." I frowned. "However, that makes little sense if the man who attacked her is the same fellow who accosted Miss Julia. But then, how is that he went no further than removing her pantaloons and did not complete his attack?"

"Perhaps the villain faced being seen if he continued his evil activity," Angelina said.

"And how would he have had a chance to strangle her, unless he did the killing before trying to..."

I swallowed. The ensuing thought was utterly unpalatable.

"That is vile," said Angelina, her voice surprisingly casual for such a disgusting subject. "But if he was that type of villain, and assuming it was he who forced himself on Miss Julia, why did he not attempt to kill Julia?"

"I have no idea," I said.

"Ah, but I have just remembered." Angelina pressed her lips together, then spoke. "I saw it once when we lived in Santa Barbara. A man had killed several women over the course of a year or so, and each time, he took some piece of the woman's clothing, mostly a petticoat, and kept those items in his adobe. What if we have a similar villain? What if Miss Lavina was strangled, then the killer took her pantaloons to keep for some reason?"

I closed my eyes. "What kind of monster are we dealing with?"

"A most terrible one, it would seem." Angelina frowned. "It would stand to reason that someone this monstrous should be fairly easy to find."

"And yet, we know that terrible people can and do hide in plain sight," I said. "And that their depravity is not necessarily visible to the eye."

"This, alas, is all too true." Angelina tapped her fingers on a nearby table. "Is it time to make a list?"

"In all probability," I said. "However, I haven't any idea who to put on it. Almost any man in the pueblo could be the attacker."

Angelina smiled sadly. "Maddie, you are obviously too perturbed at present to be thinking at your best. Give yourself a little time."

"I do hope we have it," I said, quite sourly.

However, Angelina was quite right in that I was too perturbed to be thinking with my usual clarity. I also had patients to tend to.

I made my way from the funeral home and went back to my ranch. There, Olivia had ready for me a soothing cup of warm milk liberally dosed with chocolate and cinnamon. I was better able to go about my business after my lunch and spent the afternoon occupying myself with rancho chores and visiting my patients.

It was a good thing that I had gone on my rounds. I missed another demand from Judge Gresham that I appear in his chambers immediately. I was not in any frame of mind to deal with His Honor and was quite glad that the judge resorted to sending me a note with a messenger boy.

My observations were once again needed in the case of Lavina Gaines. That was, at least what the judge claimed. I suppose that in Christian charity, I should have taken His Honor at his word, but after the inquest for Mama Jane, and in my immediate distress over Lavina, I was not as disposed to charity as I would have wanted.

Nonetheless, the clock tower was striking nine that next morning as I tied Daisy up outside the Sutton house. Both Angelina and Mr. Sutton awaited me in the workroom. I was glad to see Mr. Sutton there. I had formerly found him a dour fellow, but eventually realized that I had misjudged him. He was a short, almost stout man, with graying brown hair and whiskers. His mien was unusually somber, which, while appropriate to his calling, was in direct contrast to his wife's merrier nature. I hoped his presence that morning would lend weight to Angelina's and my observations. I knew that Mr. Sutton was in agreement with us, but with Judge Gresham, one never knew.

Three of the jury arrived before His Honor did, with Mr. Alverno in tow. The rest of the jury crowded into the room over the next several minutes. We uncovered Lavina's body, which had finally relaxed. I pointed out the bruises on the corpse's throat.

"They are the same as was found on Mama Jane," I said, glaring at Judge Gresham. "This was no more an accident than was Mama Jane's death. We have a killer on the loose in the pueblo again."

Given the violence that regularly visited the pueblo at that time, that was perhaps a bit dramatic, but I wished to make as strong an impression as I could.

"That much seems obvious," His Honor replied with great disdain. He looked at Mr. Sutton. "And it is your opinion that it was the same man who killed both?"

"It is," said Mr. Sutton. "See the drawings that Mrs. Wilcox made? The bruising is very similar."

"Perhaps if Mama Jane's death had been ruled a murder, we would have found this villain before Miss Gaines came to grief," I said, my arms crossed.

Judge Gresham sputtered. "But it was ruled a murder by person unknown."

"That was not what I read in the newspaper the next day," I said.

"Bah! They got it wrong yet again." Judge Gresham nodded at the rest of the jury. "We will hear the rest of the evidence in my courtroom. Come along."

"Oh," I said softly. It would hardly have been the first time our newspapers had published an incorrect version of an incident in the pueblo.

As the group of men filed out of the workroom, I debated following. I would have liked to hear the actual ruling, but since Mr. Sutton would be there and was likely to relate the proceedings accurately, including the missing pantaloons, I decided not to go. I would not likely be allowed to testify because of my sex, which was utterly vexing but couldn't be helped. Women generally weren't allowed to testify unless there was absolutely no one else and if they were not testifying against an American man, even then it would be unlikely.

Mr. Alverno paused for a moment, gazing at Lavina's body with an odd look on his face.

"Mr. Alverno?" I asked.

"You have no idea how put upon I am," he said, his voice so quiet I could barely hear it. "If it's not the judges, then it's everyone else who wants to know the status of their case, when they'll need to appear, summoning people who have no wish to appear. It's terribly demanding." He sighed. "However, Miss Gaines was… quite special. She was always kind, never demanded anything. It is such a tragedy."

He left and I helped Angelina prepare Lavina's body for the viewing that night. There was not much else to do. Mr. Sutton returned in time for lunch, to which I was invited. I accepted, sending a note to Olivia with the Suttons' errand boy and general helper, a Chinese lad named Tai Chin.

"Well, it isn't much," Mr. Sutton told us as we settled down to our meal. "But there is some good news. His Honor ruled the death a murder by person unknown. However, he is of the opinion that Mr. Timothy Gaines should be looked at more carefully."

"Mr. Gaines?" Angelina shook her head. "I suppose that might be, but why would he have murdered Mama Jane?"

Mr. Sutton chewed thoughtfully before answering. "His Honor thought it could be that Mr. Gaines wished to be sure he knew how to do such a thing before attempting to do so on his sister."

"That hardly makes sense," I said, allowing my disdain to flow freely. "In the first place, I have seen no sign from him that he held any particular rancor for Lavina. And in the second, there are so many easier ways to kill someone, why would he strangle her and, before that, practice on someone else to be sure he could? If he or his odious wife truly wanted to be rid of Lavina, it would have made a great deal more sense to have poisoned her. She would have died with almost no one the wiser because poison is so hard to detect."

"Nor does it make sense that her brother would have taken her nether garment," Angelina said.

"This also is true," I said. "Finally, what good would it have done Mr. Gaines to kill his sister? He certainly didn't need to. The way her trust was set up, he could have not only held onto it for the rest of her life but profited from it with no one the wiser. Perhaps a little suspicious in that one could reasonably ask why he never released it, but he could have found any number of excuses not to hand it over to her."

"At least, His Honor is willing to look into the matter," Mr. Sutton said.

"Of course." I couldn't help snorting. "Lavina was an American. Mama Jane was only an Indian."

Angelina and her husband looked at each other. They well knew my opinion of such ridiculous prejudices, and I like to believe, shared that opinion.

We had barely finished our meal when a young lad whose name I never learned knocked at the back door and asked for me. He belonged to the rather large Garcia family. The problem was yet another case of the measles. When I arrived at the Garcia's adobe, the lad's young brother looked to be having complications from it. The child was barely four years old and when I listened to his lungs through my stethoscope, he definitely had some pneumonia. I ordered beef tea and warm milk with spirits, leaving behind some angelica to that end. I also made a plaster to help with the child's breathing and promised to return the next day with a fresh one. The child's mother agreed to keep cooling compresses on the child. After that, we could but hope.

My spirits were quite low as I rode Daisy back to Rancho de las Flores, arriving there in good time for supper.

Soon after we'd eaten, I once again put on my ochre

visiting dress. Sebastiano drove me in the buggy to the viewing for Lavina. It was a terribly sad affair, and I confess I spent a fair amount of time dabbing at my eyes with my handkerchief. Mrs. Gaines, however, remained remarkably dry-eyed, even as she looked daggers at me more than once. Mr. Gaines was also stoic in the face of the loss of his sister, but there was less to be made of that.

Chapter Eight

The next morning was Lavina's funeral. The Gaines family were members of the Methodist congregation in the pueblo, and Reverend Miller led the services, first at the Gaines' home, then at the cemetery. The morning was cool and clouded over, as usual for that time of year, but it felt particularly apt as we gathered around the grave site.

I was a little surprised to see Mr. Alverno among the mourners. He seemed quite bereft, and if it was true what he had told me about Lavina being kind to him when no one else was, then it would make sense that he would be.

As we walked from the cemetery, I sought out Mr. Smith. The poor man looked utterly devastated.

"I share your grief," I said softly to him as we fell into step together.

"I know, Mrs. Wilcox." He swallowed and blinked his eyes. "You are kind to say so when you are just as grieved."

Mr. Alverno came up at that point. "Good day, Mr. Smith. How are you faring?"

"As can be expected," Mr. Smith said, looking at the smaller man with no little suspicion.

"Indeed," I said quickly. "We are all grieved by Miss Gaines' passing. Especially you, Mr. Smith, given your understanding with her."

Mr. Smith nodded. "Yes. My heart is quite broken."

"I heard you'd been meeting illicitly with her," Mr. Alverno sucked on his tooth.

"Mr. Alverno!" I snapped in spite of myself. Still, I looked at Mr. Smith.

"No, Mrs. Wilcox," he said softly. "It's quite alright. I had been meeting Miss Gaines in the afternoons close to four-thirty when she took her walks. It was the only time we could see each other." He stopped to catch his breath and blink his eyes. "In fact, when I met you that Sunday night, I'd been out looking for her. We had the usual assignation, but she never came. She wasn't at home, so I went looking for her immediately, fearing she'd come to some—" He choked.

"I don't doubt it," I said, swallowing back my own grief.

Mr. Smith shook his head. "How did this come to pass? Who could have done such a terrible thing?"

"I am trying to find out," I said.

"You are?" Mr. Alverno asked.

"Of course, she is," Mr. Smith said, drawing himself up. "Don't you remember how determined she was last fall when her field hands were killed? She found that killer, and they were only—" He paused and saw the glare on my face. He was about to remark that my two field hands were only Chinese, as one so commonly did. Fortunately, Mr. Smith obviously realized that I would take umbrage if he made such a remark and stopped himself in time. "Only field hands."

"Still, I liked to call them friends," I said. "And, yes, Miss Gaines was particularly dear to me."

"We must find her killer," said Mr. Smith, his face growing hard and determined. "I will do everything I can to help."

"As will I," said Mr. Alverno.

"Then I will be glad to have your help," I said, even though I seriously doubted that Mr. Alverno would be of much use. "I will need it. There is a potentially more dire reason that the killer must be caught. The truly difficult part is that the killer might not have had any obvious reason for attacking Miss Gaines, specifically."

"But there was someone who might have had a reason to harm Lavina," Mr. Smith said. "My former partner, Mr. Lyons."

"How so?" I asked.

"He blamed Lavina for the loss of our partnership," Mr. Smith said. "We were going to buy land for a rancho and raise cattle, maybe some sheep. Only after I met Lavina last winter, I didn't want to make her a farmer's wife, so I started working with Mr. Gaines to become a land agent. Mr. Lyons was quite enraged."

"I shall have to speak to Mr. Lyons, then," I said. I looked at Mr. Smith. "Do you know where he resides?"

"He has a room with Mrs. Davies, I believe," Mr. Smith said.

"Thank you, Mr. Smith," I replied, then sighed. "I must get back to my rancho as I have other chores to complete, so I shall wish you gentlemen good day."

I walked off, wanting to spend some time alone with my thoughts. I conceded to myself that if Mr. Lyons had been so ill-disposed toward Lavina, it made sense that he'd strangled her in a fit of rage, rather than shooting or poisoning her. It was also an observation that applied to anyone who might be the killer. Whether that would be a useful observation remained to be seen.

Once home, I changed into a riding habit, then gathered my bag, and mounted Daisy. I had to bring a fresh plaster to the Garcia boy, not to mention check on Arabella and Ruth. I had barely completed these errands when Damiano, Sebastiano and Olivia's second youngest child, came running from the center of the pueblo. He was a solid lad with earnest brown eyes and black hair that was usually in disarray. Like his father and uncle, he had broad shoulders, and at the tender age of fourteen, was just starting to grow into manhood.

"Mrs. Wilcox!" he called. He addressed me by my surname, as did all of the children on the rancho, even those who had left childhood behind and were adults.

"Yes, Damiano," I said.

"Mr. Gaines needs to see you." Damiano gasped a little from his run, then swallowed. "His boy said it was extremely urgent."

I tried not to show my disdain. "I shall make my way there now. Thank you for finding me so promptly."

"Can I follow you?" He looked exceptionally hopeful.

"Don't you have work to do?" I asked, as severely as I could.

Damiano shrugged. "I've been weeding in the vineyards all day. Tio Enrique won't let me weed anywhere else. He says I pull up the wrong plants."

"Perhaps you need to work harder on your study of botany."

"Oh, I know what plants are what. I just get bored and don't pay attention to what I'm pulling." He graced me with a most winning smile.

Sebastiano's two sons were exceedingly charming. His eldest, Reuben, had broken numerous hearts in the pueblo. Damiano seemed to be destined to do the same, especially since he had aspirations to the priesthood and would start at St. Vincent's College the following fall.

"Very well. Perhaps a small break is in order."

I walked Daisy to the Gaines' home and let Damiano hold her while I went inside.

Mr. and Mrs. Gaines were in the front parlor. Mr. Gaines struggled up from the big chair next to the fireplace as Mrs. Gaines paced.

"Finally!" she snorted as I entered the room.

"I came as soon as I was able," I replied evenly.

"What if my poor husband were gravely sick?" Mrs. Gaines snapped. "He could have died waiting for you!"

I glared at her. "Such would have been possible no matter how quickly I arrived. However, he looks hale enough to me now."

"In body, I am," said Mr. Gaines. "Please, sit down, Mrs. Wilcox. The situation is dire, but it is not an issue of my health."

I settled myself on the couch and waited while Mr. Gaines sat back down in the chair. His wife continued to pace.

"This is your fault," Mrs. Gaines snapped. "It was bad enough you encouraged dear Lavina to put herself in mortal danger, but now, thanks to you, my darling husband is facing the worst scrutiny."

"Mabel, please," Mr. Gaines shot his wife a glare, then sighed and looked at me. "I am under suspicion of doing my sister harm. It appears that Judge Gresham believes that I killed her."

"As I have been given to understand."

"Why on earth would you have put my darling husband under such suspicion?" Mrs. Gaines shrieked.

I stood and faced her. "I did nothing of the sort! His Honor came to that conclusion entirely on his own. Perhaps if your darling husband had not been so insistent on taking control of Lavina's inheritance, then His Honor might have had less reason to suspect Mr. Gaines of causing his sister's death."

Mr. Gaines gaped. "I was trying to protect her."

"And conveniently profit from that protection at the same time." I turned on him. "I assure you, Mr. Gaines, you have fooled no one. It is your good fortune, however, that your greed is what saves you now. With full control of your sister's inheritance, you had no reason to kill her."

"Unless he no longer wished to see to her care," sniffed Mrs. Gaines. "Or is supposed to have no longer wished to."

I tried to bite my tongue, but it was no use. "Or perhaps you no longer wished to. Perhaps Lavina put you into a rage, and you killed her after killing Mama Jane for no reason."

"Who?" Mr. Gaines asked as his wife gaped like a fish in a net.

"I— I— I did no such thing!" Mrs. Gaines had the good grace to sink onto the couch, putting her handkerchief to her mouth.

"Nonetheless, you were not the kindest of sisters," I said. "You kept her practically locked up like a prisoner, and I never saw you extend even the least tenderness or affection to her. Lavina, bless her, was not the sort to complain even under the worst treatment." I glanced over at her brother in accusation. "I know full well what she endured under her father, and also from the younger Mr. Gaines, because I saw it. I am glad that the senior Mr. Gaines had the decency to ask his daughter for her forgiveness before he passed away, so that she had some memory of kindness from her father."

"But I didn't hurt her," Mrs. Gaines sobbed. "There may have been a few cruel words, which I utterly rue, mind you. But I never even touched her, let alone, slapped or pinched. And I certainly did not kill her. Or that other... Who did you say?"

"Mama Jane."

Mrs. Gaines' mouth opened and closed as she tried to form words.

"I have no idea who that is," she said, finally. "Lavina's former nurse maid? Why would I kill her?"

"There is no reason that makes sense," I said softly. "It does not mitigate your cruel treatment and disregard for Lavina. But it does mean neither of you are likely to have killed her."

Mr. Gaines heaved an enormous sigh of relief. "At least, you believe us." He swallowed and looked up at me, his eyes pleading. "Mrs. Wilcox, you must help us. You are known for having found killers before. Can you please find Lavina's killer? If you do not, I am afraid I shall have to leave the pueblo, my reputation utterly destroyed. And I shall have no place to go with such a shadow hanging over me."

"Nonsense," I let out a most unladylike snort. "There are a great many places you can go with no one the wiser about your past. That is why people come here. I shouldn't like to think what your father did before coming here, or any number of people we now call respectable citizens." I took a deep breath. "In any case, I am already looking for Lavina's killer, and for reasons that have nothing to do with either of you. I might add, that while I find it unlikely that you did the deed, it does not mean that I have completely absolved you of it. Good day. I can show myself out."

I left the house feeling exceptionally out of sorts. Damiano laughed when he saw me.

"And what do you find so amusing, young man?" I said, folding my arms across my chest.

"You are angry," he said, his grin utterly unrepentent. "That means we are going to have another adventure."

"Which means you are not going to accompany me. I do not wish to risk the neck of one of such tender years."

Damiano laughed even harder and helped me into my saddle.

"I'm not so tender," he announced. "I am almost fifteen years old."

Indeed, the boy was fully as tall as I, and from the size of his hands, was likely to grow still taller.

"That you are." I couldn't help smiling down at him. "However, your father and uncle will be most put out with me if I allow you to shirk your chores."

"I think they'd rather I followed you. That way, I'm not pulling up the wrong plants."

"Indeed." I smiled softly at the youth, then focused my attention on where I should go next.

I decided to seek out Mrs. Davies and her boarder, Mr. Lyons. Mrs. Davies was a fairly young widow with dark black hair and deep brown eyes. She had four little ones, all under the age of six. Her husband had been the rare exception of a prudent miner who had come to the legendary gold fields, found a small fortune, and left with most of it, coming to Los Angeles sometime before the War. He'd buried one wife before marrying the young Miss Carranza. Fortunately, he'd left her a large house for hers and the children's keeping, and Mrs. Davies usually had three or four men boarding with her at any given time.

She was not happy to hear that I wished to speak with Mr. Lyons.

"If you wish to speak with him, that means he's either got some unspeakable disease or he's about to be in trouble."

"I speak with a great many people in neither circumstance," I said in my own defense.

"But you are looking for another killer," Mrs. Davies said. "It's all over the pueblo that you are."

I sighed. "I cannot say that isn't true. However, when I am looking for a killer, it has been my experience that the vast majority of the people I ask questions of are, in fact, innocent. I have no strong reason to suspect Mr. Lyons of ill-behavior, but how will I know for sure unless I ask him?"

"Well, he's not here." Her eyes flashed in annoyance. "He is working as a manufacturer's agent and has taken a load of something or other up to San Francisco for sale."

"When did he leave?"

"Which time?" She shrugged. "I have no idea. He comes and goes. He paid for his rent through the end of June before he left sometime last month. So he'll still have a room when he returns."

"He sounds very honorable."

"Honorable?" She laughed bitterly. "He is no better nor no worse than most fellows I take in. I insist on taking the rent in advance if a boarder is going away. I must. My first year, I lost several months' rent when the boarder took off, swearing he was going to return, and never came back. Mr. Lyons lost his first room when he went on a trip and returned after the rent was due. He swore never to do it again and has kept his word."

"Well, thank you for the intelligence, Mrs. Davies. And how are your children?"

She rolled her eyes. "They all have the measles but seem to be faring well."

"Would you like me to look at them?"

She hesitated. "I cannot pay you, and they are not seriously ill."

"You have already paid me by answering my questions." I smiled at her.

She blinked and nodded. I could see that she was a proud woman, but worried enough about her four daughters to accept charity. I didn't mind offering it. She was, after all, a widow, and our Good Lord is most concerned with the care of widows and orphans.

Fortunately, she was right. Even the little girl of two-years-old was managing quite nicely, although she was a little restless.

"As difficult as it is to manage this stage, it is a good sign," I told Mrs. Davies. "It means that she is recovering. But she needs to stay quiet a while longer until she has her full strength back, or she may sicken." I held up my hand in advance of her protest. "I understand. That will not be easy. Why not have her oldest sister play with her or recite lessons to her? It will help your oldest when she returns to school and the infant might find it interesting."

"It's worth trying." Mrs. Davies sighed. "Thank you, Mrs. Wilcox."

I left promptly so as not to burden the woman further. It was no easy thing to keep house and cook for three to four men while caring for four sick little children. I did not wonder that she had not thought of the obvious ploy of getting the elder children to entertain the younger ones.

Upon leaving the boarding house, I sent Damiano on ahead to the rancho to let Olivia know that I was on my way and would not be late for supper, barring another call.

It was a rather normal evening. We ate in the courtyard, as the weather was still warm. Anita and I listened to the younger children as they recited their lessons, then I retired to my study to update my journal.

The next morning, I again donned my brown riding habit. I did have an errand that I wished to embark upon, and patients to visit. Rodolfo had Daisy already saddled by the time I had broken my fast and helped me mount her.

I trotted Daisy toward the center of the pueblo more for

the fun of trotting than any real need to go quickly. Alas, as I neared Alameda Street, I nearly ran over Mr. Alverno. He tumbled as he scrambled away. I reined Daisy in and dismounted.

"My apologies, Mr. Alverno!" I gasped as he slowly got up. "I did not see you. Are you injured?"

He began dusting himself off. "I do not believe so."

"Oh, thank Heaven! I cannot say how sorry I am."

"It is of no consequence," he said with a vaguely affronted air. "I was coming to seek you out."

"Is there someone at the courthouse who needs me?"

"No. Not this time." Mr. Alverno sucked on his tooth with an air of contemplation rather than annoyance for a change. "I was thinking yesterday about the people who might have cause to kill Miss Gaines. Is it possible that Judge Gresham might be one of them?"

"Judge Gresham?" I made a face. "Why would he have done so?"

"I don't know. But there was that false report in the newspaper. Perhaps His Honor misled the newspaperman in an effort to misdirect you or anyone else about the affair. And he is most adamant that Mr. Timothy Gaines was responsible when we both know there are others who could have done the deed."

"That's quite true," I said thoughtfully. "Well, Mr. Alverno, it is quite kind of you to tell me. Will you be so good as to keep watch on His Honor and let me know if you see any unusual behavior?"

"Of course." The small man smiled and lifted his chest. "It is so kind of you to consider my information seriously."

I must confess, I felt somewhat abashed at that, as I'd had no intention of considering him seriously.

"There is no reason not to," I replied, nonetheless. "And I'll thank you for telling me whatever you find."

He smiled again, and I glanced at my horse. Oddly, he made no offer to help me into my saddle but hurried off back toward the courthouse. It was no matter. I could mount a horse perfectly well on my own. It was simply common courtesy for a man to offer to help me. That Mr. Alverno didn't do so only proved that courtesy had little to do with his offer to help me. Or perhaps, he, who knew so little of courtesy from those around him, had no concept of how to offer it himself. It didn't matter, I told myself, then mounted Daisy and pointed her toward the Plaza.

Chapter Nine

My first stop was at a small adobe on the Plaza end of the Calle de los Negros. The small street housed much of the Chinese population in the pueblo and had been devastated by the riot the previous fall. Still, much of it had been rebuilt, and the small storefront I entered smelled of fresh whitewash.

A wooden counter bisected the room, with an opening at the end. A table and two chairs had been placed in a corner next to the front window. Shelves lined the walls, filled with jars of all sorts, each labeled with the curious characters the Chinese used for their writing. Behind the counter, two oaken chests with dozens of tiny drawers filled the wall on either side of a desk loaded with a scale and other implements necessary for the preparation of herbs and other medicaments.

Two American men were waiting as Wang Fu finished preparing some herbs at the desk. After Dr. Gene Tong had been lynched in that horrible riot, Dr. Wang took over the medical practice that had been left behind, as well he should have. Not only had Dr. Wang been trained as a physician in his native China, he was quite an effective herbologist. We had become fast friends, and the two of us frequently challenged each other over our preferred treatments.

Dr. Wang had cut his queue that winter. It was the custom of the men in China to shave the front of their heads and wear the remaining hair braided into a long queue down their backs. As most of the Chinese who had come to America planned to return to their homeland, they kept their queues. It would be impossible to live in China without them. I did not know the entire circumstances, but Dr. Wang's family had been dishonored and he could not return home. He'd always worn Western clothes on the rancho when he'd worked for me. Now, with his new medical practice doing rather well, he decided to be more approachable for the Americans, and not only wore an American-style suit, he'd let the hair over his forehead grow and kept it cut in the American style. He was not much taller than me, and his hair was dark black, as were his eyes.

I waited patiently while he finished with the two men. Dr. Wang waited to greet me until the men had left the shop.

"Good day, Maddie," he said with a smile. We had achieved the easy familiarity of dear friends.

"It's good to see you, Fu," I replied. The Chinese have the habit of using their family names first, then their given names. "I am running low on willow bark again."

"Ah," he grunted. "The measles."

"Indeed. I hope not too many of your countrymen have been infected."

He shrugged. "There are some, but no one has died yet."

"And have you found anything that works against it?"

"No. Just the salve that I gave you for the rash."

"And I need more of that, too." I put my hand to my forehead. "Thank you for reminding me."

Dr. Wang grew even more solemn. "Maddie, I have question for you. It is difficult, but it is about your friend Miss Gaines. I know she was murdered."

"I'm afraid so," I said.

"And you are looking for her killer." He nodded. "I do not know if it's important, but a week or two before she was killed, she came to my shop. She described her condition as being difficult." He swallowed. "As in with child."

"And you have herbs that will relieve a young woman of that condition."

"I cannot keep them," he said. "The prejudices here are too harsh. But there are those who believe I do and seek them out. I do not wish you to think ill of Miss Gaines, because she was not with child. My guess is that she wanted the herbs for a friend."

"Oh, dear. I believe I know which friend." I frowned.

"Could it be that the friend who needed the herbs told Miss Gaines the name of the person who caused her problem? If so, is that possibly why she was killed?"

I thought about it. "Fu, you are absolutely right. It is entirely possible that is why Miss Gaines was killed. Thank you for telling me."

He smiled. "It is better when I do." He shrugged. "And I do hear things. After all, there are those who do not think I understand them and speak freely around me."

I caught my breath. "Fu, I have reason to believe that

there is a man in the pueblo who is forcing himself on young women and may have been the source of the problem Miss Gaines' friend had."

"There is probably more than one," Dr. Wang sighed.

"My problem is Miss Gaines did not know who that man is, and thus could not tell me. If you hear anything, it is of the utmost importance that you let me know at once. There appears to be a monster loose in the pueblo, and he must be stopped."

"I will let you know."

After that, Dr. Wang fetched me the supplies I required and I bought some others, as well.

After tending to my patients, I still had an hour or so before lunch, so I trotted Daisy out to the small hut where Mama Jane had died, and Lavina had been found. There was that bit of lace that had been torn from Lavina's dress. Angelina had been right when she'd said that it might present a clue as to who had killed Lavina. I hadn't recalled seeing the lace anywhere near where Lavina had been found, but I hadn't really looked, either.

I tied Daisy in the oak tree again and scoured the ground around the hut and under the tree.

"Hello!" a voice called from the road.

I left the shelter of the tree and saw Mr. Navarro riding his horse toward me from the south. The road where the Samples and Lomax farms met wound down that way toward the Lawrence family home and other farms.

"Good day, Mr. Navarro," I said, forcing a smile onto my face.

"What are you doing out here?" he asked as he dismounted and tied up his horse next to mine.

"Looking for something," I said simply.

Laughing, he came up to me and made free with my person.

That he felt free to do so was not, I blush to disclose, entirely unwarranted. We had formed an understanding, of sorts. However, his family had decreed that it was time for him to marry, so that he could join his father in managing their extended rancho and other holdings, and I had, and still have, no use for a husband. We had ended our understanding on cordial terms, nor had I been concerned about his fickle heart and intemperate behavior until he'd cast his eyes on my darling Juanita. Which is the reason I slapped him with all the force I could muster.

He yelped in pain and grabbed his cheek. "Maddie! What did you do that for?"

"Why do you think, you intemperate rogue?"

"There's no one around, and we're well hidden."

"And what about Miss Alvarez? Do you honestly expect me to believe that you have reformed when you accost me in this way?"

"I have reformed." He pouted.

"You have a fine way of showing it."

"Until Miss Alvarez accepts my suit, who's to care if I take a small liberty or two with a friend?"

"I care." I glared at him. "How is Miss Alvarez to trust you when you behave this way when she's not around?"

"Oh, she'll be able to trust me." He laughed. "You know

what a temper she has, and I don't want to get hurt. Or you'll find out and perform a most indelicate surgery on me."

I crossed my arms. "I most certainly will, and without benefit of ether."

He had the grace to look a little worried. "So, what are you looking for?"

"Something that may have been left behind when Miss Gaines was left here." I went back to my search, wondering what I should tell him.

I do not know if I genuinely did not suspect him of the two murders or of forcing himself on young women, or if I did not wish to believe that he could be our monster. Either way, I still thought it best to tell him as little as possible.

There was nothing on the ground to find, so I made my way to the little hut. But before I entered it, I turned on Mr. Navarro.

"You said you came out here for a love charm."

Mr. Navarro flushed. "Yes, but we both agreed it was a fool's errand."

"How did you know that Mama Jane had returned to the pueblo?"

"Father Gallar told me." Mr. Navarro rolled his eyes. "Well, he wasn't sure that Mama Jane had come back. He'd just heard the rumors. But he asked me to find out if she had, then see to it that she left again. I came out here because, well, I liked Mama Jane." His eyes suddenly began blinking. "She was always good to me, gave me sweets when I was little." He looked out at the road beyond the oak tree. "She was good to talk to. I told her about Juanita, and she decided to make the love charm for me. She told me it wouldn't work if my heart wasn't true to Juanita. She'd just sold one to someone else whose heart was black, but she needed the money." Mr. Navarro looked down at his feet. "I gave her some bread and dried meat that I had in my saddle bag."

"Then why did you lie to Mr. Lomax?"

He looked at me. "Maddie, I know you think I'm a rogue and that I trifle callously with the hearts of women. I don't really. I tease a little, but it's all in good fun."

"Until you break the heart of a sweet young woman who doesn't know the difference between teasing and serious intent." I looked at him severely but couldn't help my heart softening.

He did look a little abashed. "I don't mean to confuse them."

"And Mr. Lomax?"

"He's another policeman, like me. We have to be strong, tough men. It's not easy keeping the peace in a town like this. You constantly have to prove yourself. You can either make people afraid of you or get a reputation with the ladies." He gazed over at the Lomax farm. "Lots of people are afraid of Mr. Lomax. I'm not. But I'm not going to share my finer feelings with him. I need him to respect me, like I respect him. So, when he asked why I was visiting Mama Jane, I lied, just as I told you the other day. It seemed easier than saying why I was really here."

"And why are you here now?"

"I saw you." He chuckled as I looked at him. "I was coming from the Lawrence place. One of their little ones had wandered off and I'd found her."

The Lawrence family was quite blessed with a large

number of children, most of whom survived well into adulthood. Their eighth child was approximately eighteen months old, and the ninth had arrived only the Saturday before.

"Well, if you would be so good, I'd prefer to finish my inspection on my own," I told Mr. Navarro.

He smiled and bid me good day. I waited to enter the hut until he'd gotten on his horse. I searched along the walls and through the bed clothes left behind but found nothing.

I returned to my rancho feeling quite perplexed. There were several chores waiting for me after we ate our mid-day meal, so I focused on those in the hopes that an answer would come while I was otherwise occupied. Not that we had any inkling then of Dr. Freud's concept of the subconcious, but it did seem to often work that way.

I also sent notes to Regina and Angelina, asking them to a conference in my adobe that evening after supper, and in short order received notes that they would attend.

Regina arrived first, driving herself in her buggy.

"And how is Arabella?" I asked.

"Much better, though still coughing." Regina rolled her eyes. "But now Sophronia has the measles. I'll have you in on the morrow to check on her, although she is one my saltier girls, so I have every confidence that she'll sail through without trouble."

Regina settled herself on the sofa in my study, then looked around.

"Where is that little nuisance?"

She meant my dog ChiChi. We had, at the time, three dogs living on the rancho. Bella and Negrito were large dogs and lived outside in the yard, because however delightful dogs are, they are not sanitary. ChiChi, however, was a small Mexican dog, not even twelve inches at the shoulder, and as such, had to be kept inside lest he be eaten by a coyote. He was quite prone to biting people when he wasn't yapping his fool head off.

"He has decided he wants to live in the barracks," I said, pouring a glass of angelica for Regina from the pitcher on my desk. "I have no idea why, although he is getting rather old."

"Aren't we all?" Regina chortled.

"Indeed. However, I'm quite happy to have him there and not chewing on my shoes."

"Or us."

"Oddly, he hasn't bitten anybody in months. And he's not chewing anybody's shoes, either." I sighed. "I probably should have banished him to the barracks sooner."

I then had to get up to admit Angelina, her little wooden desk in hand, and the three of us were soon settled with plenty of angelica and good pan dulces. Magdalena and Olivia went back to their adobes after checking to see that Sofia was asleep. Lupe had been declared fully recovered that afternoon and had returned to her own bed. Juanita also retired to her room, fully expecting me to get myself out of my work dress on my own. Conferences with Regina and Angelina often lasted quite late and usually involved more than one pitcher of angelica.

I told them my thoughts regarding Mr. Lyons and the possibility that the killer had acted in rage, then added Dr. Wang's theory that Lavina had been killed to protect the killer.

"It's a most excellent theory," Regina said. "And if he

reacted in rage, perhaps it was because Miss Gaines made some attempt to bring his nefarious deeds to light."

"That would make a great deal of sense," I said, thinking, "Except that on the day of Miss Julia's funeral, Lavina told me that she didn't know who the man was. Julia had told her that she didn't dare say. Lavina thought it was because the man is married."

Angelina tapped her finger on her little desk. "What if Miss Gaines managed later to guess who this person was? Or maybe, he pressed himself on her, then she guessed it was him, and that made him angry."

"That does seem to be a distinct possibility," I said. I poured a small glass of angelica for myself, then got up to pour a second glass for Regina. "But which men in the pueblo had reason to be in contact with both Julia Carson and Lavina Gaines?"

"It could be almost anybody," Angelina said. "Maybe not in the last week or so, when Miss Gaines' family decided to keep her in. I don't think Miss Carson worked in her father's stationery store, but she was there often enough."

"There were plenty of men who were aware of her," Regina said. Her eyebrows rose. "In fact, I can think of two, in particular. Mr. Wiley, the manufacturers agent, and Judge Gresham."

"Mr. Wiley?" Angelina's eyebrows rose in shock. "He is utterly mild."

"I, perhaps, should not say this, but I have reason to know that he is quite the lusty fellow." Regina focused on sipping some wine.

I could feel the flush on my face. "Oh, dear. I suppose he

can be." I sat up straight. "But wait. He's not married. Lavina seemed sure that the man in question is."

"But she did not know that for certain," Angelina said, busily scratching down Mr. Wiley's name onto a piece of paper. "And what about Judge Gresham? He is certainly prone to rage."

I took a sip of angelica. "Indeed, he is. And Mr. Alverno made the same suggestion when he came to see me this morning. Is His Honor married?"

"Oh, yes," replied Regina.

I went back to thinking. "The problem with both Mr. Wiley and His Honor is that they have no apparent way to have been in contact with either young woman."

Regina set her glass down with a thud. "I know of someone who did. Mr. Lawrence, the schoolmaster. He was supposedly tutoring Miss Carson, according to the rumors."

"He was also tutoring Lavina at her home," I said, my brow creasing with concern. "But, again, he seems hardly the person to become enraged or to dally with young women."

"He is in frequent contact with them," said Regina.

Angelina snorted. "Regina, you assume the worst in every man."

"Darling, I see the worst regularly."

"Be that as it may," I said. "I will check, but I do believe that it is very unlikely that Mr. Lawrence is our monster."

"What about Mr. Smith?" Angelina asked, pouring a second glass of angelica for herself.

"He is too intent on finding Lavina's killer." I realized my glass was empty and set it down for the moment. "As is Mr. Alverno. Why would they be doing so much to find the killer if they did the killing? On the other hand, Mr. Smith said that his former partner, a Mr. Lyons, was quite angry with Lavina for causing Mr. Smith to give up buying property with him because Mr. Smith no longer wished to be a farmer."

"But how would Mr. Lyons have had any contact with Miss Carson?" Angelina wrote Mr. Lyons' name down, nonetheless.

I couldn't help groaning. "And do you know what else we are forgetting? The murder of Mama Jane. We have reason to believe that the same person killed both her and Lavina."

Angelina gasped. "I know someone it could be. Father Gallar. We know he hated Mama Jane."

"A priest?" Regina's laugh was low and warm. "Oh, that would be simply too rich."

"Nonetheless, he'd have a great deal to lose if it got out that he'd forced himself on Julia," I filled my glass again.

"What about Mr. Gaines?" Regina took the pitcher from me to fill her glass, as well.

I shook my head. "It is extremely unlikely for the same reason as Mr. Smith and Mr. Alverno. He even asked me directly to help him find the killer to save his miserable neck." I sipped and thought. "However, it is possible that Mrs. Gaines killed Lavina. She certainly had the most reason to want to be rid of her."

"Do you think Mr. Gaines knows that she did?" Angelina asked.

"Maybe he does," Regina said. "Maybe his marriage is not a happy one and he has asked for Maddie's help in order to rid himself of a burdensome wife."

"But if Mrs. Gaines is the killer, then what reason did she

have to kill Mama Jane?" I asked. "Nor would Mrs. Gaines be capable of causing Julia's problem."

"Unless it was Mr. Gaines who caused the problem." Regina looked thoughtful. "I'm not sure how Mama Jane's death would be a part of it." She set her glass down on the table next to the study sofa. "I know. Mama Jane's herbs. If Mrs. Gaines had learned that her husband had attacked another young woman in the pueblo, and that the young woman had sought Mama Jane out to relieve herself of the problem, then it was possible that Mama Jane knew what Mr. Gaines had done. Mrs. Gaines killed her first, in order to be sure that she was silenced, then when her sister-in-law would not stay at home, killed her to ensure her silence."

"But why did she not poison Lavina?" I asked. I debated refilling my glass but settled on nibbling at a pan dulce instead. "It would make a great deal more sense to do that, since it would be less likely to be questioned."

"And why would Mrs. Gaines take the pantaloons?" Angelina asked, pouring herself a glass of angelica.

"Ah, the pantaloons." Regina finished off her glass. "That adds a most interesting twist."

"Yes." I shuddered. "I do believe we are looking for someone who is quite depraved, indeed."

Regina let out a most evil chuckle. "That is my specialty. Perhaps I shall be able to help out more directly than I have in the past. The question will be how to do it discreetly."

"We'll leave that to you to determine," I said, then paused. "There is one other oddity. Mr. Navarro has been acting rather strangely since Mama Jane was found. He lied to Mr. Lomax about having seen her before she was killed."

"Mr. Navarro?" Angelina made a face as she wrote his name down. "He seems quite inoffensive."

"Most of the time." Regina glanced at me. "However, he can be roused into quite a rage."

"Perhaps, but you might as well suspect Mr. Lomax," Angelina retorted.

I sighed. "Actually, we probably should look at Mr. Lomax." I swallowed. "It was something his... wife told me."

Regina looked at me. "Is it possible?"

"What?" I picked at the pan dulce I'd been nibbling on.

"It's a rumor that has been bandied about and mostly discredited," Regina poured herself another glassful. "Largely because Mr. Lomax has been known to take a drink of whiskey or two. But the rumor is that he is really a Mormon and that the younger of the two women there is not the wife of his late brother, but his second wife."

Alas, my two friends know me too well. I tried to act as if I knew nothing about the true nature of Mr. Lomax's family, but both Angelina and Regina saw through it immediately.

"I cannot say," I replied quietly. "It is not for me to do so. However..." I took a deep breath. "I have been told by Mrs. Lomax that he has not been a husband to either of them since they came to California."

Regina's eyebrows rose. "A strapping, healthy fellow like that? He would have better reason than most to breach a young maiden."

"Except that the problem is that he is being honorable to the two women," I protested. "Why would he do something so despicable and dishonorable as to force himself on a young woman when all he had to do was take advantage of what is at home?"

"He got caught in a moment of weakness." Regina sighed as she looked at her glass. "It would certainly explain needing to be rid of both Mama Jane and Lavina. I know he is your friend, Maddie, as he has been a friend to me, at times, which is why I do not want to think that he is our monster. But healthy men doing without the right stimulation can become quite depraved. I've seen it happen."

Sadly, the propriety of the conversation deteriorated completely from there. The difficulty of all three of our respective professions was that we were privy to a great many unmentionable realities, and it was quite a blessing that we could talk to each other about such things. Nonetheless, it doesn't do to repeat such talk.

Chapter Ten

I arose rather late the next morning, one of the unfortunate but frequent results of an extended consultation with Regina and Angelina. Juanita brought my breakfast, and I ate while still in bed. She also brought a list of patients asking for my care, most of it involving more measles.

I also need to speak with two people regarding Lavina and Mama Jane's murder. Regina had asked to speak to Mr. Wiley and Judge Gresham, as she was most likely to come across them and would be able to speak quite frankly. Angelina decided that she would talk to Mr. Navarro and Father Gallar (and I pitied the poor priest). That left me with Mr. Lyons and Mr. Lawrence. We were undecided what to do about Mr. Lomax.

Once I finished eating, Juanita helped me into my brown riding habit. I briefly debated putting it aside in favor of a lovely dark green habit I had, made of linen and wool. However, with as many patients as were waiting, it seemed likely that my lovely dress would acquire yet another noxious stain. I made a mental note to visit my dressmaker at some point in the day to order a third riding habit in advance of the brown habit falling apart, as it seemed fated to do.

"Are you going out to find this new killer?" Juanita demanded as she buttoned up the back of my dress.

"I must," I replied. "He has been preying on innocent young women. It will only continue if he is not stopped."

"Why can't you let Mr. Navarro do the searching? He is better able to defend himself."

I sighed and put on my hat. "Juanita, it is entirely possible that he is the killer."

Juanita sniffed and blinked back tears.

"Juanita, dearest, are you afraid he might be?"

"I have no reason to think so." She swallowed. "I know he visited Mama Jane the day she was killed, and then he lied about it to me. I could tell. But I don't think he killed her. He was most affected by her death."

"Or, perhaps, you don't want him to be guilty?"

Juanita hung her head. "That could be."

"I do not want him to be guilty, either," I said softly. "However, we cannot let what we wish were true get in the way of stopping this most vicious killer."

"I know."

I left her, gathered my things together and went outside. Rodolfo had saddled Daisy and waited for me to mount. Damiano was already astride one of the mules. He insisted when I questioned him that because he was so bored on the rancho, and of no good use, his parents had said he could enjoy a day of following me about. Yet, he had a good-sized pistol stuck in his belt, and his parents, aunt, and uncle waited in the yard, giving me annoyed looks in lieu of reminding me to avoid making people want to kill me. Alas, they knew well that a monster was loose in the pueblo and needed to be caught as soon as possible.

Elena was also in the yard, looking even more annoyed than her parents. With Sofia mostly recovered and Lupe gone from the sick room, Elena knew that the only reason her brother was going with me and not her was because I was on the hunt for another killer. She had no interest in such searches, but bitterly regretted not being able to see patients.

My heart softened. "Elena, I have too many patients this morning. Would you mind checking a few for me?"

Her eyes brightened. Most of the children I sent her to were in the later stages of the disease. I also made a point of sending her to Mrs. Davies' house, with orders to tell Mrs. Davies that Elena needed practice seeing patients, and since Mrs. Davies' children seemed to be managing well, it would be a good opportunity.

I also reaffirmed where she was and was not allowed to go. I was still uneasy in my mind about the more unseemly aspects of our vocation, and how I was going to introduce them to her.

With Elena dealt with, Rodolfo helped me mount Daisy, and off Damiano and I went. As we came to the road leading to the plaza, both Mr. Smith and Mr. Alverno hailed me together.

"Good day, gentlemen," I said.

Mr. Smith helped me dismount from Daisy, but Damiano stayed mounted.

"Good day, Mrs. Wilcox," Mr. Smith said. "I take it that you are still on the hunt for Lavina's killer."

"I am," I said. "Have you spoken with your former partner, Mr. Lyons?"

"He's not at his boarding house?" Mr. Smith asked. "Then I do not know where he is. He has taken up work as a manufacturers agent, or so I've heard."

"Yes, he has," I said.

"Mrs. Wilcox," Mr. Alverno butted in. "Have you spoken with Judge Gresham yet?"

"Not yet, but I expect I shall soon." I looked at both of them, debating how much to say, but then realized that Mr. Alverno already knew about what I wanted to ask. "Do either of you know of any connection Miss Gaines might have had with Mama Jane?"

"The Indian who died?" Mr. Alverno shuffled his feet.

"Yes." I watched both of them carefully. "I have reason to believe that the same person killed both her and Miss Gaines."

Mr. Alverno sucked on his tooth again. "There's no way to say for certain. Besides, what would Miss Gaines have been doing talking to that old witch?"

I glared at him. "Mama Jane was a good woman and deserved better than she got!"

Mr. Smith looked puzzled. "Wait, wasn't Mama Jane that old Indian lady who used to make charms and simple cures? I have no idea why Miss Gaines would have talked to her, but I heard you could find her out near the Lomax place."

"Which is right next to one of those Negros' farms." Mr. Alverno raised his eyebrows. "Oh, you know what they say about them. Perhaps that is how Miss Gaines came to grief."

I glared again at Mr. Alverno, who this time quailed. "I

know well what is said about colored people. It is irrelevant. Mr. Samples is a hard-working man trying to build a good life for his wife and children. I'll thank both of you to keep your accusations in that regard to yourselves. We do not want another riot, do we?"

I knew they placed little value on Mr. Samples' life, but the riot the previous fall had been so horrific, it was likely that the fear of another such event would silence both men. It certainly silenced Mr. Smith, who had been drawn into the terrible lynchings and was thoroughly ashamed that he had been, and I had good reason to believe that Mr. Alverno had been involved as well.

The two men swallowed nervously.

"I do have patients to see this morning," I said. "But thank you, gentlemen, for offering your thoughts."

Mr. Smith helped me back onto Daisy, and I went to see my first patient. The problem was that Mr. Alverno did have a point about Mr. Samples, not in reference to the prejudicial assumptions people often made about Negros, but because Mr. Samples lived in close proximity to Mama Jane and had found Lavina. Still, there seemed to be little reason for the man to have killed either, especially Lavina.

As I passed down the Calle Primavera, I noticed Mr. Mahoney's saloon and another thought occurred to me. He'd known Julia Carson and seemed to have had a high regard for her. He'd also been widowed a good many years, and it was possible he had slipped in a moment of weakness. I was glad we hadn't mentioned his name the night before. It was a secret of the deepest sort that Mr. Mahoney was actually Regina's brother. I winced. The two held each other in deep affection, but Regina did not wish to see her brother's reputation tarnished by hers, and it was all too likely in the pueblo. But it also meant that Regina would have an insight into her brother's behavior that the rest of us would have great difficulty finding out.

It was early yet, and the nature of Mr. Mahoney's business was such that he would not be abroad at that time. So, I went on and visited my first three patients. The first was a field hand with a cut on his arm that had gotten so infected there was little I could do except amputate it. I had his fellows take him to the hospital while I dealt with a case of consumption in a young man and dispensed some unguent for an old woman with the shingles, then I headed back to the hospital and spent the rest of the morning and well into the afternoon, amputating the field hand's arm. Fortunately, Elena had heard I'd be doing the surgery and had hurried to the hospital, as well, and was quite helpful.

As I washed up after the surgery, Damiano appeared. He'd had the good sense to ride back to Rancho de las Flores as soon as I'd gotten to the hospital and had convinced his mother to send along some bread, cheese, and chicken for Elena's and my mid-day meal.

As we ate in the nun's refectory, Elena mentioned that Mrs. Lawrence's new little one had developed a croup.

I sighed. "I hope it's not the measles."

"I don't think so," Elena said. "But I would rather you took a look at her."

I thought. "As it happens, I'd like to speak with Mr. Lawrence, anyway. I'll go after we finish our lunch."

With Damiano again at my side, Elena and I parted ways, and I rode out to the Lawrence family's home.

In addition to his work as schoolmaster, Mr. Lawrence had about seventy acres of grapes and beans that he worked. His two oldest sons were getting to be of an age where they could help out, and often did. Still, there was so much work to be done on the place. Furthermore, the house was a rambling shack that had begun as a simple adobe. Mr. Lawrence had added rooms to it in a higgledy-piggledy way as his brood grew. Sometime the summer before, a group of citizens had done the family the supreme kindness of repairing and rebuilding much of the house. After all, Mr. Lawrence was a very good and kind schoolmaster, but not much of a carpenter.

Mrs. Lawrence and the new little girl were in the front of the house. I listened to the infant's chest, and although she was coughing, it wasn't serious.

"Do any of the other children have the measles?" I asked Mrs. Lawrence.

She had nut-brown hair, a fair complexion, and an incredibly calm mien. She sat, doing stitching that she took in to add to Mr. Lawrence's meager earnings.

She laughed quietly. "Ours were the first to get it. They had all recovered by the time the baby was born."

"And both you and Mr. Lawrence have had the disease."

"Yes."

"Has anyone else been here?"

"No one besides Miss Ortiz."

I thought carefully. "Well, the cough does not seem serious, although we both know how quickly that can change." I rummaged in my bag. "I have some drops that could help. Just one every few hours."

"Thank you, Mrs. Wilcox."

"Is Mr. Lawrence about?"

She smiled. "No, he's not. He's at his school, probably tutoring some new youths with the hopes of them passing the teacher's test. He was quite upset when Miss Carson died, and then Miss Gaines."

"I believe he was tutoring Miss Gaines for the test, wasn't he?"

Mrs. Lawrence nodded with a sigh. "He had high hopes for her. In fact, he was working with both her and Miss Carson."

"Oh. I understand that he was working with Miss Gaines at her house."

"Yes." Mrs. Lawrence's eyes opened wide. "But there was not the least impropriety, at either Miss Carson's or Miss Gaines' houses. Mr. Lawrence made sure that the young women worked together, and that Mrs. Carson or Mrs. Gaines was nearby at all times. I'm sure they will tell you the same."

You might wonder that Mrs. Lawrence became so quickly worried about me thinking there might have been something indelicate going on, but it was such a common conclusion in those days that one would defend even the most innocent look a man cast upon a young woman.

"I'm sure they will," I said, not voicing my doubts about Mrs. Gaines.

I excused myself shortly afterwards and made my way back

to the center of the pueblo. In the back of Mr. Mahoney's saloon, Annie and Alice were hard at work, pulling fresh bread from their oven, adding the final spices to the stew and the soup, and otherwise preparing for the night's business.

"Papa is in his office," Annie told me. Both she and her sister were much alike, as they were twins, tall, with full auburn hair. Their figures had filled out and were pleasingly proportioned. Annie's hair was generally falling in her face, and seldom stayed pinned. It was how I told the two girls apart.

Mr. Mahoney was pleased to see me and gave me the lone chair in the office.

I smiled softly and began my unpleasant mission. "Mr. Mahoney, I need to take you into my confidence."

"Gladly," Mr. Mahoney said.

"It is regarding both Miss Julia Carson and Miss Lavina Gaines." I pursed my lips trying to find the most delicate way to say what I needed to. "There may have been some impropriety involved."

Mr. Mahoney went pale. "Not with Miss Julia!"

"Well, yes, unfortunately. I believe her to be an innocent victim."

But Mr. Mahoney had already leapt to his feet and rushed from the office to the front of the saloon. I waited a few minutes, until Annie came to the office door.

"Mrs. Wilcox? What is happening? Tom just came back and told us that Papa is upset."

"Oh, dear. I had to ask him a most distasteful question."

Annie blinked. "Was it about Miss Julia Carson?"

"Yes. Why do you ask?"

"Miss Carson." Annie swallowed. "On the day she died, she came to visit with Alice and me. Only she didn't come to visit. She came to warn us that there was a man in the pueblo who was behaving in a most vile way."

"Did she say who?"

"No. She didn't dare, she said. Only that if anyone asked us to step behind a block or a store, or to go to the back of the store, under no circumstances were we to go."

"I would think you wouldn't anyway."

Annie winced. "Well, sometimes, a grocer or a tradesman wants Alice or me to go to the back of the store because it's easier to load our cart there. It's not unusual and there has never been a problem. But Julia said there had been for her." Annie sniffed. "And then she died. Then Miss Gaines was murdered. Alice and I don't know what to think."

I stood and put my hand on her shoulder. "You are right to be cautious. There is a monster loose in the pueblo, and we do have reason to suspect that Miss Julia's death may have been related to Miss Lavina's. You should ask your father to watch in the alley whenever you leave."

Annie sighed. "He does when he's here. It's just that I think he has found a woman he is courting."

"Courting?"

"Yes." Annie blinked, then giggled. "We can always tell when Papa is looking for a wife. He suddenly starts going to the barber's every other day and gets very quiet about where he's going and is often gone at strange hours."

My heart caught, but I had to ask. "How long has he been courting this lady?"

"Just for the past three weeks or so."

"And you have no idea who."

She shook her head and a lock of hair fell next to her nose. "No. He won't even say that he is, let alone who." She shrugged as she pushed the lock behind her ear. "It's his way."

"I see." I patted her shoulder again. "Well, Miss Annie, I'm grateful that you thought to speak with me. If you hear anything about a man being impolite or forceful, you are to get the name and come tell me immediately. Will you?"

"I will, Mrs. Wilcox. Thank you for hearing me. Not everyone believes it when someone complains about such things."

I shuddered. "I'm afraid not, but it is not to the credit of the disbeliever. Which is why I wish to know also if someone behaves badly with you or Alice. I will believe you."

"Thank you, Mrs. Wilcox."

I left the saloon and looked both ways in the alley behind it. It was empty, but for Damiano reading a small book while standing next to the mule.

We returned to the rancho in good time for supper, which I was barely able to finish before being summoned to the Carson's home because Mrs. Carson was ailing. I will admit to feeling somewhat annoyed by the summons. Having cured Mr. Carson's dyspepsia some years before, I had become their favorite physician. However, they had the exceedingly aggravating habit of forgetting that I required payment for my services. They were certainly wealthy enough. In addition to his successful stationery store, Mr. Carson had several acres of land around the pueblo that he rented out to some of the rancheros in the area to provide additional grazing for their herds. It was odd that those who had the least, such as Mrs. Davies, wanted to be sure that I had my fee.

Nonetheless, I put aside such less than charitable thoughts as I walked to the Carson home, finally alone. It was not yet dark, and I reminded Sebastiano and Enrique that they could send someone after me if it got late. I walked with a goodly stride, reveling in being alone. But as I approached the house, I paused. The Carsons had suffered a terrible tragedy, and it behooved me to be sensible of it.

Indeed, Mr. Carson's rotund figure seemed to have become less round even in the week and a half since his daughter's death.

"It's Mrs. Carson," he told me when I arrived. "She will not leave her bed."

"She is deep in grief," I said. "Such manner of hysteria is not unusual."

"Hysteria." Mr. Carson paled, obviously thinking that I wanted to place his wife in an insane asylum.

"There, there." I patted his arm. "It is most likely of a temporary nature, brought on by her sorrow. Let me see her, and then I shall be better able to see what steps, if any, should be taken."

As Mr. Carson had said, Mrs. Carson lay in her bed, not quite asleep, but not truly aware, either.

"Mrs. Carson?" I asked, softly.

There was no response. I reached over and gently shook her elbow. She looked up at me sleepily, then sniffed and looked away.

"Mrs. Carson, your husband is quite concerned."

"I wish to be left alone," she whispered.

"I don't doubt it," I said. "Pray forgive the intrusion."

She sobbed softly and I left the room.

Downstairs, Mr. Carson looked at me anxiously. "Well?"

"Is she taking nourishment?"

He sighed. "She has lost much of her appetite, but we can generally get her to take some soup and water."

"It is most assuredly grief, then." I considered carefully. "You might try some small doses of spirits, such as whiskey or angelica, although they can worsen the condition."

"What about laudanum?"

I shook my head. "Absolutely not."

"But that is what is given for the vapors, isn't it?"

"I know I differ from my colleagues in this respect, but I firmly hold that laudanum is the worst thing you can give a woman for the vapors. I have yet to see it help. If anything, it seems to make it all the worse. And still worse yet, it can cause a craving for it so strong that many women eventually die of it."

Mr. Carson looked at me skeptically, then swallowed. "I have heard of women becoming dependent on it."

"Exactly. Do you wish that for your wife?" I gazed at him.

He looked away.

"Mr. Carson," I said, my voice as severe as I could make it. "I know that I am only a woman, and when a great many medical men swear by the use of laudanum for the vapors and hysteria, I can understand why you question it when I say otherwise. However, I know of a woman in the pueblo whose sister suffered greatly, thanks to being given laudanum. Would you like to hear her testimony? I am sure I can arrange it. And I know of several others, as well. I assure you, laudanum has its uses, but not in cases such as this."

Mr. Carson stuttered and coughed. "But we've been giving it to her. That's what you do for the vapors."

"No wonder she's all but catatonic!" I snapped. "And why didn't you say so in the beginning?" I took a deep breath. "Nonetheless, discontinue the use immediately. She'll probably be quite sleepy for a day or two yet, and given her grief, it's quite likely she'll keep to her bed for a while longer. And never mind what I said about giving her spirits. They can make the effects of the laudanum worse."

"I was just trying to do my best for her," Mr. Carson whispered.

"I apologize for my display." I sighed. "I'm sure you were caring for her in the best way you could, and it's a very common practice. It just is not a very good one, and not everyone seems to understand that."

I took another deep breath, then looked at him, wondering how much he knew about the real circumstances of his daughter's death. Alas, I could not find a way to ask him about it, though.

I pushed a soft smile to my lips. "In any case, please be sure to discontinue the laudanum. If she gets worse, you can always return to it. I shall come by in the next day or two to check on her again. And please let me know how she fares in the meantime."

Mr. Carson nodded.

I left, quite unsettled by my own temper. It was so desperately unfair that the men always got more regard in these matters, never mind that the practice they insisted on was so very harmful. Of course, most men at that time were quite ready to diagnose any problem a woman had as mere hysteria, never mind the actual disease or condition. It was most aggravating.

Chapter Eleven

The next morning dawned with the usual dark skies for that time of year. My anger at Mr. Carson and medical men, in general, had not abated, sadly. Poor Elena came to me to confer on her progress the day before and was quite downcast, herself.

"Mrs. Jones' baby, the two-year-old," Elena said. "He'd caught the measles, but then began shaking and convulsing right in my arms and died." She sniffed. "There was nothing I could do."

"I know," I said, giving her a solid embrace. "There so often isn't, is there?"

Elena had certainly seen such an event before, although I had always been with her. However, she was quite tender-hearted. I suddenly bristled, and Elena drew back in fear.

"No, no, Elena," I said. "I am not in the least angry with you. You are a wonderful physician, and part of what makes you such a wonderful physician is your tender and sweet nature. What has me angry is that most of our male colleagues would insist that your tender heart is what makes you unfit to be a doctor." I put my hands on her shoulders and looked straight into her eyes. "You are not, under any circumstances, to believe them."

She smiled, her eyes still watery. "I know, Mrs. Wilcox, and I do believe that I am a good doctor, no matter what the men might say." She took a deep breath, then blinked. "But then, the baby died. It was so sad. Her only son, and I couldn't help thinking that if you'd been there, you'd have known what to do."

"Did you try the potassium bromide?"

She shook her head. "The poor thing had died even before I could get the syringe out of my bag, let alone mix the solution."

"Then you did the very best anyone could have done. You know as well as I do that there are times when our best efforts do not help. That doesn't stop us from trying, nor does it help us feel better when we lose someone. In fact, I am still unsettled by Julia Carson's death. There was nothing I could do then, either."

She nodded. We both donned our work clothes shortly after, then I retired to my study to work on writing up our notes for the past few days. It was Saturday again. After our luncheon, I took Elena with me, and made a point of praising her work at every chance. The praise was not only well-earned; it had the usual salubrious effect. By the middle of the afternoon, Elena's confidence had been fully restored.

We were heading toward the Plaza on New High Street when Regina saw me and waved. It was very unlike Regina to acknowledge me on the streets, never mind that most people in the pueblo knew that I saw to the care of her young women, and thus had, if not a respectable reason to know Regina, at least a charitable reason. At the same time, young Oscar Tejas came running up.

"It's Mama's time!" he called.

"I'll go, Mrs. Wilcox," Elena said, her eyes bright.

"Please do." I smiled, my heart full.

"I'll return to the hospital when I'm done." She ran off with the boy as I offered a silent prayer that all would go well.

It was just what Elena needed, and of all the work we did, her greatest gift was in delivering babies. Indeed, she would turn out to be better at it than I was.

I turned as Regina hurried up to me.

"Thank God, I found you," she gasped. "Poor Sophronia is failing badly. Her fever is so high. The other girls are looking for you, too. We are beside ourselves."

Regina turned toward her house, which was nearby. I went slightly ahead of her since I knew the way, my mind firmly focused on the fever. It seemed as though the blast from the shotgun came out of nowhere. It had to have been somewhere on the street behind us, but I had no time to consider where, as Regina suddenly sagged on top of me.

"I've been hit!" she gasped.

She was not only considerably taller than me, she weighed a great deal more and I was barely able to keep on my feet. I tried to turn and see but couldn't.

"Where?" I cried.

"In the back." She gasped. "I think I can walk."

"Good. It's not far to your house. Do you wish to go in the back?"

"Yes."

We struggled, but soon got Regina into her house where her maid helped me get her upstairs and into her bedroom.

"Sophronia," Regina gasped, leaning over the bed.

Her bustle had been shredded by the blast.

"Buck shot," I said. "You'd best get undressed, and I'll be back to get it out as soon as I've seen to Sophronia."

"Undressed?" Regina gasped, her eyes wide in fear.

"How else am I going to get the buckshot out of you? Do you want me to call one of the other doctors?"

"No!" Regina's hand flew to her jabot.

"Then do as I say." I softened. "Dearest, you know that I am aware of what you really are. You are still my friend, and there is nothing about your bare form that I haven't already seen on many others, as well you know. Now, get undressed and I shall return as soon as I know Sophronia's condition."

I hurried back downstairs to the sickroom to find that Sophronia's condition was very dire, indeed. She trembled and coughed. Her flesh was completely speckled by the rash and her fever burned. Her lungs were so badly congested, I was surprised that she was still breathing. Indeed, it was not long before her breath ceased altogether. I sighed deeply. I knew Elena's pain from that morning all too well and felt it again.

But I did have another patient who needed me almost as badly. Weary, I picked up my bag and went upstairs.

Regina lay face down on her bed. Her nightdress had been pulled up to expose her back and nether limbs, where the blast had mostly hit. There was some blood, but it didn't look overwhelming, and I was quite glad to find that while there were quite a few wounds scattered across her shoulders all the way down to her nether limbs, they were all quite small, and only a few looked like they would require sutures.

"I suppose there is something to be said for corsets and bustles," I said. "Yours seem to have deflected the worst of the blast." I reached for my bag. "I'll give you some morphine for the pain."

"No!" Regina glared at me.

"But getting all that shot out and stitching you back together is going to hurt quite a bit."

"Mortification of my wretched flesh." She sighed. "It's got to count something toward expiating my many sins."

I sighed. There wasn't much I could say. She knew well what I thought of her profession. In turn, I knew well that she and her young women had little choice in taking it up.

"Besides," Regina said. "We need to consider our next steps, and I cannot afford to fall asleep on a Saturday night."

Regina cursed loudly and extensively as I dosed the wounds with carbolic acid.

"It's only going to hurt worse," I told her. "Are you sure you don't want some morphine?"

"I want a great deal of it, but it's Saturday night."

"I'll give you a little then." I got the bag and put together the solution. "Just enough to take some of the sting out."

Regina looked at my syringe and shuddered. "That thing is terrifying."

"Hardly. Regina, you have faced many a man with a knife bigger than this needle." I gave her the injection.

"This is utterly humiliating."

I cleaned a small pair of forceps with the acid and went to

work. Regina couldn't help twitching here and there but bore the pain with considerable fortitude.

"As I see it," she said while I poked. "The questions are who was shooting at us, which of us was he shooting at, if not both, and why?"

"Why seems simple enough," I said, dropping a bit of shot into a china bowl. "One of us asked one too many questions of the wrong person. Or the wrong person heard us asking said questions."

There was a knock on the door and the maid peeped in. "Mrs. Medina, Mrs. Sutton is here and would like to talk to you and Mrs. Wilcox."

"Oh, bring her in," I said.

"And please bring in the rest of the pueblo to look at the freak!" Regina yelped.

"Hush now! There is nothing freakish about your body, and again, there is nothing about it that Angelina has not seen before. We need her, and it is always possible that the monster who shot you could shoot at her next."

Regina snorted. Angelina appeared a moment later.

"Oh, dear!" she gasped.

"As I told you," Regina snarled.

"What?" Angelina looked at me.

"Our darling Regina is humiliated by having her secret bared."

Angelina's retort was... quite indiscreet, and even Regina chuckled, only to yelp as I went after a somewhat deeper bit of shot.

"I am so sorry, dearest," I said.

"How badly is she hurt?" Angelina asked.

"Not very. This looks like the deepest bit of shot I've found. Wait. This one is… Angelina, can you bring that lamp over, please?"

Poor Regina couldn't help a further howl, but I retrieved the shot and dropped it in the china bowl.

"Why didn't you get her drunk?" Angelina asked me.

"It would take too long," I replied.

"So, who was shooting at you?" Angelina asked.

"We haven't the faintest idea," Regina said. "As you can see, we were shot at from behind."

"Both of you?"

"I was slightly ahead of Regina when the gun went off. She took the full brunt of it."

Angelina looked at me crossly. "And what about you?"

"I don't understand." I bent to my work, completely puzzled by Angelina's question.

"Did any of the buck shot hit you?"

I stood up and shifted my shoulders and nether limbs. "I don't think so."

Sighing, Angelina circled around me, holding the lamp.

"Here! You've got at least three holes in your skirt." She grabbed the hem and lifted it.

"Angelina, I am trying to work."

"See to her care, Angelina," Regina said. "I could do with a respite from the torture."

Sighing, I stepped back and let Angelina inspect me for wounds. There was one scrape, but it had already stopped bleeding and would only require a bandage. I inspected Regina one more time and determined that only two of the wounds needed sutures. The next half hour was not a happy one. Poor Regina continued to refuse the morphine. Angelina tried to distract her with sips of whiskey, and I stitched as quickly as I could. But sutures are quite painful, and while Regina did her best, she found herself crying out several times.

"There. I am done," I announced, stepping back.

"And none too soon," Regina wept. "I will now get dressed—"

"You will do no such thing!" I snapped. "You need to rest and let your wounds heal."

Angelina and I finished bandaging Regina, then the two of us pulled up chairs next to the bed.

"We need to consider," Regina said. "Who shot us and which of our questions provoked the attack?"

"I seriously doubt it was mine," I said. "Mr. Lawrence was, apparently, quite circumspect with both Julia and Lavina. He only worked with them when they were together and when either Mrs. Carson or Mrs. Gaines was at hand. As for Mr. Lyons, he is still away from the pueblo."

"I did talk to Mr. Navarro," Angelina said. "But he didn't have much to say. He is just as perplexed as anyone else about the two murders, although he does agree with us that it was probably the same person who killed both. He wasn't acting guilty or evasive either."

"I did speak to Mr. Wiley about Miss Carson," Regina said. "It was quite simple, as it was obvious that he was quite enamored of her. It would appear that he is merely grieved by her passing, but that could also mean that he is feeling guilty, as well." She paused to take a sip of whiskey. "Also, I did manage to start a discussion last night amongst the men as they were waiting in the parlor. We were talking about some of the odd things we'd seen, and I couldn't help asking why someone would take a lady's pantaloons?"

"What did they say?" Angelina asked.

"They were befuddled by the idea." Regina didn't quite shrug, thanks to the three small holes in her shoulders.

"Dare I ask who was there?" I asked, not expecting an answer.

"Mr. Wiley, Mr. Hewitt, and Mr. Carson." It must have been the morphine that had loosened Regina's tongue. She never named who visited her house.

"Mr. Carson?" I looked at Regina. "I spoke with him at his house last evening after supper. He'd called me to look at Mrs. Carson. He seemed quite affected by his grief."

"Oh, he is." Regina shifted herself to relieve some discomfort. "I think that's why he was there. He did arrive quite late, which is why he was waiting. Oh, and Judge Gresham was in the house, but engaged."

I forbore to ask who else had been in the house.

"And today you got shot at," Angelina said, pulling her list from her reticule.

"But was it me that was the target?" Regina's eyes fell on me. "I know the questions you have been asking seemed rather inoffensive, but it is well-known that you are seeking out this killer."

"Why would the killer attract attention to himself by shooting at me unless he had reason to believe that I knew considerably more than I do?" I took a small bit of whiskey from the bottle on the chest of drawers. "Although, I did startle Mr. Mahoney earlier today when I asked him about any impropriety concerning Julia Carson. He ran from the office and was quite upset."

"My brother?" Regina's eyebrows rose as she considered. "He seems highly unlikely to have forced himself on anybody, and he certainly doesn't need to."

"His daughter Annie said that he is courting somebody at the moment."

Regina laughed full-out. "No. He is not interested in courting anybody. He has taken another lover is all."

Angelina gasped. "Do you know who?"

"He wouldn't tell me, although the odds are excellent that she's a married woman." Regina chuckled. "I have no idea why he prefers it that way, but he does not want another wife, of that, I am certain. When he was first widowed, when the girls were small, he considered remarrying for their sakes. Fortunately, there were enough neighbor ladies to care for the girls until they got old enough to help in the saloon kitchen."

"Annie said something else, though," I said, remembering the conversation. "The day Julia died, she had come by to warn Annie and Alice that there was a man in the pueblo behaving in quite an evil fashion. Julia did not dare name him but told Annie that if she or her sister were asked to go behind a block or adobe, or to go into an alley with someone, they were not to go."

"We need to find a way to talk to the young ladies of the pueblo," Angelina said. "I will take that on."

"As will I, as I have occasion," I said.

"I will speak to my brother about Miss Carson," Regina said. "That is a rather odd reaction, indeed."

The clock on the bureau struck the hour of six.

"Oh, dear," I said, getting up. "It is getting quite late. I'd best get to the hospital. The fights should start at any time now."

"I'll stay with Regina for a while," Angelina said. "Miss Sophronia is not going to go anywhere."

"What?" Regina gasped.

"That's why I came," Angelina said. "My men took her to the parlor, and I will see to it that she has a nice burial."

"Oh, no. She was so salty."

"I'm so sorry, darling," I said. "There was nothing to be done."

Regina blinked, her eyes full. "What a ghastly event. Why isn't there more we can do about such diseases? I know the measles is mostly a nuisance, but we can prevent variola. Why can't we prevent measles the same way?"

I gave her bandages one final check. "Perhaps someday. But there are worse diseases to conquer first. The consumption, cholera, typhoid, malaria. All of those kill far more people than the measles do. But perhaps, when we've conquered those others, we'll be able to find a way to stop the measles."

Regina let out a very unladylike snort and gestured to Angelina to give her yet another small glass of whiskey. As I had pointed out earlier, however it might have eased Regina's pain to have gotten her inebriated, it did take a considerable amount of time, let alone spirits, to achieve that end.

Chapter Twelve

I was grateful that, for a change, there were no surgeries required of me that Saturday night. Elena and I still stayed quite late at the hospital. The good sisters provided cots for each of us, and we slept rather soundly, only rousing ourselves in the hour just before dawn to go home.

Once there, I slept soundly, then managed to get up in time to go to church and came home to quite the tongue-lashing from all the women of my household. After all, I had done it again, getting someone angry enough at me that he wanted to kill me and not only wanted to, but had tried yet again, and how I was still alive was a miracle, but even the Blessed Mother was going to get tired of saving my miserable hide one day and there were not enough saints in Heaven to intercede on my behalf, and if I didn't take more care in how I went about my inquiries, I was going to need Angelina's services, assuming I hadn't gotten her killed, as well.

Luncheon was somewhat strained, as a result, but fortunately, I was able to convince the ladies that I could manage on my own that day.

That afternoon, I did go on a quick round of several patients, including Regina, then rode Daisy out to the Lomax place to check on Mrs. Ruth. It had been some time since I'd seen her and was happy to see that she was almost well and had even taken up some of her usual duties.

"It isn't fair to Sabrina to leave it all on her," Mrs. Ruth told me with a soft smile.

"You care a great deal for your sister wife," I said quietly.

We were, again, alone in the small adobe.

Mrs. Ruth nodded. "I could not have wished for better. Her heart is pure. She is so kind and gentle and is so patient with the children. And she is kind to me, too, never seeing me as a rival."

"Given what you have told me, it seems odd that you do not see her as one."

Mrs. Ruth blushed. "There is no reason to." She swallowed again. "It must seem quite odd to you, Mrs. Wilcox, being one of two wives. But it is how Sabrina and I were raised. It is all we know. We have been blessed in Mr. Lomax, that he is the kindest of husbands." She frowned. "Sabrina went to the market yesterday and heard an odd conversation. She does not know between whom. But there is a rumor that Mr. Lomax might have killed Miss Gaines."

"And on what are they basing their suspicion?" I asked.

Mrs. Ruth shrugged. "I do not entirely know. It may be because we keep so closely to ourselves. I fear that they might have deduced that we are Mormons."

"And Miss Gaines' body was found next to your farm." I sighed, then looked at her. "Do you think he could have?"

"What?" Mrs. Ruth gaped in horror. "Are you...?"

"No." I put my hand on her arm. "I must ask in order to be sure your husband is innocent, not because I believe him to be guilty."

"My husband will not lift a gun to defend himself." Mrs. Ruth glared at me, utterly indignant. "Why would you even consider the possibility that he would do such a thing?"

I pressed my lips together. "I wouldn't. I merely had to be sure."

I left soon after, feeling quite unsettled. Alas, I was anything but sure about Mr. Lomax. It was quite frustrating. Mrs. Ruth was absolutely correct in that Mr. Lomax was well-known for keeping the peace in the pueblo and settling disputes without violence. It was a rare occasion, indeed, when he drew his gun. But Lavina and Mama Jane had been strangled, an act of rage. It was hard to imagine the laconic and calm Mr. Lomax becoming so enraged that he would do such a thing, let alone be so troubled by his passions that he would force himself on a young woman.

I went on about my rounds, then returned home, and spent the evening most uneasy.

The next morning presented me with a rather unhappy possibility in terms of how to find our monster thanks to a routine visit to a long-time patient, Mrs. Olson. The visit was sorely overdue. Mrs. Olson was a kind and virtuous woman, noted for her charity toward the children in the pueblo. Would that her husband had been so virtuous. He had died of syphilis the winter preceding, and not surprisingly, had passed the disgusting and miserable disease on to his wife.

Like him, she had developed constitutional syphilis, and I had been treating her with small doses of mercurous chloride, which was the standard treatment.

Alas, like many such treatments, it was not terribly effective. Indeed, I was somewhat suspicious that Mr. Olson had actually died of mercury poisoning, as the symptoms were remarkably similar. My colleague Dr. Skillen, a homeopath, had said that he'd had some success curing syphilis with a bark called cundurango. As I'd had little success with the mercury that I'd given Mrs. Olson, I had procured some of the bark from Dr. Skillen in the hopes that would cure her.

It may be that you are thinking that syphilis cannot be cured, and, indeed, it has been proven that the many neurological diseases that some patients eventually develop are, in fact, caused by the bacterium. But that would not be discovered for almost forty years after the time of which I write. It is true that the symptoms usually abate on their own after constitutional syphilis develops. But we thought the patient had been cured.

As I gave Mrs. Olson some of the concoction I'd prepared, I began to wonder. Syphilis wasn't as common as, say, tuberculosis, but we saw it often enough, in spite of the various attempts by patients to hide it. It didn't seem unlikely that our monster had contracted the dread contagion. Rage was often associated with the disease, and given how it was transmitted from patient to patient, it was possible that it might provide a trail we could follow. The question would be how to discover who might have it.

I realized as soon as I left Mrs. Olson that Regina would be the best person to ask about who was afflicted with the disease and who wasn't. I needed to see her, anyway, to check on her wounds, and was glad that Damiano was not with me. I rode Daisy through the pueblo toward her house, wondering if she would have an answer.

Regina was sitting up in her bed when I arrived and happy to see me.

"The tedium of it all," she complained, sipping some tea that I was fairly certain had been laced with angelica. There was a small decanter sitting on the table next to her bed with a liquor that looked remarkably like mine. "But you were right about resting. I can barely move, let alone get dressed."

She had managed some of her usual ablutions, but then Regina was most scrupulous about hiding her oddity. Indeed, even the collar on her nightgown reached the bottom of her chin and was tied closed.

"I know resting can be tedious," I replied. "But it's the best thing for you."

I went about checking her wounds and was pleased to see that all but one were healing cleanly, including the two that had been sutured, and even the one that was a touch infected was only a little red and not giving anything up. I pressed it to be sure, then rebandaged her. As I did, I shared my thoughts about the possibility that our monster had syphilis.

"That would account for the rage," Regina said. "Some otherwise quite mild fellows will sometimes develop that kind of raving during the worst of that miserable scourge." She shuddered. "I insist that each of my ladies inspect their men and call me if there is the least chancre or discharge."

"I am well aware of that," I said with a sigh. Even those inspections did not guarantee that a young woman wouldn't develop the disease. "However, have you any idea who might currently be suffering from it? It might lead us to the monster."

Regina thought for a moment. "Maddie, dearest, that does put me in a most difficult position. I must stay discrete. My entire business depends on it. Are you certain that our monster has it?"

"No." I sighed deeply. "Worse yet, I'm simply guessing that he might."

"Well, if you can find some way to ascertain that the monster does have it, then I might be able to convince some of my gentlemen to play stool pigeon on their fellows for you."

"Perhaps I will ask Angelina if Miss Julia showed any signs of the affliction on her body," I said after a moment's thought. "Would that be enough for your plan?"

"It might."

Regina also told me that I could look for another sign that a man was so afflicted. It was not a useful sign, however. In fact, it was quite a common practice for men in the pueblo to ease their discomfort by scratching that region of their person, although most tried to avoid it when ladies were present. Nor did it necessarily mean that syphilis was behind the behavior.

Which is why, as soon as I was done with Regina, I made my way to the funeral parlor and Angelina. Given that Sophronia had been buried that morning and the quiet Saturday night that we'd had, Angelina was at liberty for the moment and happy to speak to me. As soon as I made my request, she pulled down a large accounts book and opened it on the one of the empty tables in the preparation room.

"When we talked after Mama Jane's funeral, I examined Miss Julia a little more carefully," Angelina said. "She was definitely expecting. Whether her self-probing worked or not, I didn't really ascertain. Because of what you said about someone forcing himself on her, I did a drawing or two in the hopes that it might help find the monster. But I don't recall seeing anything."

I looked over the drawing. "What's that?"

"I'm not sure." Angelina peered more closely at the drawing. "It could be just her shape, but you're right, it could be a chancre."

"We'll not likely know for certain." I smiled grimly. "However, that may be just what we need." I explained what Regina had said regarding asking about the disease. "Thanks to this, we have reason to believe that our monster does have the dreaded scourge. I don't know how we'll discover who does and doesn't have it in the pueblo, but at the very least it is something to be looked for."

"Hopefully, Regina will be able to tell us something." Angelina suddenly smiled. "Or maybe my darling Edgar will have a way to talk to some of the men."

"Your husband might, indeed, prove helpful that way." I frowned. "Do you mind making him a part of this sordid mess?"

"No, nor will he mind." She looked a little abashed. "I tell him everything. He seldom has much to say about it. Still, he listens very well."

"How very unusual," I said.

Angelina smiled and nodded. "It is, and I am so glad of it." She gazed back at the large volume. "Maddie, perhaps we are going about this the wrong way. Wouldn't it be better to find out who can account for where they were on the Sunday that Miss Gaines died? Once we know who can't account for their whereabouts, then it might be easier to find out who among them has the disease and who doesn't."

"That would make asking questions a great deal easier," I said. "But Lavina wasn't found until Monday morning. That seems to be a great deal of time to consider, especially when a good many people would be in their beds for part of it."

Angelina flipped a page or so ahead in the accounts book. "But we do have an idea of when she died, roughly between three and six o'clock that Sunday."

"How can you be so certain?" I asked.

"I can't." Angelina pulled another, smaller volume, bound in black leather, off her shelf. "But here are my studies of rigor mortis. There are always variations and some of them are very common. However, more often than not, the body begins relaxing approximately twenty-four hours after death. And it was not so warm that the rigor would have come on early. In fact, the conditions were ideal. Miss Gaines' body began relaxing between four and five-thirty that Monday afternoon. We know that Miss Gaines went for a walk shortly before her supper on Sunday."

"Which would have been about four o'clock, if what Mr. Gaines told me was correct," I said.

"So then, four o'clock is approximately the last time she was seen alive." Angelina looked at me. "My guess would be that the killer met up with her very soon after she left for her walk. If he killed her in a rage, then it would not make sense that he would hide her away for a while before killing her. It would have happened very shortly after he came across her."

"And if Mr. Smith is not the demon who did this, and I have good reason to believe he isn't, then the killer must have come across her before her four-thirty assignation with him." I began pacing. "That does make things somewhat easier and will give us a reasonable and modest question to ask." I shuddered, then thought. "If we believe that this began with Miss Julia, then perhaps we should talk to Mr. Carson."

Angelina gasped. "You don't think..."

"No!" I swallowed, horrified. "I was thinking that perhaps Miss Julia confided in her parents about who forced himself on her." I blinked as Angelina's suggestion took hold. "But I do suppose it was possible that her father did the deed."

"Why would he do such a terrible thing?"

"It does happen." I tried to ignore the bile as it rose in my throat. "Before I went to medical school, I apprenticed with a lady doctor in Boston. A young girl, perhaps fifteen, came to us looking for relief from her condition. She had tried purging it with water and it hadn't worked. I spent some time with the girl and found out that her father was responsible. The doctor I was working with said that it was not common, but that she'd seen it several times before."

"How terrible."

"Indeed." I sighed. "Sadly, you and I are fated to see the worst of the human condition by virtue of our vocations, as is Regina." I reached for my bag. "Nonetheless, I must put aside my suspicion for the time being and will try to assume the best of Mr. Carson until I have good and solid reason to believe otherwise. It will not do the young women of the pueblo any good to cast such a vile aspersion on a probably innocent man without sufficient evidence that he is not."

Mr. Carson's stationery store was not far from the funeral parlor, so I left Daisy tied up where she was and walked to the store. The man behind the counter, Mr. Drew, was quite old and somewhat frail.

"I'd like to see Mr. Carson," I told him. "Is he in the store today?"

"Eh?" Mr. Drew asked, putting his hand to his ear.

"Is Mr. Carson in the store today?" I asked more loudly.

Mr. Drew jerked his thumb to the back of the store and did not protest when I went behind the counter and in that direction.

Mr. Carson had a large, comfortable office behind his store. More clerks worked in the large office on the other side of the hallway that led to the back of the block in which the store and offices were located.

Mr. Carson sat glaring at some paper on his wide, dark wood desk as I entered. He sighed when he saw me, but got promptly to his feet, and offered me a chair in front of the desk. I sat down and pressed my lips together.

"I've come to ask after Mrs. Carson," I said, partly because I did not know how else to begin and partly because I did want to know how she fared.

He tugged at his white beard. "She is better. We got her to dress and go down to the parlor yesterday."

"I'm glad to hear it."

"Still…" He looked rather annoyed with me. "She remains

very sad and will not leave the house or receive visitors. She will barely speak to me."

"Mr. Carson, it has not even been three weeks. Of course, she is still grieving. It will possibly even be the full year of mourning before she is ready to return to society."

"Hmph! You are, of course, right." He frowned. "There yet seems to be something... I have no idea how to say this, but I have reason to believe that you think there might be a connection between my daughter's death and that of Miss Gaines."

"Should I ask what that reason might be?" I said, watching him carefully. There was good reason to believe that he'd made that deduction from the discussion the previous Friday night at Regina's.

Mr. Carson sputtered. "It was, eh, a mutual acquaintance, Mr. Wiley. We were having a drink together."

"Indeed." I sighed. "Well, you are right, Mr. Carson. I do fear that there might be a connection between the two deaths." I paused. "I know this will not be easy to consider, but did your daughter speak to you about a man she feared?"

Mr. Carson went pale, then his face flushed with anger. "You will not impugn my daughter's memory!"

"I have not the slightest interest in doing so," I replied, feeling somewhat angry, myself. "However, there was someone she was afraid—"

"Do not even imply it!" He leapt to his feet. "In fact, this interview is finished."

I gathered my bag up. "Very well, then. Good day."

I made my way through the store, feeling quite nettled and

almost worried. That Mr. Carson had heard that there was a connection between his daughter's death and Lavina's did not bode well. As for him assuming I meant the worst when I asked about Miss Julia's fear of a man, it was not entirely surprising. I have already remarked upon the ready assumption that a young woman had caused her own downfall.

Chapter Thirteen

As I made my way back to where Daisy was tethered, I was surprised to see Mr. Alverno nearby, apparently waiting for me.

"Oh, Mrs. Wilcox," he exclaimed. "I am so glad to see you. I have found out that Mr. Lyons is in the pueblo. In fact, he is even now having his luncheon at the Bella Union Hotel."

The hotel was not far from where we were, but I untethered Daisy and walked her there, with Mr. Alverno by my side the entire way. I was quite puzzled by his behavior, but I thanked him quite nicely as I re-tied Daisy in front of the hotel.

"You have been quite helpful," I told him. "However, I do not wish to keep you from your work. I dare say all three of the judges would be quite put out with me if I did."

Mr. Alverno sighed. "They are always put out."

"That may be. However, if I must come before either Judge Trafford or Judge Widney, I would much rather be in their good graces than not, and I have enough trouble keeping Judge Gresham's good opinion of me, as it is."

Mr. Alverno sighed again but left. As I entered the hotel and made my way to the restaurant, it suddenly occurred to me that I had no idea what Mr. Lyons looked like. This left me little choice but to ask the maitre d'hotel, a solemn man with coal black hair. If I was reluctant to do so, it was because the gentleman, while perfectly polite, still managed to make one feel as though one were utterly beneath his notice. I asked after Mr. Lyons and was taken to his table accompanied by a smirk that I longed to slap off the maitre d'hotel's face.

Mr. Lyons was a small, wiry man, with dark brown hair, a neatly trimmed beard, and a clean suit. He leapt to his feet the second I approached.

"Pray excuse the intrusion upon your meal," I said, as the maitre d'hotel seated me at the table.

"A pretty woman is no intrusion, ma'am," he said. "And who do I have the honor of entertaining?"

"My name is Mrs. Wilcox." I smiled, bracing myself for his recoil, after all, I did fear that my reputation had preceded me. "I have a vineyard and winery in the pueblo."

Mr. Lyons smiled quite prettily. "And I believe you are a physician, are you not?"

"Yes," I said, utterly charmed against my will.

"Please dine with me," Mr. Lyons said, putting up his hand to summon the waiter.

"Why, thank you." I couldn't help consenting, even though I dreaded the tongue lashing I would get from Olivia for missing the meal she had undoubtedly prepared for me, and for my temerity in eating in a restaurant when her food was so much better.

The waiter appeared and Mr. Lyons quickly ordered for me, keeping one eye and his smile aimed in my direction.

Alas, my vanity is possibly my greatest weakness. I like to think that I was still quite attractive at that time, never mind that at thirty-three years old, my dewy youth was well behind me. I took great pains to keep my skin as milky white as it had been when I'd been taken from my home in Boston over twelve years before, and I had largely succeeded. I took care with my hair dressings and if my riding habits were more sensible than decorative, well, I had my work to thank for that.

Nor was I insensible to the pleasures of being courted. It did not matter that I had not the least interest in remarrying. I could not help but enjoy the attentions of a courtly gentleman or even the occasional charming scoundrel.

"I'm told I have you to thank for this most excellent angelica," Mr. Lyons said, indicating his glass.

"That's quite kind of you, Mr. Lyons," I said, feeling the soft flush cover my face.

"As it happens, I was hoping to make your acquaintance." Mr. Lyons leaned forward, then leaned back as the waiter brought me a glass of angelica and set a lovely dish of lamb stew in front of me.

"You were? And may I ask to what end?" I sipped as delicately as I could from the glass. I would have complimented him on his choice, but given that it was my wine, I feared that might be a little too self-aggrandizing.

"Mr. Wiley and I are forming a partnership," Mr. Lyons said. "We finalized the terms this morning."

"He has said nothing to me of this," I said, feeling nettled in spite of the fact that Mr. Wiley was under no obligation to have let me know any of it.

"Well, I'm sure he didn't want to worry your pretty little head over it." Mr. Lyons suddenly gulped as I glared at him.

"Mr. Lyons," I said, "you should know, as well Mr. Wiley does, that when a man tells me I needn't worry my pretty little head, that is precisely when I must."

He gaped for a moment, then sat back and laughed, full and hard.

"Mrs. Wilcox, I salute you." He shook his head in merriment. "Mr. Wiley did tell me that you are quite an astute woman of business and not one to be trifled with."

"He is entirely correct." I offered a stern smile as an olive branch.

"I can see that." Mr. Lyons chuckled again, then turned his attention to his own luncheon. "It will be quite the pleasure working with you, ma'am." He looked at me for a moment. "And yet, you sought me out."

"As I understand it, you have not been in the pueblo for the past few weeks."

"I have been traveling quite a bit of late." He nodded. "Trying to better my fortunes."

"Then you might not be apprised of the tragedies that have struck our fair village over the past two weeks. There have been two cruel murders, one two weeks ago today, and the second a week ago this past Sunday. Two women."

He looked aghast. "What kind of dog would hurt a woman?"

"I have no idea. But I believe you knew at least one of the women, a Miss Lavina Gaines."

"Miss Lavina?" He appeared quite affected by the news. "My former partner was quite sweet on her." He shifted, his face acquiring a most guilty look. "Mr. Efrem Smith. We, eh, were friends as well as partners until we had a falling out this past spring. Over Miss Lavina, as a matter of fact."

"So I have been told." I smiled softly at him.

Mr. Lyons shook his head and sighed. "What terrible news. Poor Miss Lavina. She was such a nice young thing." He looked up at me. "And to think we had a falling out over her. The worst of it is, Efrem was right. There ain't no real money in farming and ranching, just hard work."

"I don't understand," I said. Myself, I was doing rather well, but when I'd thought about it later, that had more to do with my winery business than the actual farming, and not only am I an astute woman of business, I did make very good wine that commanded excellent prices.

"Well, it's kind of a long story." Mr. Lyons had finished most of his repast and I still had plenty of mine, so I nodded to indicate that he should continue. "I grew up in Texas, on a small rancho, but a year or two before the War, my pa took sick and died, and we lost everything. I left my ma and my sisters in the care of my older brother and went off to seek my fortune. It meant one less mouth to feed, and if I was successful, life would be easy for them. I was only thirteen, but I caught on with a cattle driver and we went up North. During the War, I was mostly in the territories, scraping together whatever work I could find, and finally landed in Salt Lake

City, where I met Efrem. He came from a poor family, too, and together we decided that we could pool our resources and buy a good-sized bit of land. I'd take over the ranching, since that was what I knew, and he'd take on the farming, since that was what he knew. We'd heard there was plenty of land in California, so that's where we went. Got here about four years ago and signed on with Mrs. Costa."

"That's where I met Mr. Smith," I said. "The month after the riot."

Mr. Lyons shuddered. "Yes, I heard about that event. I was with Mr. Costa selling hides at the time."

"I see."

"Anyway, it was hard work, but we scrimped and saved as best we could. I could tell Efrem was wanting to settle down real bad. Any pretty little thing that caught his eye, he started courting her. He was getting real anxious about buying our land. He needed a house to bring a bride to. Then he fell hard for Miss Lavina, and she fell for him. He started working with Mr. Gaines then, and said he was making more money faster doing that than anything. So, one day, I asked him what about our ranch and farm that we'd been dreaming about for so long? Efrem flat out told me that he wasn't going to make Miss Lavina a farmer's wife. She wasn't bred to it and didn't deserve that." Mr. Lyons swallowed. "All our dreams gone in a puff of smoke. I don't mind saying I was angry. Efrem had already left the Costa ranch to work here in town with Mr. Gaines. Mr. Costa, he doesn't trust agents, you know."

"Actually, I do, in fact, know that." I smiled at him.

Mr. Lyons looked puzzled for a second, then went on. "At the same time, he was getting awful tired from selling his hides up and down the state. So, a month or so before Efrem and I had our parting of the ways, Mr. Costa sent me to the Anaheim Colony with a load and was so happy with the price I got, that he gave me some of the money. I took another load up to San Francisco, back in March, and the next thing I know, I'm Mr. Costa's agent. In April, not only did I have Mr. Costa's hides to sell, I got another rancher, Mr. Bautista, to give me his. I took the whole load up to San Francisco, and got an even better price for them."

"It would seem that you have quite the business acumen," I said, finishing my stew.

He nodded. "Mr. Wiley's been looking for a partner to expand his business, especially for the wool in the area, so last month, I took a load up to San Francisco for him. Got a very good price and he paid me handsomely." Mr. Lyons chuckled. "I gotta say, I like this work much better than breaking my back chasing cattle on a ranch."

"When did you return to the pueblo?" I asked.

Mr. Lyons blinked as he thought. "I'm not rightly sure. It was sometime the week before last. Or maybe the week before that."

"And you've been here the whole time?"

"No." He laughed and shook his head. "I've been back and forth between here, the Anaheim Colony, San Buenaventura, and San Gabriel. Got some folks out those ways wanting me to agent their goods, too."

"I see. Where were you the Sunday a week past?"

"Oh, I was in the Anaheim Colony. I'd just got there, I think. Wanted to get to business first thing Monday morning."

I smiled. "Well, I am afraid I do have other business to attend to. It was very kind of you to stand me to a luncheon."

"More than happy to, Mrs. Wilcox." He stood as I got up. "It was a real pleasure talking to you."

I wished him a good day, then went out to the street, at a bit of a loss as to what to do next. However, the block across the street gave me an idea. Mr. Wiley's office was not far away, and I was fairly certain that he had not taken a trip anywhere.

Mr. Wiley seemed pleased to see me, but then he usually did.

"However," he said, after seating me in the chair in front of his desk. "I do not have any money for you today."

"I didn't expect that you would." I decided not to perambulate around my reason for being there. "I met Mr. Lyons at luncheon today."

"Oh." Mr. Wiley smiled weakly. "Am I to assume you are not happy with the new arrangement?"

"I see no reason to be unhappy at the moment. Mr. Lyons seems quite capable."

Mr. Wiley chuckled. "You found him quite charming, I'm sure."

"That is neither here nor there, although I would have liked to have had some warning that you were considering a partner."

"I wasn't." He shrugged. "At least, not until a few weeks ago, when I heard that Mr. Costa had decided to trust him. I've been wanting to represent Mr. Costa's hides for years. They're the best in the pueblo. By securing Mr. Lyons as my associate, I get Mr. Costa's trade, as well. I do believe it will be to all our respective benefits."

"No doubt." I paused. "I have one concern, though, not immediately related to Mr. Lyons. I was speaking with Mr. Carson earlier today, and he told me that he'd heard that I believed there to be a connection between the deaths of Miss Julia and Miss Lavina. And while he did not specifically say that you'd said so, he very strongly implied it."

"That's extremely odd." Mr. Wiley's face flushed a deep red. "Yes, Mr. Carson and I were having a drink together, and I do not doubt that you know very well where." He blinked. "Mr. Hewitt was there, as well. There was a discussion about some of the odd things we'd seen, and you can imagine our hostess had seen some very odd things." He paused and blinked at me. "Perhaps I shouldn't say so, but she seemed most curious as to why a man would take a lady's nether garment."

"I see." I swallowed back my embarrassment, as well.

"The odd thing is, I have wondered whether the two deaths were connected." Mr. Wiley's brows knit in thought. "That evening I realized that Miss Gaines was not only your friend, but a friend of Miss Julia's, and it does seem a rather strange happenstance that both deaths occurred so closely together." He looked at me. "But I never said so to Mr. Carson. I wonder how he came to that conclusion and why he would say that it was from me."

"I wonder, as well." I looked out of the window of his office. "Are you still very grieved over Miss Julia's death?"

"I am afraid so." He sighed very deeply, indeed. "Mrs. Wilcox, you might have wondered why I do not wish to marry. The truth is, I would dearly love to have a wife and children. However, three times I have become engaged to be married and each time the young woman in question died before we could get to the altar." He looked at me, his eyes growing full with tears. "I was in love with dear Miss Carson. She was so utterly charming and sweet. I was about to speak to her father about courting her when she, too, died." He sighed again. "I must be cursed somehow."

"Dear Mr. Wiley." I smiled at him softly. "I do not believe in curses, and I sincerely hope that you will find your wife."

He chuckled. "Just not in you, my darling Mrs. Wilcox."

"Absolutely not." I laughed gently, as well. "I will grant that you are more tempting a fellow than most, but I have no use for a husband."

"And while I cherish our friendship, I should not at all like to have you for a wife."

I smiled, then suddenly frowned. "I do need to ascertain your whereabouts on Sunday afternoon, a week past. June second, to be precise."

"Oh." He blinked. "I was at home all day, at least until the shots were fired for the dispensary fire."

"That's right. You're one of the volunteers." I got up and Mr. Wiley scrambled to his feet. "Well, I must wish you good day. Thank you for talking to me."

As I left, Mr. Wiley held me back.

"Mrs. Wilcox," he asked. "It now occurs to me why you asked about that Sunday evening. That was when Miss Gaines disappeared."

"I'm afraid so, Mr. Wiley."

He frowned. "Surely you do not believe that I had anything to do with her murder."

"I do not know what to believe, Mr. Wiley." I looked down at my hands. "You have always been quite kind, to be sure." I looked up at him. "I cannot explain why, but I must ask you not to discuss either Miss Carson's death or Miss Gaines'. Nor any conversation you might have had in Mrs. Medina's parlor."

"I won't. I assure you."

I smiled sadly and hurried out.

It was true that Mr. Wiley had no inclination to rage, however exuberant he might have been. I, perhaps, should not have asked him not to talk about the deaths and the conversation at Regina's. However, I had decided that if he kept silence, then there was more reason to trust him. That might not have been the most logical or appropriate decision, but then, there was part of me that did not want Mr. Wiley to be guilty.

Chapter Fourteen

The next morning found me once again at the Clocktower Courthouse. I had spent the night before wracking my brains trying to make sense of the few bits of information that I had. Finally, I decided to speak to Judge Gresham in the hopes of prying some information out of him.

The problem was that I was going to have to be particularly circumspect in how I did so. I could afford a certain, shall we say, frankness with Mr. Wiley thanks to long association and friendship. Judge Gresham may have had some association with me; however, there was no friendship and very little trust.

For once, Mr. Alverno was actually helpful and arranged for me to speak with His Honor promptly. I think the clerk was hoping that I would accuse the judge of killing Lavina, but I had no such plan.

His Honor rose as I entered the room and offered me a chair in front of his desk.

"What can I do for you today, Mrs. Wilcox?" he asked brusquely as he settled himself.

"You can answer some questions." I blinked at the sunlight streaming in through the window behind him. "Are you aware that there is a man forcing himself on young women in the pueblo?"

"What?" he sputtered. "We do not tolerate that sort of abomination here!"

"Of course not," I said, somehow managing not to roll my eyes. "No one tolerates that sort of thing. It does not, however, prevent it from happening. I gravely fear it may have had something to do with the two murders, however."

"And how so?" The judge's bushy gray eyebrows squeezed together. "Do you have any proof that Miss Gaines had been, eh, forced upon?"

"Well, perhaps some..." I thought about how to explain what I'd found. "There's a... nether garment missing. And there was some lace torn from her dress."

"That is not proof that some man forced himself on her."

"Who else would take it?"

He cleared his throat. "You examined the body."

"I did, and found no... eh, sign that she had been... eh, fully forced upon."

"Then upon what are you basing this spurious claim?" His voice almost rang with triumph.

"Miss Gaines was, in fact, murdered," I replied, my voice rising in spite of myself.

Judge Gresham sputtered. "Need you impugn the poor young woman's memory with such tawdriness?"

"How is it impugning her memory when she was violated by a monster who is probably preying upon other young women in the pueblo?"

The judge snorted. "It is well known that a young woman violated in such a way generally incites that violation herself."

I leapt to my feet. "However well-known it may be, it is an utterly false assertion. No woman wants to be forced upon, and innocent young women who are kept ignorant of the ways of men and women are often led into believing themselves trollops simply for smiling kindly and sweetly at the very men they are supposed to attract in order to gain husbands. If men are so much stronger and wiser than women, then why is it they are not able to restrain their baser instincts? Why must you blame the young woman when she is wholly innocent and preyed upon by a depraved monster?"

His Honor hemmed and hawed for a minute. "You may, in fact, have a point. I will keep this conference between us, however."

"And if you hear of anyone who might be engaged in such depravity or has that bit of lace or the... nether garment, I would appreciate it if you let me know." I watched as his eyes widened. "Your Honor, I am a lady, and hope to bear myself with that dignity and care at all times. However unfit and unsuitable such a topic is and might be, it is still, sadly, an all too frequent occurrence, and will continue to be so as long as men like you are afraid of offending delicate sensibilities. I assure you, mine are not all that delicate, nor does that make me any less a lady. I am not a hoyden or a trollop, and I will take great umbrage if you choose to characterize me that way. Nor will you tarnish the memory of a perfectly lovely and innocent young woman simply because some man chose to visit upon her the worst kind of evil!"

With that, there was nothing else to do, but sweep from the office, which I did. It is also sadly true that I must number my temper amongst my faults. After vanity, it is possibly the worst.

"Mrs. Wilcox." Mr. Alverno scuttled up to me as I walked into the corridor leading to the stairs. "Mrs. Wilcox."

I stopped and turned. "Yes, Mr. Alverno."

"I take it your interview with His Honor did not go well."

That my temper was still flaring I could not help, but I realized very quickly that I did not wish to take it out on the hapless clerk.

"No," I said finally after taking a deep breath. "It did not."

"Could it be because he...?" Mr. Alverno looked back at the office.

"I have no way of knowing, Mr. Alverno." I sighed deeply.

"He keeps saying that it was Mr. Gaines."

"That seems highly unlikely. Mr. Gaines, himself, asked my aid in finding the killer."

"His Honor says that Mr. Gaines did so in the hopes that you would think just that."

I looked at the clerk, feeling decidedly annoyed. "Of course, His Honor would think so. I am a mere woman. However, I do hope that my perspicacity is well enough renowned that it would make no sense for a man to ask me to find the guilty party if he, himself, is the guilty party. If I were a doddering fool, perhaps. But why would he think that, even if I am a woman."

"Perhaps if he wished to distract you?"

"Possibly." I looked back at the judge's chambers. "Or if he were that foolish." I looked back at the clerk. "Well, good day, Mr. Alverno. This was but one of many errands I have today."

I left the building feeling exceptionally annoyed. I was no closer to finding the malefactor I sought. His Honor had been impossibly obtuse and immune to reason. I took a deep breath in the hopes of soothing myself, then turned my mind over to my next few tasks.

Given that I had several people that I wished to speak to, and that I had spent as much time the day before walking Daisy as riding her, I decided that I might as well walk that day. I visited a couple of patients, then made my way to the Gaines home.

I was somewhat surprised that Mrs. Gaines had me admitted, especially after she haughtily informed me that Mr. Gaines had yet to arrive for his luncheon.

"It is good of you to see me then," I said.

She sat daintily in a chair next to the fireplace and with some reluctance indicated that I should seat myself on the nearby sofa.

"How might I help you?" she asked.

I thought about how best to begin. "There is some good news about your sister-in-law's death. We have been able to ascertain a likely time that it happened. However, it is now incumbent upon me to discern where all the related parties were at that time."

Mrs. Gaines' eyes widened. "Surely you are not accusing Mr. Gaines? He came to you for help."

"I am fully cognizant of that, Mrs. Gaines." I forced a

smile to my lips. "In fact, it is in that capacity that I am here now. If I am able to say that Mr. Gaines was clearly in the company of someone else during the critical hours when his sister went on her walk, then no one can accuse him of the deadly deed."

"He did not kill his sister!" Mrs. Gaines snapped, quivering with rage.

"I did not say that he did," I replied as evenly as I could. "Nor do I particularly think so. However, if we can clearly state that he was with you that afternoon, or better yet, with some guests, perchance, then it will be a great deal harder for the gossips in the pueblo to claim that he did."

"Oh." She blinked her eyes, then pulled a handkerchief from her sleeve and dabbed at her cheeks. "Pray forgive me for such a display. You have no idea how difficult it has been. First, to be so vilified for simply trying to care for poor Lavina in the best way we knew how, and now to come under such scrutiny and suspicion when we are utterly innocent of the deed."

"You, as well?" I asked.

"Of course, me." She shuddered and sniffed again. "Everyone insists on believing that I had no regard for our dear sister, that I would have been happier without her presence. But nothing could be further from the truth. I dearly loved Lavina and only wanted the best for her."

"There was the matter of the will," I said softly, watching her carefully.

"Yes, there was." She sat up straight, the umbrage wafting off of her. However, it was not directed at me. "It was utterly unfair. You, perhaps, might have some idea of how harsh Father Gaines was with my darling Timothy. He was dreadfully cruel to my husband, who did not deserve it."

"I had thought there was some rapprochement shortly before your father-in-law's passing."

"There was." Mrs. Gaines blinked and dabbed at her nose this time. "It hardly made up for the years and years of debasement that Timothy suffered under him. Timothy was satisfied, however, until the will was read. What vicious monster would do such a thing as to leave half his fortune to an unmarried girl when she had a brother perfectly capable and happy to care for her? I even told Father Gaines repeatedly that I had nothing but the most tender concern for our sister. Lavina would have been in the best of hands. Timothy was cut to the quick! The poor thing. His own father didn't trust him to take care of his sister. Can you imagine?"

"I suppose I must."

Mrs. Gaines snorted. "We had to put Lavina's fortune into a trust. It was the best way to protect her."

"She was eminently sensible."

"Was she?" Mrs. Gaines glared at me. "What about that farmer, Mr. Smith?"

"He was working with the senior Mr. Gaines to prove himself."

"And you know very well what comes to pass when a young man makes himself over to win his lady love. The day after the wedding he goes right back to his true nature and his poor bride is hung out to dry. I have no doubt that Mr. Smith would have turned dear Lavina into a farmer's wife, a drudge, slaving away in poverty." Mrs. Gaines pursed her lips in disgust. "Lavina deserved a husband of breeding and culture. Timothy and I had several good candidates ready for her."

"Here?" I asked.

It was another of my failings, I'm afraid. What most of the Americans in the pueblo considered good breeding and culture was not what I thought of as such. It was one of the many reasons I did not care for Los Angeles, even as it became more and more my home. However, I was not alone in my disregard for the men in the pueblo.

"In San Francisco," said Mrs. Gaines with a sniff. "I have cousins who have made good fortunes and would have supported her quite nicely. That's why we had to keep her at home. I explained it to her. This town has a terrible reputation for violence and ruffians, and that horrible riot last fall did not help in the least. I had to protect her to assure my cousins that she was completely modest and had been kept safe from any malefactors in the town."

I bit my tongue, remembering that Lavina had told me something completely different. It also suddenly occurred to me that Mrs. Gaines' disregard for the men of the pueblo did not entirely make sense.

"Pray forgive me, Mrs. Gaines," I said slowly. "If you do not find the men here suitable as husbands, how is it that you came be to be married to one?"

She began to shudder with rage, then suddenly broke down.

"They did not want me!" she sobbed. "They said I was too grasping, too meddlesome. I merely wanted to be a good helpmate, but they wanted girls who were small and dainty. Not some ugly giant like me."

"There, there," I said, feeling somewhat nonplussed. "You and Mr. Timothy seem quite companionable."

"We are of one heart." Mrs. Gaines' sobs abated, and she wiped her eyes and nose. "But I was forced to come here to get a husband."

I sighed. I knew well her disdain for the pueblo. I had felt it many, many times, myself.

"At least you are blessed in a husband who suits you," I finally said. "I was not so blessed in mine."

"Did you find him here?"

"No." I looked at her as I tried to find the right words to describe my situation. Many people in the pueblo knew the basic facts of how I had come to be there, but only my friends knew how harsh those facts had been. "I was married in Boston, where I am from. The late Mr. Wilcox decided to bring me here."

"Did he not survive the trip?"

"Oh, he survived that, and lived long enough to buy Rancho de las Flores, but not much longer than that."

"How terrible! You poor thing."

"I have managed." I smiled weakly.

She seemed to take my smile as being brave in the face of grief. It was anything but. Mr. Wilcox had dragged me there in 1860, almost immediately after our marriage. Upon arrival, he bought the winery and vineyard, then was conveniently struck by lightning while riding one Sunday. I suppose I shouldn't describe Albert Wilcox's death as convenient. He was, after all, one of God's creatures. But he was a dreadful man, utterly lacking in tenderness or kind regard. That he had died so soon after buying the rancho had only been the kindest of blessings as far as I was concerned, especially after I was able to show the court his letter promising me all of his property when he died.

We were interrupted by the arrival home of the young Mr. Gaines. Mrs. Gaines greeted her husband happily, then scurried off to the kitchen to see to his lunch.

"I hope you are well, Mrs. Wilcox," Mr. Gaines said with some trepidation.

"Quite well," I said, getting to my feet. "As I was explaining to Mrs. Gaines, we have ascertained a probable time during which your sister came to grief. I am hoping you can say that you and Mrs. Gaines were at home that afternoon until supper."

Mr. Gaines sighed deeply. "I cannot. I presume Mrs. Gaines was, but I was not at home that afternoon."

"Oh? Where were you?"

Mr. Gaines gaped and hawed for a moment. "I do hope you will not think ill of me. However..." He swallowed. "I was in my office working on accounts." He winced and held up his hand to forestall my response. "I know. Working in such a way on the Lord's Day." He sighed. "However, one of my clerks had run off the week before, leaving the accounts in a complete mess."

"One of your clerks? Not Mr. Smith?"

"Oh, no!" Mr. Gaines smiled quite enthusiastically. "Mr. Smith has been an enormous help in our business. He saved us from buying a terrible property not too long ago when he pointed out that there was no nearby zanja to irrigate it. His farming experience has been quite helpful." Mr. Gaines looked back toward the dining room of the house. "It is possible that he will return to farming some day, as Mabel fears. That is why she did not favor his suit. If he does, however, I do hope that I can call upon him even then to help evaluate properties. He is uncommonly good at it."

"Was anyone else at the office with you?" I asked.

He shook his head. "I'm afraid not. I did not wish to be seen. It is bad enough that my father's reputation was as a miser. I do not wish to be excoriated in such a way."

"No doubt. Well, thank you, nonetheless. I must be on my way."

"Would you care to stay for luncheon?"

I shook my head. "No, thank you. I missed my lunch yesterday, and Mrs. Ortiz will be quite put out with me if I miss it again."

I left, feeling quite put out, myself. Neither Mr. nor Mrs. Gaines had fully absolved themselves by virtue of being in company during the critical hours, and what I had learned from them was interesting, perhaps, but of little use to my inquiries. As I walked back to my rancho, it occurred to me that Mrs. Gaines had not lied to me.

That is not to say that I believed that she had any true consideration for Lavina's well-being beyond keeping her husband's hands on Lavina's money. However, Mrs. Gaines had clearly convinced herself that she did want the best for her sister-in-law. Furthermore, Mr. Gaines was more concerned that he would be judged badly for working on a Sunday than he was about the act, itself. Not that it was that great a sin, but I suppose he felt it important to look pious, even if his behavior was not. I sighed. The two certainly were well-matched.

As it turned out, I was late for my lunch, and Olivia was decidedly annoyed.

"And who tried to kill you today?" she demanded as she set a plate of chicken in front of me.

"No one," I said, sighing. "I was merely detained while speaking with Mr. and Mrs. Gaines. In fact, I declined to eat with them because I knew that you had my lunch ready."

"It's a good thing you did." She flopped into the chair next to mine. "They would have probably poisoned you. It would not be the first time."

Alas, it wouldn't have been.

"Olivia, what am I to do?" I looked at her. "There is a monster loose in the pueblo who preys on young women. Am I to leave him to go about his business only to have him ruining innocent girl after innocent girl, and quite possibly killing them, too?"

She sighed. "You're right, Maddie. And the worst of it is, no one else in the pueblo will be able to find him. But I can't help worrying about you. You take no care for yourself."

"I take care. I am very cautious."

She snorted. "And yet you go into the home of the very person who could be doing this."

"I am fairly certain Mr. Gaines is innocent. He did ask for my help."

"And what about Mrs. Gaines? Are you so sure about her?"

I sighed. "I'm afraid not."

"And what about Mr. Lomax? You went to his home on Sunday."

"Mr. Lomax?" I stopped eating long enough to look at her. "What makes you think Mr. Lomax may be part of this?"

She winced. "I don't, but there are rumors in the pueblo. Maria brings them back. You know that."

"And what are the rumors about Mr. Lomax?"

"That they're Mormons and that Mr. Lomax wanted to take Miss Gaines as his third wife. She wouldn't marry him, and that's why he killed her."

"What nonsense!" I snapped. "You know Mr. Lomax."

"I'm not saying that I believe it." Olivia rolled her eyes. "But you asked what the rumors were. Those are the rumors. However ridiculous they are, that's what people are saying."

I drummed my fingers on the table. "How utterly unkind. And undeserved, I assure you. Mr. Lomax is not a Mormon."

Olivia's eyebrows rose. It is true that I had stretched the point in that Mr. Lomax had been a Mormon, but no longer adhered to that sect, and I do not doubt that Olivia had seen right through me. But there was little else to be done. I did not want Mr. Lomax and his family exposed to the kinds of nastiness that often occurred among the Americans in the pueblo toward those who were different. We'd seen too much of it the previous fall, and while it was very unlikely Mr. Lomax would be lynched, there was tremendous potential for vandalism or other torments.

After my dinner, I went to the winery to see to the wines, and all was in order there. Sebastiano, Enrique, and I spent some time in conference, since it appeared that we were going to have another drought year that summer. Fortunately, we made our plan in good time, for yet another summons sent me walking back into the main part of the pueblo, this time to the home of Mrs. Glassell.

In many ways, she was the twin of Mrs. Carson, stout,

medium tall, and extremely fond of gossip. Her husband, Mr. Glassell, was a prominent attorney in the area who owned vast swathes of land, both northwest of the pueblo proper and in the Anaheim Colony, and presumably along the route the new proposed railroad would eventually go. I never found out for certain that he did, however, Mr. Glassell was on the committee devoted to convincing the railroad people to terminate the second transcontinental railroad in Los Angeles.

Although no one in the Glassell home was ailing, I came to almost wish someone had been. Mrs. Glassell was not happy with me.

She sat in the throne-like chair next to her fireplace in her front parlor, which was filled with bibelots and badly done paintings on the wall. She wore a pink-sprigged lawn tea dress that did not favor her and had her huge carpet bag next to her on the floor. I had good cause to be wary of the carpet bag, since Mrs. Glassell was prone to carrying possibly the largest pistol I had ever seen.

"Why are you besmirching the memory of poor Julia Carson?" she demanded as I entered the room.

"I am doing no such thing," I replied. I sat down on the huge rose-figured sofa. "Who told you that I am?"

"It is of no consequence. Have you no concern for poor Mrs. Carson's feelings?"

"I have a great deal of concern for them. But—"

"And what makes you so certain that Julia was…?" Mrs. Glassell blinked, trying to find the right words.

"Mrs. Glassell, I am a physician and there are certain signs of that condition that I saw upon the poor girl, myself."

Mrs. Glassell gaped. "You knew about that part?" She suddenly sobbed. "Oh, dear! This is so terrible."

I kept my voice as soft and soothing as I could. "Yes, I know."

"She was innocent!" Mrs. Glassell shrieked, pulling a handkerchief from her sleeve. "The monster forced himself upon her. I am certain of it."

"As am I," I said firmly. "There is no reason to believe that Julia Carson was anything but virtuous. I don't know how it has gotten out that I believe that what happened to Miss Carson is quite possibly connected to the death of Miss Gaines. That is why I wish to know who told you about the situation. Perhaps it will lead me to the monster who did this."

Mrs. Glassell sighed. "It was Mr. Glassell who told me. He is quite peeved that you are going in that direction. It is so unkind to the Carsons. Haven't they been through enough?"

"Will it ease their grief if the monster strikes again because we hesitated to find him in order to spare their feelings?"

"But people will say that she brought it on herself."

I couldn't help groaning. "I know what people say. It is ridiculous! And, dear Mrs. Glassell, if there were any other way to find this monster, then I would most certainly pursue it. I was hoping to avoid harming poor Julia's reputation. It disturbs me greatly that the rumors have gone in that direction."

"So, what are you going to do?"

"I have no idea." I could feel my brow creasing as I thought. "You have a daughter of that age, do you not?"

"No. Both my daughters are grown. Still, I have my granddaughters. Maizie is a little young but has connections among

Julia's associates." Mrs. Glassell glared again at me. "You do not propose to send her in the way of this evil man?"

"Oh, Heavens no!" I fidgeted with the stitching on the back of my glove. "However, Julia had warned two other girls in the pueblo to be wary. Perhaps she let something slip to someone else. Or perhaps some other girls have come across the man but have not fallen prey yet."

"We can but hope."

"In any case, I would not be surprised if the word has gone out among the young people without we adults being any the wiser."

"To be sure." Mrs. Glassell sniffed and worried her handkerchief. "I have seen it happen any number of times. Young people are always so certain that they know more about the world than their parents do."

"As we did when we were young."

Mrs. Glassell glanced at me as if to correct me but obviously knew that I was right. I stood.

"I am so sorry for what has happened," I said. "But if you could speak with your granddaughters and let me know what, if anything, they say, that would be a help. In the meantime, I must find out who told everyone about my concerns."

Mrs. Glassell had her maid show me out, and I walked aimlessly toward the Clocktower Courthouse. As I passed in front of that edifice, loud screaming erupted from behind it.

Chapter Fifteen

The young woman who had screamed was Dolores Ayala, whose father had an exceptionally fine apricot orchard. The moment I saw her behind the courthouse, I immediately thanked Our Most Merciful Savior that she was not in immediate peril, although what she had found was exceptionally ghastly.

The corpse lay in a trash heap. It belonged to a well-rounded man, but it was not immediately obvious who, as the face had been obliterated thanks to a shotgun blast. Others gathered, and young Dolores' mother took the girl into her care. I bent to the body on the ground.

"I thought he was a drunk," Dolores gasped to no one in particular. "I went to wake him, and he had no face!"

I turned the corpse's head slightly and saw the cauliflower ear.

"It is Judge Gresham," I said, also addressing no one in particular.

"Looks that way," said a familiar, quiet voice.

I turned. Mr. Lomax stood over me, his face grim. Mr. Navarro also ran up.

"What happened?" Mr. Navarro asked as I immediately began looking around the trash heap.

"Judge Gresham has been shot and killed," I said. "How and why he was left here, I do not know."

"How do you know he was left here?" Mr. Navarro asked.

"Don't see any blood," Mr. Lomax said, then he looked at me. "Is that what you're thinking?"

"Yes, I am." I looked carefully at the ground around the trash heap. I could see no sign of a body being dragged or of the gore that would most assuredly have been dropped. "But how could someone have brought a body here in the middle of the day without being seen?"

Sighing, I looked up at Mr. Lomax, and just beyond him I saw a smear of something just below the windows on the second floor of the building. Mr. Lomax turned and saw the same thing I had.

"Which of those windows belongs to Judge Gresham's chambers?" I asked.

"The one right above us," said one of the junior clerks. He was a dark-haired lad who looked to have freshly finished a short course of study at St. Vincent's College. "Hey, look at that brown spot just underneath it," he added, noticing the dark blood stain that I and Mr. Lomax had seen.

That the spot had turned brown already told me that it had been left at least an hour or so before. The clock in the clocktower began tolling four in the afternoon.

"When was the last time anyone saw Judge Gresham?" I asked the small crowd that had gathered.

The junior clerk laughed. "I didn't see him all morning. I heard him yelling at Mr. Alverno again, though. We were all leaving for luncheon."

"Did you hear what he was yelling about?"

The junior clerk shrugged. "Does it make any difference? The judge is always yelling or screaming at someone. The rest of us run the second it starts. We don't want to get yelled at, too."

Fortunately, Mr. Sutton's men came running up just then. I left the body in their care and hurried into the courthouse with Mr. Lomax and Mr. Navarro both on my heels. As I strode into the corridor, Mr. Alverno scrambled to his feet and looked up at me anxiously.

"Is it true?" he asked with a worried frown. "They are saying that Judge Gresham was shot. Is it true?"

"I'm afraid so," I said.

I went straight to the door to the judge's chambers, which was closed.

"You can't go in there!" Mr. Alverno snapped in terror.

Mr. Lomax stepped in front of the clerk. "I don't see why she can't."

I went into the chambers and found exactly what I expected to find. The judge's chair was turned toward the open window. The back of the chair had the traces of the gore I would have found in the alley had His Honor been shot there. The wall on either side of the window held the same.

"He was shot here. Then killer turned his chair and tipped him out of the window," I said. "There is no doubt of it. But how is it that a shotgun blast would go unremarked in a busy courthouse?"

"It's not so busy at noontime," Mr. Lomax said.

Mr. Navarro laughed. "Everyone rushes off to his luncheon the second the clock strikes twelve, if they haven't left before then."

I nodded, realizing that it was, indeed, true. It was most inconvenient for those in the pueblo who had business with the court but who could not leave their place of employment except at lunchtime.

At that moment, Mr. Alverno slid into the room and gasped.

I turned to him. "I understand that His Honor had words with you right at lunchtime."

"I didn't do anything!" Mr. Alverno squeaked.

"I didn't say you had," I replied. "However, one of your fellows said that he heard the judge yelling at you as they left for their luncheon."

Mr. Alverno turned pale. "Oh, no! He always yelled at me. You can't be accusing me...!"

"I am not accusing you of anything," I said sternly. "I merely wish to know what His Honor was upset about."

"Oh." Mr. Alverno trembled, then sucked his tooth. "Oh. It was nothing. He was like that. Constantly berating me for absolutely nothing."

"I am well aware of that," I said. I had kept my voice stern even as my heart wrenched for the poor little man. I looked around the room again. "I'm afraid there's little more to be found here." I looked at Mr. Lomax and Mr. Navarro. "Do you wish me to inform the judge's widow?"

"We'll see to it," Mr. Lomax said. He glanced at Mr. Navarro and nodded.

I left the courthouse with both of the police officers but made my way to the funeral parlor whilst they went on to, presumably, Judge Gresham's home. Angelina was in, but there was not much to be discovered from the corpse. It was all too obvious what had killed him and given that we had a very good idea of when he had been killed, little to consider beyond that.

Angelina sent a note to Regina with Tai Chin, requesting a conference that evening and I waited only long enough for the answer, which was in the affirmative, to arrive.

As I made ready to leave for my rancho, Damiano arrived at Angelina's workroom door.

"I'm here to see you safely to your next visit," he announced, then chuckled. "Although, I think you'd better head back to the rancho."

I couldn't help groaning. "They are worried, aren't they?"

"They should be," said Angelina, not smiling. "First, Regina is attacked with a shotgun, which could have been aimed at you, and now Judge Gresham is killed with one?"

"Shotguns are hardly uncommon in the pueblo," I replied testily.

"But most people prefer rifles or six-shooters," Angelina said.

I sighed and took my leave. As it happened, I'd planned on returning to the rancho after speaking with Angelina. Therefore, I decided not to forestall any tongue-lashings and walked with Damiano back home.

Maria, Magdalena, Olivia, Anita, and Juanita were all

waiting for me in my front parlor, their faces solemn, and for once, not all speaking together.

"Maddie," Anita said, "You must catch this monster."

"Of course, but..." I was nonplussed to say the least. Usually, the women of my household were dead set against me searching out killers.

"Elberta Alonso," Maria said. "She told me today that another girl has been attacked. She would not say who. You know what people think about girls that way. Señora Alonso only told me because she was hoping you'll put a stop to it."

"That will be hard to do if no one is willing to say who has been attacked, let alone who their attacker is," I replied.

"You can talk to Señora Alonso," Magdalena said. She was married to Enrique and was tall with dark hair and a face that generally smiled. She was utterly serious at that moment, however.

I untied my bonnet. "Do you think she will speak with me?"

Juanita took the bonnet and my gloves. "We think so."

"She was very upset," Maria said.

"I do not doubt it," I replied. I looked the women over. "Do any of you have any idea who could be forcing himself on the young women of the pueblo?"

Anita's laugh was short and bitter. "There are lots of men who could be. Even the best gentlemen think nothing of taking liberties with us Mexican women."

"Mr. Larson, the grocer?" Maria said. "He does every time I am in there. I know you told me not to go there anymore, but it doesn't make any difference. Mr. Carson. Mr. Loya. Mr. Gambrino. They all do it."

"And often enough, they take liberties with the American

young women, too," Juanita said. "Then they claim that we ask for it with our smiles. But if we are sour and pull away, then we are being cold and unwomanly."

"Mr. Carson?" I asked suddenly.

"Ay. He is the worst!" Maria gasped. "It's bad enough that the deaf old man pretends not to see me. But if Mr. Carson is in the store, I will not go in unless there is another woman or two in there, as well. Otherwise, he will chase me to get what he wants."

"Why haven't you said anything about this?" I asked her.

"What good will it do?" Maria snorted. "The men won't believe us, and they won't listen to you, either." She shrugged. "And we still need paper and flour and sugar and other goods. We have our ways of getting around these fools."

I sighed. "But the fact that there are so many of them will make it quite difficult to discern which of them is the man who killed Miss Lavina and Mama Jane."

Which is exactly the conclusion that Angelina, Regina, and I arrived at later that evening as we sat in Regina's bedroom. Regina was feeling quite her normal self but remained bedridden partly on my say so and partly because she couldn't get a corset on over her wounds. Angelina sat with her little wooden desk on her lap, frowning at her list.

"It would seem that a great many men in the pueblo had some sort of contact with either Miss Julia or Miss Lavina," Angelina said. "And several of them had contact with both."

"But how many of them would have reason to shoot the judge?" I asked.

Regina chortled. "Quite a few, I would imagine. His Honor was known to accept the odd bribe or two, albeit in cases that he deemed as being of no consequence. And he did seem to favor the weaker party many times."

"Nor is it by any means certain that his death has anything to do with our search," Angelina grumbled. "After all, Mama Jane and Miss Lavina were strangled."

I frowned. "I just thought of something. There was no indication that Mama Jane had been violated or any such attempt made."

"True," said Angelina. She took a sip of the angelica all three of us were drinking. "But the marks on her throat were the same as on Miss Lavina's."

"Oh, that's right." I sighed and emptied my glass. "But perhaps we should ask ourselves who would want to shoot both Regina and Judge Gresham?"

"That is assuming that I was the desired target," Regina said. "It could just as easily have been you lying useless in your bed."

"You are hardly useless," Angelina said even before I could.

"Perhaps it is more of consequence that it has gotten out that I seek a connection between Miss Julia and Miss Lavina," I said. "I can't think how that came about."

"Oh, I can," Regina said. "You mentioned it to my brother."

"Mr. Mahoney?" I closed my eyes, then groaned. "Do you know why he reacted so oddly when I told him that there may have been some impropriety involved?"

"Two reasons," Regina said. "One was that he was utterly shocked that you would mention such a thing. The other was that he was horrified that anyone would accuse Miss Julia of an impropriety. And if Miss Julia were coming under such an accusation, then he was worried that Annie and Alice would come in for worse. Miss Julia considered them friends, as you know." Regina snorted. "It is so ridiculous that people would be so quick to accuse even my dear nieces, who are exceedingly proper. My brother has never let them anywhere near the front of that saloon and has taken great pains to make sure that no one is able to get to the back. What more could he do to protect his girls? But, alas, many of even our finer citizens have very small minds, indeed, and are quite prone to assuming the worst in everybody."

"As I know all too well." I closed my eyes. "But I told Mr. Mahoney that I wished to take him into my confidence. Why would he have then spread it about?"

Regina's eyebrows rose. "That is most certainly not like my brother."

"If he was so shocked, perhaps he said something without realizing it," Angelina said.

"That is more likely," Regina said.

"I suppose that would be the case." I poured another glass of angelica. "But if he did, why did Mr. Carson suggest that it was Mr. Wiley? Mr. Wiley told me that he had said nothing of the sort to Mr. Carson, although after your conversation last Friday, he did say that he began to wonder if there wasn't a connection between the two deaths."

"Lies upon lies," Regina intoned.

"True," Angelina said, pouring some angelica for Regina, then for herself. "I do believe I know why Mr. Carson said it was Mr. Wiley, though. Mr. Wiley was very sweet on Miss Julia, and Mr. Carson did not approve."

Regina took the glass from Angelina. "That would make sense. I have detected some enmity between the two men, but that does not mean either of them were responsible for the deaths. Now, if someone had shot at Mr. Wiley, then there would be good reason to be suspicious of Mr. Carson."

"Which means..." I pondered, then blinked my eyes against the tears. "Oh, good Heavens, I have no idea what it means."

Angelina frowned at her notes. "Perhaps if we look at the men that we think might be our monster, maybe we can find a connection to Judge Gresham."

"If His Honor were the only death, I could readily be suspicious of Mr. Alverno," I said. "However, while he held Mama Jane in disdain, it was no worse than the disdain he holds for everyone, and he seemed quite fond of Lavina."

"Neither Mr. Carson nor Mr. Wiley seemed to have any connection to the judge besides the occasional meeting in passing," Regina said.

"Mr. Lomax and Mr. Navarro worked with him as police officers," Angelina said. "And they were frequently asked to be jurors for inquests."

"They were also right there when His Honor's body was found," I said, then frowned. "The problem is, there is no reason to be suspicious of them being in the neighborhood of the courthouse. If anything, that is one of the places one would most likely expect to see them."

"What about Mr. Smith?" Angelina asked.

"It's possible he has appeared before the judge in some matter or other, but I know of none," I said. "The same could be said for Mr. Lyons, Mr. Samples, and Mr. Lawrence."

"And Mr. Lawrence could not have killed the judge," Angelina said. "He was at his schoolhouse all day today preparing students for the teacher's exam."

"How do you know this?" Regina asked.

Angelina shrugged. "I could see him. The schoolhouse is across the back alley from my workroom and study. He and the students even ate their lunches there."

"And he is the person we least suspect of forcing himself on Miss Julia," I said. "Angelina, have you had a chance to speak to Father Gallar?"

Angelina looked exceptionally peeved. "He will not talk to me. But he does leave the church several times a day. No one knows where he goes."

"Which is deeply suspicious but hardly conclusive." I shook my head to clear it. "We have no clear way of discerning anything, especially given that we are potentially searching for two different malefactors. It is my opinion that we should end this conference while we are still relatively sober so that we can continue asking questions tomorrow without a headache."

Angelina slipped away to call Tai Chin, who was waiting in the kitchen. Some minutes and another glass of angelica later, the maid summoned Angelina and me to the back, where Tai Chin led us to the street and the Suttons' buggy. Mr. Sutton got down from the seat and helped us ladies into the back, then drove me to my rancho.

The next morning, I rode Daisy into the pueblo, with Damiano on the mule following me as I made a few rounds of patients, then went to visit the Alonso adobe up on Calle de Eternidad. Damiano held the beasts as I knocked.

Mrs. Alonso, a care-worn woman with dark gray hair, opened the door. She wore a simple, but very clean dress and spectacles.

"I'm Mrs. Wilcox," I told her. "My housemaid, Mrs. Mendoza, said that you wanted my help."

She pursed her lips but let me into the small adobe. "Please. Sit down."

There was a small sofa and two well-used chairs on either side of a fireplace. The floor was dirt, but the walls were bright white. There was a small cabinet near the door with a photograph in a frame. Mrs. Alonso saw me looking at it.

"My late husband," she said as I perched on the edge of the sofa.

"I'm so sorry. Has he been gone long?"

"Long enough. I have good sons, though, and they support me." She sighed deeply, then sat in one of the two chairs. "You have come about the man in the pueblo who is hurting our girls."

"Yes. Do you know who he is or might be?"

The old woman shook her head. "Nothing. The girl I am thinking of is too afraid to say. She said that he will not only hurt her, but will ruin her friends, as well."

"Which would be all too easy, I'm afraid." I looked at her. "How is it that you know what has happened?"

Mrs. Alonso swallowed and closed her eyes. "She is my granddaughter. Her mother, she married an American. She said our girl was suffering somehow. I could see that, too. So, I kept her here at my home and finally, after a terrible nightmare, my granddaughter told me about an evil man who forced himself on her."

Mrs. Alonso began crying, and my eyes were full, as well.

"And you have no idea who he is."

She squeezed her eyes shut and shook her head.

"Is there any way that I can speak with your granddaughter?"

"Not easily. We sent her to San Buenaventura to live with my other daughter and her husband. There no one knows her, and she can live without worrying that her shame will be revealed."

"What shame?" I couldn't help saying. "She has done nothing wrong. I know that there are those who will not see it that way, and you were right to send her elsewhere. But we need to know who this monster is so that we can stop him from ruining other young women. If she identifies the man, she will be safe where she is, and I, personally, will see to it that no other young lady is harmed by him."

Mrs. Alonso nodded. "My son goes to visit them today. I will send a note. We can but hope she will tell us something."

I thanked the old woman, then left. As I left the adobe, I saw several men hurrying up toward the northwestern part of the pueblo. Several boys followed, and I stopped one as he ran past.

"What is going on?" I asked.

"They're going to arrest the Negro farmer for murdering Judge Gresham!"

Chapter Sixteen

Damiano and I galloped our mounts to the Samples' place by another route and arrived well ahead of the men on foot. We dismounted, tied Daisy and the mule to the rail in front of the small adobe, and went straight inside. Fortunately, the Samples family had already left. I wasn't sure, but I thought I saw their herd of sheep on Mr. Lomax's property, just to the south.

Eight men strode up to the front of the adobe, at least three of them wearing Sheriff's stars.

"Ma'am, what are you doing here?" their leader demanded. He was a tall man with light brown hair and beard.

"Trying to avert a miscarriage of justice," I said calmly.

Needless to say, I did not feel particularly calm. The men looked at each other.

"Who are you?" the leader demanded, adding a rather foul epithet.

"Mrs. Madeline Franklin Wilcox."

"She's that lady doctor," one of the other men called.

The leader expectorated to his left side. "I have a warrant here, Ma'am. It's legal."

"Unfortunately, it won't do you any good," I replied. "Mr. Samples and his family have gone."

"See?" someone else yelled. "I knew he'd done it."

I glared at the group. "Based on what, may I ask?"

"He was at the courthouse yesterday afternoon," the leader said.

"At what hour?" I asked.

"What in tarnation difference does that make?" the leader asked.

"Judge Gresham could not have been killed before the hour of noon because he was heard speaking to one of the clerks." I smiled. "He could not have been killed after one o'clock because the clerks and other judges would have returned from their luncheons by that point and heard the blast of the shotgun."

"Well, the fellow's gone, ain't he?" one of the deputies said. "Why would he have run if he weren't guilty?"

I sighed deeply. "You truly have no idea why? He is a colored man and fully apprised of the prejudices against him, nor is he likely to trust a court system that will not even let him testify in his own defense. You have already decided that he is guilty on the basis of him simply being at the courthouse the same day. Would you hang one of your fellows on that basis? I think not. Indeed, I think you would be bending over backwards to exculpate him. Mr. Samples has taken quite a reasonable course of action to protect himself and his family. I would like to know, however, who decided that Mr. Samples was responsible for His Honor's death."

The leader shook his head and pushed forward. The men followed, but there was naught to be done. The adobe was truly empty of anything worth having. I waited for the men to leave, then signaled Damiano.

As we rode back into the pueblo proper, my mind was decidedly unquiet. As much as I did not wish to believe that Mr. Samples was behind the killings, he could well have been. He lived quite close to where Mama Jane's hut was. Lavina had been found there, by him, no less. Moreover, I had no reason to believe that he had cause to be angry with Regina. He might well have been over something involving his wife's sister, Sybil, who was Regina's assistant. I couldn't say what his argument with Judge Gresham might have been, but while Mr. Samples was not prone to violence, if anyone threatened his family, I had no doubt that he would have defended them.

That thought, in itself, gave me pause. Mr. Samples did not carry a shotgun. He carried a rifle, a small one, to be sure, but it was a rifle, of that I was reasonably certain. I suppose that it comes as no surprise that my knowledge of guns was decidedly cursory, but I did like to think that I could tell the difference between a rifle and a shotgun. But even if I were not mistaken about his weapon, it was entirely possible that he had a shotgun as well.

It was also entirely likely that he was innocent but had knowledge of Mama Jane's or Lavina's deaths that he was not aware of. Indeed, people see all manner of things and seldom think about them, and occasionally what they've seen becomes quite important. Unfortunately, with Mr. Samples and his family having disappeared, it would be difficult, if not impossible to question him further.

But then it occurred to me that I might know someone who could help. Mrs. Biddie Mason was a Negress in the pueblo who had managed to amass a considerable amount of land and was even wealthier than some of our premier citizens. We didn't cross paths often, but I knew her to be an honorable woman and, understandably, of considerable standing among the colored people in the pueblo. Daimiano and I made our way down Calle Primavera to her house there.

She agreed to receive me in her front parlor and offered me tea and biscuits, which I accepted gratefully.

"I am here about the Samples family," I told her. "I believe Mr. Samples to be innocent, but he might have some intelligence that will point me to the true malefactor in the killing of Judge Gresham."

"And if the true malefactor is found, then it would, by necessity, exonerate Mr. Samples," Mrs. Mason said, thoughtfully. She was a stern-visaged woman with gray hair that she wore pulled tightly back.

"It would, indeed."

Mrs. Mason nodded. "Mr. Samples is not in the pueblo, but I know how to contact him." She looked at me with some wariness. "I know you to be a kind-hearted woman, but I must be careful."

"As you should," I replied and took a deep breath. "Please take any and all precautions you feel necessary to protect Mr. Samples."

"I will do what I can," Mrs. Mason said.

I left shortly afterwards, feeling somewhat at a loss as to

what to do next, but then I realized that I should pay a condolence call on Mrs. Gresham, assuming that she was open to receiving.

She was not only open to receiving, but as soon as I was settled in her front parlor and served refreshments, she removed her veils and tossed them aside with a sigh of great relief, then ran her hands along her graying brown hair.

"Mrs. Gresham!" I gasped.

I had come across her from time to time, but barely knew her and not to any extent that I could expect such intimacy.

She snorted, her brown eyes lively and twinkling. "I have little use for such false propriety, and I would think that you, of all people, would understand."

"I— I think I would understand," I said, trying not to gape. "However, you quite startled me."

"Well, I suppose I might have." Her smile was bitter. "But the only use I have for widow's weeds is so that people will not see my lack of tears for my late and unlamented husband. And given how little I care about the opinions of others in this benighted cesspool of a town, I don't know why I bothered in the first place."

"Oh." I took a sip of tea and considered.

She looked at me shrewdly. "I have been given to understand that you are of the same opinion regarding your late husband."

"What have you heard?" I asked, my eyebrows rising.

"Most recently? Only that you showed more grief at Miss Lavina Gaines' funeral than you did at your husband's. Not that any of those ridiculous biddies in town would have had the decency to assume that you were facing your bereavement with great strength and dignity, and how could they have seen how you were faring under your weeds, I ask you?"

"It is true that they couldn't have, but they generally assume the worst of everyone." I toyed with the biscuit sitting on my saucer. "Then again, it is true that I used my veils for the same purpose as you."

Mrs. Gresham laughed. "I do not doubt it in the least. I had the misfortune to meet your Mr. Wilcox shortly after you arrived in the pueblo. It was at some party or other. He paid me several unwanted attentions."

I smiled in spite of myself. "You were hardly the only one who received them."

"That is the one blessing I can lay at the feet of my husband." Mrs. Gresham shuddered. "Phineas could be quite cruel and showed me next to no regard, but he never embarrassed me in front of the pueblo's chattering hens. I suppose his frequent visits to Mrs. Medina's house might count as an embarrassment, except that so many of their husbands visit rather regularly, as well."

"Not to question your veracity, but I am curious as to how you know this."

"Phineas said so, usually while fulminating on what dreadful gossips their wives are. He seemed to think that is what motivates the men to seek companionship elsewhere, which of course begs the question as to why he went. I have always kept to myself and do not say anything about anyone."

"Indeed, you don't," I replied. I looked at her carefully. "Still, while you are not grieving overmuch, I must offer some condolence, even if it's only on the loss of the support of your husband."

Mrs. Gresham laughed gaily. "I am actually better off without him that way. We have considerable property, all of which I have managed for years since he couldn't be bothered, being far too busy as a judge. He was also prone to making foolish investments, some of which cost us dearly, not to mention his preference for high living. I do prefer being comfortable, but darling Phineas was quite the spendthrift. He also kept a mistress in considerable comfort."

I swallowed as the flush took over my face. "How interesting. Eh... What about your children?" I tried to recall how many she'd had.

"I have only the one daughter who lived and she is well married, living in San Diego, and all the happier for not being anywhere near her noxious father. As Phineas had no near relatives, he was forced to leave everything to me, too, and failed to even mention the dear girl in his will."

"Oh, you've read it."

"I kept quite the sharp eye on it, too." She shuddered again. "I did not want to have to fight for my rights, and according to Mr. Simpkins, my lawyer, I should not have to. Fortunately, as far as we know, Phineas only left a few gambling debts."

"You are well off, indeed."

"More than that. I have a perfectly delightful lover—"

"Mrs. Gresham!" I gaped.

She looked at me curiously. "Truly? You find that so shocking?"

"Well, not that you have a lover, but that you are so forthright about it. Usually, one is exceedingly discreet about such things."

She sighed. "If I must be, it is only until the will is probated. It's why, I suppose, I am bothering with widow's weeds. Why give Judge Widney the least reason to suspect that I was not the good, devoted wife and helpmate? Not that there is anybody to contest the will that I know of, but greed will out, as I'm sure you know."

"All too well," I squeezed back the tears that had suddenly rushed to my eyes as I thought of how Lavina had been robbed of her inheritance.

"I suppose I should ask for your discretion," Mrs. Gresham said, suddenly wincing. "I have probably said far too much, but then it is such a relief that I no longer must present myself as His Honor's adoring wife so that the rest of the town will respect the ghastly old creature. You cannot imagine what a burden that has been. Now, I am free to pursue my own interests and carry on with Mr. Mahoney with impunity."

I couldn't help chuckling. "I cannot say how, but I had heard he'd taken a lover."

"He might have yet another," Mrs. Gresham said, laughing. "But I care not. If he has, then there is less reason for me to marry him. Not that I would." Her smile grew rich with mischief. "It is my intention to become as notorious as possible. That way, I shall be left alone with my books and my properties, and the occasional attentions of one or more good men."

I felt myself flushing again. "I can see where you might wish to do so."

She looked at me. "You might try taking a lover, yourself."

I choked. "Mrs. Gresham, while I appreciate your very shocking perspective, for myself... How shall I say this? Given my vocation, I must comport myself as the lady I am at all times. It is hard enough being taken seriously as a woman in a man's profession."

"You poor thing." She reached over and patted my hand. "I understand completely. I had a feeling you would be in sympathy with me, and I am glad to find that you are. Would you care to come to tea occasionally?"

I smiled in spite of myself. "I do believe I would. And thank you for being so forthright with me."

I left soon after. It was growing close to lunch time, so I sent Damiano back to the rancho with the message that I would be there as soon as I could after one more errand and went on to Mr. Mahoney's saloon. I was somewhat concerned that he would not speak to me, but Alice quickly sent me back to his office when I arrived. Mr. Mahoney gave me the lone chair, as usual, and settled onto his whiskey box.

"I should be out front," he sighed. "But I do fear that I owe you an apology for the other day."

"I understand completely," I said. "It is a most difficult topic to discuss, but regrettably, necessary at this time."

"I know. But my poor girls, they are so grievously maligned and only because they are tarred by my profession, never mind that my saloon is home to many of the Common Council's meetings, not to mention the railroad committee, and many other major works in the town. My girls are virtue, itself!"

"I know, and it is utterly unjust that they should be maligned so." I again fidgeted with my glove. "However, Annie did tell me that Miss Julia had warned her against a man in the pueblo but would not name him."

Mr. Mahoney nodded. "Both Annie and Alice told me the same. It's a terrible thing when decent girls can't go about their business without fear of attack."

"It is. And there was the dreadful shooting yesterday." I looked at him. "I ask only that I might forestall any nasty rumors, but you were here during the luncheon hour, were you not?"

"I was, indeed." Mr. Mahoney snorted. "And it was a busy day, too. If Judge Gresham had been here, I would have said that the whole courthouse was. Judge Trafford and Judge Widney came and ate together. All the clerks were here, although Mr. Alverno ate by himself, as he usually does. Then there were the businessmen." Mr. Mahoney paused and looked at me. "Is there anyone in particular that you're asking after?"

I couldn't help smiling. "What about Mr. Wiley?"

"No. He doesn't usually eat here. He prefers the American Hotel. I think it's closer to his office."

"I wonder if Mr. Lyons was there, as well."

Mr. Mahoney shrugged. "I'm not sure who Mr. Lyons is."

"What about Mr. Carson?"

"He eats his luncheon at home, I'm told, although he will come in of an evening or two."

I thought. "What about Mr. Gaines or Mr. Smith?"

"Smith? Efrem Smith?"

"Yes."

Mr. Mahoney nodded. "He and Mr. Gaines dined together, as they frequently do."

"And Mr. Lomax or Mr. Navarro?" I took a deep breath and held it.

Mr. Mahoney shook his head. "Didn't see either of them."

I let my breath out and frowned. "Oh, dear. Well, it doesn't mean anything for certain." I stood. "Thank you so much, Mr. Mahoney."

He rose and showed me through the back door, pausing first to check the alley. Fortunately, there was only Daisy waiting patiently for me. Mr. Mahoney helped me into the saddle. As I walked the horse around to the street, I found Mr. Alverno crossing it on his way to the saloon. He saw me and signaled me to stop.

"Yes, Mr. Alverno?" I asked from my saddle.

He sucked his front tooth. "How fares your inquiry into Miss Gaines' death?"

"Well enough," I said slowly. "How are you and the rest of the courthouse faring in terms of Judge Gresham's death?"

He shrugged. "Well enough, I suppose. I can't help but wonder why he was shot. I really did think that he killed Miss Gaines, but if he did, why was he killed?" He frowned. "There are others, too, who might have. Father Gallar was preaching against Mama Jane, and if you think that he might have killed her, why wouldn't he have killed Miss Gaines?"

"True enough, but why would he have done so?"

"I suppose..." He sucked his tooth again. "Perhaps Miss Gaines knew something about Mama Jane's death. And the priest does disappear several times a day."

"Do you think Father Gallar killed Judge Gresham?"

"He could have." Mr. Alverno frowned. "If His Honor thought that the priest was responsible for killing Miss Gaines..."

"It does seem possible." I smiled at the clerk. "Well, thank you, Mr. Alverno. I will definitely be considering this."

He didn't seem entirely happy with my response but went on to the saloon and his lunch.

The odd thing was that as I trotted Daisy back toward the rancho and my own lunch, I thought I saw Father Gallar ducking into the small copse next to where Alameda Street met the road that led to Rancho de las Flores. I reined Daisy in, not insensible to the fact that I was already late for my lunch and as such was due for a tongue lashing from Olivia. Still, I dismounted, and with one hand holding Daisy's reins and the other my gun, which I'd pulled from my bag, I slowly walked over to the copse.

Father Gallar emerged and started when he saw me.

"You would draw on a priest?" he demanded.

"Not normally, no," I said. "However, when I see someone sneaking into a group of trees near my rancho, I am forced to be on my guard lest that person use the trees to cover their own fire. I did not know for certain that it was you and therefore of no concern to me."

I was not, in fact, being entirely truthful, as I had been very certain that I'd seen Father Gallar. However, I thought some diplomacy was in order.

"How could you not know?" he snorted.

"I did not see you clearly," I said. "Nor would I expect to find you in such a place. Why have you come here?"

He hemmed and hawed. Behind him, in the trees, I heard soft mewing. I went ahead into the copse. At the base of one of the oak tree,s a tiny enclosure had been built of rocks with numerous chinks in the walls and a flat board on top that had been weighted down with another rock. More mews erupted from inside the rocks. I reached for the rock on top of the board, but Father Gallar reached it first.

"They are barely six weeks old," he said gruffly. "But they are quite active."

There were three striped, gray kittens in the little rock enclosure. Father Gallar was quite correct about their activity, for as soon as the board had been lifted, they all scrambled to escape their little den. I grabbed one by the scruff of its neck as the priest got his hands on the other two.

"They are so sweet and cunning," I gasped, my heart lifted at the sight.

Father Gallar smiled softly. "They are." He glanced at me. "I have quite the weakness for such creatures. Their mother was killed by a coyote, I imagine. I found them under the church. They couldn't have been more than a couple weeks old. I brought them here and nursed them by hand."

"But why hide them? Certainly you could use a mouser or two at the church?"

"We have such. In fact, I do believe that our old tom cat is their father. They look just like him. However, tom cats will kill kittens and, indeed, had killed one of the others in the litter." Father Gallar looked at me and sighed deeply. "And I am the pastor there. I cannot appear weak. Playing papa to kittens does not give me the authority I need. My people depend on me. I cannot fail them."

I looked at him, then petted the kitten in my hand. "Of course, you cannot. But how is tender concern for the least of the kingdom failing your people?"

He shook his head and sighed. "You cannot understand. You are not Catholic, nor are you a man."

He smiled softly, holding two of the kittens in one hand and stroking their heads.

"Father, I must ask, not because I assume the worst in you, but because I wish to clear you of any wrongdoing. Where were you late in the afternoon on Sunday two weeks ago, June the second?"

He almost chuckled. "Here, I would imagine. It's quiet here, and far from the cares of guiding such an unruly flock as I have." He looked at me. "You have heard about the Irish."

There was a brotherhood of Irish Catholics in the pueblo that was involved in some dispute, although I had paid it little mind.

"Then I suppose that if I offered help with nursing the little ones, it would force you to spend more time with that unruly flock." I smiled at him, feeling somewhat mischievous.

He did laugh at that. "It would. But..." He looked at me. "If I send you word that the little ones need their feeding, and I cannot do it, could you? They drink cow's milk and are eating a little chicken, too."

"I will happily do so and without saying whose little ones these are." I got up and brushed the dead leaves from my riding habit. "Good day, Father Gallar."

Chapter Seventeen

"Kittens?" Angelina asked, utterly incredulous.

"Sh," I hissed as Reverend Elmwood cleared his throat.

We were at the back of the front parlor of the Gresham home. As we'd waited for the pastor of the Congregational church in the pueblo to begin the service that next morning, I had told Angelina about my meeting with Father Gallar, although I had not quite finished my observations when Reverend Elmwood began his usual meaningless sermon on the text of "Well done, good and faithful servant." The casket bearing the body of Judge Phineas Gresham was closed. Angelina is quite good at making all manner of corpses presentable for their funerals, but she cannot recreate a face.

"Later," I whispered.

Several heads turned our way. I re-focused my eyes on Reverend Elmwood, but I had heard this sermon many, many times and could almost recite it. I must confess that the good reverend was quite the thorn in my side. However, I had been raised as a Congregationalist and did not wish to forswear that practice for the Methodist congregation, even though I found Reverend Miller more bearable.

As we walked to the cemetery behind the funeral wagon bearing the casket, Angelina and I watched the crowd grow. Mr. and Mrs. Hewitt had been at the Gresham home, as had the other two judges and their wives, plus all the clerks. However, I saw Mr. Lomax join the cortege, along with Mr. Wiley and Mr. Handly, my insurance agent. Mr. and Mrs. Glassell had been in the home, but Mr. Carson joined the pair in the cortege.

There were no close relatives, let alone male ones, so Judge Trafford took Mrs. Gresham's arm. Her daughter was expected at any time, probably by stagecoach, which generally took a couple of days, including one overnight stop.

There really was no way to continue our conversation on the walk to the cemetery or during the service at the graveyard (which was mercifully brief). With Mr. Sutton at hand as the mourners began to disperse, it was easy for Angelina to join me some feet from the grave.

"Kittens?" Angelina asked again. "I would never have thought it of him."

"Nor would I," I conceded. "I am supposed to be keeping this to myself. Alas, just because it seems as though the good father was occupied in an act of charity that fateful Sunday, it does not mean that he was."

"To be certain." Angelina frowned. "So, what do we do now?"

"That is the essential question."

I smiled as Mrs. Hewitt sent her husband on his way and approached us.

"Good day, Mrs. Wilcox, Mrs. Sutton." Her smile was a touch on the grim side. "So, have you found out who killed His Honor?"

I smiled back. "And what makes you believe that we are searching for the killer?"

"Why wouldn't you be? After all, I am told you are searching for Miss Gaines' killer, as well, and dragging poor Julia Carson's name through the mud in the process."

"Miss Carson was completely innocent," Angelina said, her eyes flashing. "There is a monster preying on our young women. Would you rather let him go about it unabated because of people who will think the worst of a young lady rather than blame the vile man who is doing such things?"

Mrs. Hewitt stepped back. "I suppose there is that to consider."

"I am trying to ascertain who spread the news about the possible connection between the two deaths," I said as gently as I could. "I understand that Mr. Hewitt was having a drink with Mr. Carson and another gentleman of the pueblo when the subject of the two deaths came up."

"You're assuming he would have remembered the conversation," Mrs. Hewitt said bitterly. "And you cannot possibly suspect him of being this terrible monster for the same reason."

Mr. Hewitt, unfortunately, was not known for his sobriety. Indeed, Mrs. Hewitt secretly ran their very successful buggy manufactory as her husband was generally too far in his cups to manage the business himself.

"Which is why I do not suspect him," I said. "But perhaps he said something that might point us in the right direction."

She frowned. "I will think on it. I do not believe so, but I suppose it's always possible. Good day, Mrs. Wilcox, Mrs. Sutton."

She turned and headed back into the pueblo. I looked at Angelina.

"Perhaps we should be thinking about Mr. Hewitt," she said.

"His state of dissipation is such that I seriously doubt he caused Miss Julia's problem," I answered.

"But he could have killed Mama Jane or Miss Lavina." Angelina shrugged. "I haven't the faintest idea why he would, but I suppose it is possible."

We moved toward the cemetery gate only to find Mr. Alverno waiting.

"Mrs. Wilcox, I have heard something that could be most important to your inquiries," he told us. "It is Mr. Lomax. It is said in the pueblo that he is a Mormon."

I pulled myself up straight. "And if you or anyone else is saying so, then they are spreading a most malicious rumor."

"I can't help what's being said," Mr. Alverno replied, sulking a little. "Besides, that does not mean he couldn't have killed Miss Gaines. Perhaps he wanted her as his third wife."

"That is assuming he is not well aware of the laws against polygamy in this state," I said. "And I can assure you that he is."

Mr. Alverno sucked his tooth. "Well, I did just see him bump up against Mr. Smith. It almost looked as though he were putting something upon Mr. Smith's person."

"I will endeavor to find out what happened," I smiled at

Mr. Alverno. "Now, if you will excuse us, we must make our way back into the pueblo."

"As I must. Good day."

Angelina and I waited just long enough to be sure that Mr. Alverno was, indeed, headed back to the courthouse, or at least, in that direction.

"What an appalling little man," Angelina said.

"He is unpleasant, but he was quite fond of Lavina, and as such, is determined to help me find her killer."

"Good day, Mrs. Wilcox, Mrs. Sutton." Mr. Smith tipped his hat as he walked past us.

I saw something fluttering from his suit coat pocket. "Mr. Smith, pray forgive me, but what is that in your pocket?"

"What?" He looked down at his pocket. "What's this?"

He pulled a bit of black lace out and looked at it, utterly bewildered. Angelina and I looked at each other, then Angelina took the bit from him.

"It's the lace from Miss Lavina's dress," Angelina said. "Look. There are even a few jet beads left."

"How did that come to be in your pocket?" I asked Mr. Smith as I took the bit of lace from Angelina.

Mr. Smith paled and swallowed. "I have no idea, Mrs. Wilcox! None! It wasn't there this morning."

I looked at him, half afraid to ask my next question. "Was Mr. Lomax in the close vicinity of your person at any time this morning?"

"Well, we were all packed around the graveside," Mr. Smith said. He frowned. "And I do think Mr. Lomax was right next to me at one point or another. Why do you ask?"

I looked at Angelina. "This doesn't make the least bit of sense." I looked at Mr. Smith. "Half the pueblo was standing next to you at one point or another."

Angelina pressed her lips together. I looked at her, then Mr. Smith.

"If you don't mind, Mr. Smith," I said, holding up the lace. "I would like to keep this for the time being."

"By all means, Ma'am." Mr. Smith blinked his eyes and sighed.

"Then we will wish you a good day," I said and nodded at Angelina.

We headed back toward the funeral parlor.

"Good Heavens!" Angelina snapped as we went into her study. "It was just as that little toad said."

"I did mention the bit of lace to Judge Gresham," I said, sinking down onto the sofa. "But how would Mr. Lomax have heard about that? It was said in chambers and His Honor said that he would keep it in confidence, although that may have been because he was embarrassed by my mention of the pantaloons. I'm afraid I was embarrassed enough, myself."

Angelina moved her little desk on wheels into position, then sat in her favorite chair.

"Unless the judge asked Mr. Lomax about the lace or the pantaloons," she said. "Then Mr. Lomax killed the judge and decided he'd better find a way to get rid of the lace."

"But why would Mr. Lomax have killed Mama Jane or Lavina?" I blinked back my tears. "It is true that he has the same proximity to Mama Jane's hut that Mr. Samples does, but that doesn't mean he killed either one of them."

Angelina looked at me. "But Mr. Lomax does have a reason to perhaps force himself on a young woman."

"That is true." I sniffed and began weeping. "I hate thinking such terrible thoughts about someone I have called a friend. Everything about Mr. Lomax seems so honorable and kind."

"It does." Angelina's brow knit together. "Could it be that little worm, Mr. Alverno?"

"But why? He liked Lavina, and said she was kind to him. Why would he harm someone who was kind to him when he knew so little kindness? And he was in Mr. Mahoney's saloon having his lunch on the day the judge was killed." I pulled my handkerchief from the sleeve of my visiting dress. "The worst of it is, there are simply too many possibilities and no way to get any firm answers."

"We will find a way, Maddie." Angelina's smile was weak, and I could see that she was getting discouraged, too.

I took one last sniff, then stood.

"Then let us do so." I tucked my handkerchief back in my sleeve. "In fact, I shall go seek out Mr. Lomax immediately." I paused. "Angelina, have you ever seen Mr. Lomax with a shotgun?"

"I haven't even seen him carry a rifle."

I frowned, thinking. "Did His Honor have a shotgun in his office?"

"He might have." Her eyes lit up. "I will see to finding out."

"Yes, please do. However, regarding Mr. Lomax, it seems odd that he would shoot the judge with a shotgun when he carries a six-gun as a matter of course."

"If he didn't want people to know he'd shot the judge."

Angelina shrugged. “But what difference would it make what he shot him with? Everybody carries six-shooters.”

I left the funeral parlor and walked over toward the courthouse. I found Mr. Lomax walking along the Calle Principal from the Plaza.

“Have you a moment, Mr. Lomax?” I asked him.

“I do.” He sighed, his entire demeanor still very reserved. Nonetheless, there was a pain in his eyes that I felt in my very soul.

I shook my head. “You are aware of the rumors, then.”

“Of course.” He looked at me. “It is very kind of you to lie on my behalf.”

“I do not believe I have lied,” I said. “As you have told me, you no longer adhere to the tenets of the Latter Day Saints, which would mean that you are no longer a Mormon.”

“That’s true enough.” He squeezed his eyes shut. “Folks seem to think that because Sabrina has not remarried that I must be keeping her as my second wife.”

I could not help letting a small snort escape my lips. “I can think of many reasons why a widow would not wish to remarry, not the least of them, devotion to her late husband. Have you tried that excuse?”

“Not yet, but I thank you for it.”

“Mr. Lomax, where were you during lunchtime on Tuesday?” I looked at him, trying to hide my worry.

“In the Zanjero’s office.” He sighed. “Mr. Samples and I were both there from a little before the noon bell rang until after one.” He half-smiled at me. “You trying to save Mr. Samples?”

"Yes," I said. "But why were you there? It's the middle of the month."

The Zanjero was the water overseer. His job was to be sure that the zanjas, or ditches, were in good repair and to sell the citizens whatever water there was available. The rules stipulated that we pay for our water subscriptions on the twenty-fourth or twenty-fifth of the month.

"Mr. Samples' zanja had become blocked again."

It was not an unusual occurrence, and it was most kind of Mr. Lomax to use his power as a policeman to convince the Zanjero to send his deputies out to repair the problem. Not many would do such for a colored man. I pulled the bit of lace from my reticule.

"What's that?" Mr. Lomax asked, looking slightly puzzled.

"Why don't you tell me what you think it is?"

"It's a bit of lace off a lady's gown." He frowned. "If you're showing it to me, then there's a reason."

I sighed. "Yes. Mr. Smith found it in his pocket, and someone said that you'd put it there."

"Figures." Mr. Lomax pressed his lips together. "It's exactly what I've been worried about. Someone threw a bunch of cow dung on our adobe last night, too."

"Oh, no."

"I've got to find a way to put Sabrina aside." He choked and trembled. "But how can I just give her up and my children, too?"

"We'll find a good man, and... I don't know." Exasperated, my eyes swept the several blocks on either side of us. But then I saw a sign in a window. "Mr. Lomax, isn't there a parcel that borders on the north edge of your property that's for sale?"

"What good is that going to do?"

"I don't know yet, but I do believe I see a ray of hope. If you'll excuse me, Mr. Lomax. Oh. Wait. Can you account for your whereabouts on Sunday, June second?"

He thought. "Was that the night of the dispensary fire?"

"Yes."

"I was doing guard duty at the jail until suppertime. It was a very busy Saturday night."

I smiled, feeling the weight of my fears lifting off of me.

"That is good to know. Yet another ray of hope. I must bid you good day."

He nodded and tipped his hat. I hurried off to Mr. Gaines' office. It was in a block down the street from where I was. The sign I'd seen belonged to another land agent, but it had been enough to give me an idea.

Mr. Smith was there, frowning over an account book, when I entered. He leapt to his feet.

"How can I help you, Mrs. Wilcox?"

"You can find us a space in which we can speak privately," I said softly. "Something has occurred to me."

"There's the empty office," he said, leading me to the small room.

I shut the door. "There is a large piece of land just to the north of Mr. Lomax's place."

"I know. It's the piece I'm going to buy." Mr. Smith looked at me warily. "It's too far from the Zanja Madre to be prime farmland."

The Zanja Madre, or Mother Ditch, was the canal that had been dug from the Porciuncula River generations before to bring water to the various farms and homes in the pueblo.

"The piece you discouraged Mr. Gaines from buying."

Mr. Smith winced, then smiled guiltily. "I might have had my own ideas about it."

"Were you going to take up farming after you married Lavina?" I could feel my voice grating.

He sighed. "It is what I know and what I like. But I did not want to turn Lavina into a farmer's wife. I was going to keep a house in town and work as a land agent, too. There's a lot more money to be had with only half the work. No reason I can't do both."

"On that land? If it's not good for farming…"

"That." He chuckled. "Can you keep a secret?"

"I should hope so."

"There's a big old stand of oak trees right in the middle, with all sorts of grasses and bushes and the like. It's in a bit of a hollow, too."

"As in, there's water there."

"And it's just outside the town limits, so the Zanjero and his men won't be able to do much about it if I dig a well." Mr. Smith grinned. "And the county men won't know the difference or care much, anyway."

I pursed my lips together. "That may be, but it, unfortunately, will not help Mr. Lomax."

"How do you mean?"

I looked at him. "I must take you into my confidence. If I can keep your secret, will you keep this one?"

"Sure."

I thought for a moment. "I have been told that you are from Utah."

"Yes, ma'am, I am."

"Then you are familiar with polygamy."

Mr. Smith chuckled. "I am. It's not that common, mostly just the more important elders. My father only had one wife, but my uncle had two."

"Have you heard the rumors about Mr. Lomax?"

"I have." Mr. Smith shuddered. "That's why I'm not claiming to be Mormon. Not that I believe in it anymore. I go to the Methodist church now." He looked at me. "You think Mr. Lomax is?"

"He's not anymore, either. But he is trying to be as honorable as he can regarding his two wives. Not to mention his tender heart. You wouldn't think it to look at him, but he is very sentimental about his children and loves them all deeply. Poor thing. He, understandably, does not want another man raising his babes, nor will he separate them from their mother."

"He's going to set aside the older one?"

"Oh, no. She's the one he wants to keep. It's the younger wife, Mrs. Sabrina."

Mr. Smith's eyes widened. "Most men would not do that."

"It's as I said, he is trying to be as honorable as he can, and he says he does prefer Mrs. Ruth. But he is on the horns of a terrible dilemma. I was thinking that if I could find a way to purchase that bit of land to the north of his, I could find a good man who would be willing to work it with Mr. Lomax, leaving him free to be as close to his children as possible and still be able to provide for Mrs. Sabrina's wellbeing."

Mr. Smith shook his head. "It's still possible that Mr. Lomax killed Lavina, you know."

"He was at the jail that entire afternoon until suppertime. At least, that's what he told me just now."

"Doesn't mean he was."

I sighed and glared at Mr. Smith. "And it doesn't mean that you didn't kill her. I have only your word for it that you began your search when she failed to arrive for your assignation."

He gasped, and I suddenly began to fear that I had said absolutely the worst thing possible.

"Why…? Why would I kill her? I loved her, almost to distraction, I loved her." His eyes filled and he turned away and pulled out his handkerchief.

"I know." I got mine from my sleeve, as well. "And she loved you so much." The tears slid down my cheeks. "Oh dear. Pray forgive me for such a display."

"That's all right, Mrs. Wilcox." He made quite a loud sound as he blew his nose. "But you can't believe I'd have done anything to harm even one hair on my darling Lavina's head."

At that point, I had no idea what to believe yet I did not think it would be wise to say so. Then another question began to form in my head.

"Mr. Smith, how is it that you began your search for Lavina so quickly?" I looked at him, again feeling worried that I should not be asking such a potentially damaging question. "You did tell me that you had started looking for her when she didn't appear for your usual meeting. You said she wasn't at home but failed to mention how you knew that. Mr. and Mrs. Gaines were hardly likely to tell you if she was there or not."

"Lavina would leave me a signal that she had gone on

her walk." Mr. Smith sniffed and blinked, and I was gravely afraid that we would both begin to weep again. "She'd drop a handkerchief on the ground next to her back door. Mrs. Gaines never saw it. I'd walk by around four-thirty. If the handkerchief was there, I knew I'd find Lavina at our meeting spot. If it wasn't, I knew that she hadn't been able to get out of the house. The handkerchief was there that afternoon, but I couldn't find Lavina."

He shut his eyes but somehow managed not to shed more tears. I wish I could have said the same. I dabbed at my eyes.

Mr. Smith finished wiping up his eyes. "There was Mr. Lyons, too. Have you had a chance to talk to him yet?"

"I have. But he said that he was in the Anaheim Colony that day. He had to be ready for something the next morning, as I recall."

"On that Sunday?" Mr. Smith looked perplexed. "But he wasn't. He was right here in the pueblo. I know. I went straight to him, worried that he'd done something to harm Lavina. He said he didn't know where she was."

Chapter Eighteen

I think it would be stating the obvious to write that I was very angry. I was not particularly perturbed that someone very charming had lied to me. To be honest, I had almost come to expect that from charming men. But that so much time had been wasted thanks to his prevarication raised my ire considerably.

I made my way to Mr. Wiley's office. Mr. Wiley, in turn, accompanied me to his warehouse next to the train depot, where Mr. Lyons had a small desk in the far corner of the large room filled with goods of all kinds, including several barrels of my wine. Mr. Lyons, himself, sat at the desk, frowning over an account book and shaking his head. The second he saw me and Mr. Wiley, he scrambled to his feet.

"Good day, Mrs. Wilcox." His smile seemed quite genuine.

"We shall see about that," I said. "Why did you lie to me this past Monday?"

He looked surprised. "Lied to you? About what?"

"About where you were on June the second. You told me that you had gone to the Anaheim Colony, and I have just learned that you most certainly were here in Los Angeles." I glared at him.

"When was June the second?" He stroked his chin. "Was that the night of the dispensary fire? Because I was here for that. I was in the Anaheim Colony… When was that?"

"Oh, for Heaven's sakes," stammered Mr. Wiley. "You have a record of your travels, don't you?"

Mr. Lyons looked at Mr. Wiley nervously for a moment, then nodded. First, he patted his chest, then slid the accounts book and some papers around on his desk.

"Ah. Here it is." He smiled weakly at me. "I am learning to keep better records."

"I insisted upon it before we finalized our partnership," Mr. Wiley said, glaring at Mr. Lyons.

Mr. Lyons flipped through the small diary. "Here it is. Oh. That was May twenty-seven that I had that meeting in the Anaheim Colony. Must have been then that I was thinking of." He smiled at me. "Hard to remember sometimes."

I pursed my lips together. "Yes. I suppose it is." I looked at Mr. Wiley. "Thank you for assisting me."

I left the warehouse feeling quite peeved. If Mr. Lyons had lied deliberately, he had done a masterful job of explaining it. I debated taking Mrs. Davies to task for misleading me in the same way that day I had spoken with her, but then realized that I had not asked her if Mr. Lyons had been at home the afternoon of Lavina's death.

Then I realized that if Mr. Lyons were in the pueblo on the fateful day, it was entirely possible that he had killed Lavina. I decided to pay Mrs. Davies a visit after all.

She still looked tired but told me rather happily that all of her daughters had fully recovered.

"That is good news, indeed," I said as we stood in her doorway. "The last time I was here and was asking about Mr. Lyons, I failed to ask you if he was here the Sunday of the dispensary fire. Was he?"

Mrs. Davies blinked as she thought about it, then shook her head.

"I am so sorry, Mrs. Wilcox. I do not remember." She looked behind her for a moment, then back at me. "I remember that night, hearing the gunshots and the clocktower ringing. But I seldom know who is and isn't here on Sundays. I take the girls to early mass, then visit my family for most of the day. The men eat the bread I put out in the morning for their breakfasts, or find somewhere else to eat. And for supper, I have soup on the stove, more bread on the table, and the men serve themselves. It is a day of rest."

"It is," I agreed, feeling rather out of sorts.

I thanked her and left, pondering what to do next. If I could trust Mr. Smith's account, and I was beginning to fear that I could not entirely, he had met with Mr. Lyons shortly after he'd discovered Lavina missing. Then I also realized that if Mr. Lyons was in the Anaheim Colony on May twenty-seven, then it was not likely that he was in the pueblo on the night that Mama Jane was probably killed, although he could have been, especially if he'd left the colony soon after his meeting and killed Mama Jane later that night.

That did bring to mind the one man I believed may have been the last person, besides her killer, to have seen Mama

Jane alive. I hurried back to the Calle Principal, hoping to find Mr. Navarro in that vicinity. He was actually at the jail house.

"Good day, Mrs. Wilcox," he said, grinning.

"Mr. Navarro, when you purchased your charm from Mama Jane, what time was it when you left her?"

He looked at me, utterly puzzled. "I'm not sure. It was close to time for supper, as I recall. Why do you ask?"

"And where were you in the afternoon before we began to search for Miss Gaines?"

"I was with my family. In fact, I was going to my room at the boarding house when I first saw you and Mr. Smith."

"What about this past Tuesday? You were right there when we found the judge."

Mr. Navarro's eyes widened. "Surely you don't think I had anything to do with these deaths?"

"I don't know what to think."

"Well, I couldn't have killed the judge." He swallowed and nodded back at the jail cells behind him. "I was bringing that fellow in there back from El Monte that morning. I didn't get back here until after three of the afternoon. I remember hearing the clocktower tolling the half hour as I left the jail. And I certainly didn't kill either Mama Jane or Miss Gaines." He sighed and slumped his shoulders. "I suppose I would say that even if I had. But I assure you that I didn't."

I looked at him and sighed. "Well, at least you are not attempting to harm my person."

"Are you even sure that His Honor's death is connected to the other two?"

"No." I couldn't help glaring at him. "There is no reason

to believe that it is, except that I was in conference with the judge that morning, and others may have known about it and feared the worst. Someone did try to shoot me the Saturday before. Or possibly me. In fact, you may wish to take care. If I do come to grief, there will be quite a few people looking at you as the possible culprit."

I left the jail house feeling even more out of sorts. Mr. Navarro was completely right in that there was no reason to think that Judge Gresham's murder was connected to Lavina's and Mama Jane's. If anything, there seemed to be more reason to believe that it had happened independently of the other two.

As I walked home to my luncheon, I couldn't help but grow more and more morose. Even assuming the shooting of Judge Gresham was related to the shooting that had resulted in Regina's bed stay (and again, there was no real reason to believe that the two incidents were related, except for my presence), both the judge and Regina had accrued quite a collection of enemies over their lifetimes simply by virtue of their respective professions.

I ate my meal completely preoccupied, never mind that my entire household surrounded me, eating as well. We ate outside as we usually did, resting in the shade of the oak tree in the yard.

"Maddie, are we going to check the wines for blending today?" Sebastiano asked me.

I couldn't help groaning. "I had completely forgotten about that."

Sebastiano chuckled. "I have several combinations here you can taste."

"You'll have to change clothes first," said Juanita. "Wine stains do not come out readily."

I looked down at my ochre visiting dress. "Once again, you are right, Juanita. Sebastiano, I shall return as promptly as possible."

Juanita followed me inside my adobe to my bedroom.

"You are sad, Maddie," she said, undoing the hooks on the back of my dress.

"I am afraid so." I shut my eyes, then slid out of my visiting dress as Juanita pulled out my brown riding habit. "I am no closer to finding the monster that forced himself on Miss Julia and quite probably killed Mama Jane and Miss Lavina. There is quite possibly someone trying to kill Mrs. Medina. And everyone expects me to find Judge Gresham's killer."

"You cannot solve every crime in the pueblo," Juanita said. "It doesn't matter what everyone expects you to do."

"I have no intention of trying to solve every crime in the pueblo," I said. "I couldn't possibly, as you have pointed out." I sighed and pulled the riding habit on. "It's simply that if I do not find the monster preying on the young women, then they will continue to be hurt and possibly die ridding themselves of any resulting quickening, or be killed as Miss Lavina was. If I do not find out who tried to kill Mrs. Medina, then it is entirely probable that someone will be aiming at her again and might succeed this time. We have been acting as though the person who aimed at her was trying to stop me and my questions. But the more I think about it, the more I am inclined to believe that it may not have been connected to the other murders, after all. And the same for the judge's murder."

Juanita took her brush to the visiting dress as I adjusted the front of the habit.

"Do you really care about finding who murdered the judge?" she asked.

I thought about it. "No. I don't, really. The problem is that when a killer succeeds at murdering someone, it is often only the start of more murders, as we have learned to our sorrow."

"But that doesn't mean you are the one who must find the judge's killer."

"And who else is going to? Our police officers are not up to the job, except for Mr. Lomax and Mr. Navarro, and it is entirely possible that one of those two might be the guilty party." I stopped. "Wait. Mr. Lomax told me he was in the Zanjero's office the whole of the luncheon hour." I sighed. "But that is assuming he was, indeed, there, and not lying to me about his whereabouts. I already know that Mr. Navarro lied."

"He wouldn't." Juanita gasped.

"He did lie to Mr. Lomax about Mama Jane. Mr. Lomax saw him talking to her on the afternoon she died, then Mr. Navarro said later that he hadn't seen her."

Juanita shook her head. "My Ernesto loved Mama Jane."

"So he has led me to believe." I sank down onto my bed. "Oh, Juanita, I do not wish to think him guilty of such terrible things. I do not wish to think Mr. Lomax is guilty. Or Mr. Wiley."

"What about that clerk, Mr. Alverno?"

"Given the way Judge Gresham treated him, one would have to be suspicious of Mr. Alverno, but Mr. Mahoney said that he was in the saloon eating his lunch when the judge was killed."

Juanita sat down next to me on the bed and put her arms around me.

"Oh, Maddie, it all seems so terrible and overwhelming, but you will find who the killer is. I know you will."

I patted her hand. "And I am so grateful for your confidence in me. You have been a good friend, Juanita, especially when I needed one."

"We will always be friends, Maddie. Now, go. You've got wines to blend and people to talk to."

It took but an hour to confer with Sebastiano regarding the wines. We did not always agree on such matters, although it was an infrequent occasion when the disagreement became heated. However, that afternoon, we were largely of the same mind, and the small disagreement was settled quickly and amicably.

From there, I returned to the pueblo to see to a new case of measles. The patient was a young girl of eight and was managing quite well. I left a little salve for her, hoping against hope that the disease had run its course for the time being.

As I walked, it occurred to me that the gravest matter I faced was that of the monster. Regina could stay inside her house as needed, and there would be others looking into the death of Judge Gresham, assuming they didn't continue to blame Mr. Samples for the deed.

It being after the school day was done, I thought I would speak to Mr. Lawrence, if only to eliminate him as a possible culprit. So, I ventured to the adobe which housed his particular school, and found him working with two young men and three young women preparing for the teachers exam which was to happen soon. He smiled at me and left the students to their reading for the moment.

"It is good to see you, Mrs. Wilcox," he told me as I led him to the street and far enough away so that the youths would not hear me.

He was a tall, gangling man, with dark hair and bright eyes hidden by spectacles that constantly slid down his nose.

"Mr. Lawrence, I have a matter of the most delicate nature to ask you about." I swallowed and flushed a little. "Perhaps you have heard about it already, but there is a monster loose in the pueblo."

"I have, I'm afraid." He sighed. "I have even heard some parents whispering that it might be me."

"Oh, no!"

He chuckled. "I am not worried. I know I am blameless, and my several students will stand up for me."

"This monster attacked Miss Carson, and I do fear that he might have killed Miss Lavina and Mama Jane."

"Mama Jane, too?" Mr. Lawrence shook his head. "How terrible. There is so much violence in the pueblo, it worries me. I can't help thinking about taking my family elsewhere. But the violence doesn't seem to affect the children and other decent folk."

"The vast majority of the violence doesn't," I conceded. "We do get enough murders here, but almost always it's between combatants or other shiftless types seeking to do harm. But in terms of the monster currently preying on our young women, do you have any idea who he might be?"

"No." He frowned as he thought. "I'm afraid that I did see

some signs that Miss Julia may have been... She was such a charming and pleasant girl. But then, about the middle of April, she became somewhat lackluster, not so most people would have noticed. She also became rather nervous around me, and I knew I had given her no cause to be so. I began to wonder then whether she had been attacked. There was no way for me to ask. I was going to have Mrs. Lawrence speak to her but had to wait for my wife to come out of her confinement, and by then, Miss Julia had died."

"Can you think of anyone in the pueblo that Miss Julia had contact with that might have attacked her?"

"There are plenty of men who could have."

"But not so many who have regular contact with a young woman of Miss Julia's years."

"True." Mr. Lawrence pushed his spectacles up his nose. "However, she was just old enough that a number of fellows had their eye on her. Mr. Wiley was one. I would see him gaze after her when they met on the street as Miss Julia went home from school or from her father's store."

I sighed. "That does bring to mind one other terrible possibility."

"Her father?" Mr. Lawrence frowned but did not appear to be overly shocked. "I don't think so. I have seen enough to believe that it has happened before, and of those three times, none of the girls in question behaved quite like Miss Julia did."

"How is it that you're not horrified by the possibility?"

Mr. Lawrence shuddered. "Oh, I am horrified by the thought. It is a terrible, terrible thing. But as you know well, my dear Mrs. Wilcox, that does not mean it doesn't happen.

There is little enough that I can do, and it is exceedingly frustrating, I assure you. I do try to provide safe haven for any children who fear their parents, for whatever reason, but very, very few will accept it. We both do our best to alleviate the suffering we see all too often. But there is only so much that we can do."

"You are right, Mr. Lawrence." I smiled. "I thank you for your tender heart. Sadly, it is all too rare."

"Indeed. But thanks to yours and your stalwart nature and great courage, our pueblo is all the better."

"You give me far too much credit but thank you." I paused. "I have been told that Miss Julia was warning the other girls that such a monster was about and to not accept any untoward invitations. Perhaps one of them might have an idea who the cur might be. If you hear anything, will you let me know?"

"Immediately."

"Thank you, Mr. Lawrence, and good day."

"Good day, Mrs. Wilcox."

I left Mr. Lawrence both saddened and encouraged. His kind words meant a great deal, especially when I was feeling so lost and bewildered. I was also saddened by the thought of Mr. Wiley looking longingly after Julia Carson. I thought I knew why he had been. He had been quite open about his tender regard for her. Still, his gaze had been noted, although not with the usual ill-mannered suspicion, another aspect of Mr. Lawrence's character for which I was exceedingly grateful.

As I left the schoolhouse, I realized that Angelina's house was right there. I stopped in only briefly as she was quite busy. Two of our oldest citizens had passed away, one the night before, and the other later that morning, and there were two funerals to prepare for. However, she did ask if I had spoken to Mr. Lomax, and I repeated what he had told me, then what Mr. Navarro had said. She said that she would check at the jailhouse to see if she could verify both of their stories. I moved on.

I found Mr. Wiley alone in his office and was glad of it. He smiled as I seated myself in front of his desk.

"I hope you are not too displeased with Mr. Lyons this morning," he said quickly. "He is quite a good agent, even if he does need to learn how to manage the trade a little better."

"I'm not concerned about that." I sighed. "I am concerned about your finer feelings for Miss Julia Carson, however."

Mr. Wiley's eyebrows knit together in puzzlement. "How do you mean? I had nothing but the highest regard for her."

"Well, someone forced himself on her," I said, my tone quite acerbic in spite of myself. "And I have found out that she was warning other young women, as well. Are you the monster that she warned against?"

"Me?" Mr. Wiley's face turned ashen. "No! I can't even bear to think of such a thing. Who could have done something so very terrible to such a beautiful angel? She was so kind and so pure."

"Odd that you haven't heard the rumors about it. Tongues have been wagging faster than puppy tails since it got out about the connection between Miss Carson's death and Miss Gaines'."

"I pay that gossip no mind," Mr. Wiley snorted. He

stopped. "Do you really think there is a connection between the two deaths?"

"In some ways, the same man may be responsible for both, and that of Mama Jane."

"You mean the Indian woman? I thought she died of dissipation."

"Mama Jane did not imbibe spirits of any kind." I glared at him. "You only assume that she died of dissipation because that is what you believe about Indians when there is no good reason to. Such an assumption is unjust in the extreme and will not help finding who killed her and Miss Gaines."

"Why are you so certain that the same villain killed both?"

I thought for a moment. "That is something I must keep to myself for the time being. But I assure you, I have good cause to do so."

I got up and Mr. Wiley scrambled to his feet.

"Mrs. Wilcox," he said. "I did not harm Miss Carson. I did no more than gaze fondly upon her. I promise you, I did no more than that."

I took a deep breath. "I do hope for your sake, Mr. Wiley, that you have just told me the truth."

Chapter Nineteen

I slept very badly that night. I tossed and turned, and when I did sleep, my rest was shattered by nightmares. Worse yet, I fell asleep sometime just before dawn and overslept myself.

Needing something of a lift, I decided to wear my best dark green riding habit of linen and wool, with velvet ruching on the basque. However, in recognition of the sun, I set out a nice bonnet instead of the matching hat.

As Juanita helped me dress, I received a message from Mrs. Alonso. Her granddaughter refused to name the man who had attacked her.

"Why, in Heaven's name, would she not say anything?" I groaned as Juanita did up my back. "Has she no care for her friends?"

"That's probably why she won't say anything," Juanita said. "She wants to protect them."

"But we can protect them. Why does she believe that monster and not her family?"

"You know as well as I do that it takes only the least

whisper to ruin a young lady's good character." Juanita shook her head and turned to straightening my bedclothes. "Besides, she probably feels very ashamed and wonders if she was, indeed, complicit in her own ruination. We are told often enough how that can happen. A smile that is too warm, waving a fan at the wrong time. Even a slight tumble that bares an ankle can be seen as the sure sign that she is a trollop."

"You are absolutely right." I couldn't help letting out a snort. "It is so unjust and exactly why I must take such pains to always behave as a lady. And yet, it was a man who violated that poor young woman, a man who could have chosen not to harm her, but to treat her with all due courtesy, no matter how coquettish she was. When are these men going to be held to account for their horrible behavior?"

"I have no idea. But if anyone can get them to behave, you can."

"I deeply wish that were the case."

The difficulties that morning continued with three different patients. One young girl with a fever suddenly began vomiting as I examined her, though, fortunately, it all missed my lovely habit.

Sebastiano had a few more wine blends for me to try at luncheon, which, while quite a pleasant chore, did not help me feel any more awake. We conferred and decided that the blend we'd chosen the day before was still the best of the lot.

After luncheon, I made my way to the Carson home to check on Mrs. Carson. I was admitted to her front parlor and served tea and biscuits. When Mrs. Carson came in, she looked a pale ghost of her former self. She had lost considerable weight, and her yellow tea gown hung on her like a tent.

Her hair, always sprinkled with gray, seemed to be mostly that color. She smiled at me blankly, then sank onto the sofa.

"I am glad that you are here," she said.

"I am glad to be here, but not so glad about your appearance." I looked at her. "How have you been faring?"

She shrugged listlessly. "Not well, I'm afraid."

I began a regular exam, listening to her heart and chest. Her pulse was steady, and her heart sounded normal, as did her lungs.

"Are you drinking beef tea?" I asked.

"Yes. Twice a day. I am quite tired of it, but Mr. Carson told me you'd said I should, so I do."

"How are your spirits? You seem quite sad."

"I have lost my only daughter." She sniffed.

"And yet you are not wearing a mourning gown."

She snorted. "This is the easiest thing to put on, so I do. If I must leave the house, then I have my weeds. But there is no point in leaving. They are saying such horrible things about my girl."

"I know that she was virtuous."

Mrs. Carson's voice caught. "But she wasn't." She blinked and looked away. "She was, as they say, in the family way. How it happened I do not know exactly."

"I was aware of that." I sat down next to her and patted her hand. "I had seen the signs of it."

"If I could get my hands on the cur that seduced her..."

"She was not seduced, Mrs. Carson. I have good reason to believe that some monster forced himself on her."

Mrs. Carson shook her head. "Mrs. Wilcox, I thank you for saying so. But if you knew about her condition, then you had to know that she was willing. When a woman is forced, she cannot conceive."

"That is absolute rubbish and nonsense," I said angrily. "A woman who is forced most certainly can conceive. I have seen it more than once, and in one case, was witness to the ravishment."

I did not care to say more, as it was my late and unlamented husband who had done the vile deed, forcing himself on our housemaid a day or two before the lightning found him. I also helped the poor girl rid herself of the problem that resulted when that became apparent.

Mrs. Carson blinked. "Are you certain?"

"Absolutely. I am a physician. I know these things."

"Oh, no!" Mrs. Carson broke down in sobs. "I blamed her. She swore that the man had been most cruel and that she tried to push him away. But he overpowered her, she said. And I said that could not be or she would not be... Oh, dear."

"There, there, Mrs. Carson." I reached over and sadly patted her shoulder. "I am sure you were doing the best you could in a terrible situation."

"But she died. We were trying to get rid of it, you know. I used a knitting needle. It's the best thing, I was told." She looked at me. "But you know that already, don't you? That I used it?"

I sighed and blinked my eyes. "I found the needle and kept it. I wished to spare you the pain of knowing what had happened."

"Oh, what you must think of me!" Mrs. Carson's sobs grew in force.

I will concede that I was somewhat reluctant to embrace

her, for I was not at all sure it would be received well, but I put my arms around her, anyway, and held her as she cried.

"My poor Mrs. Carson. You did the best that you could under the most trying of circumstances," I said softly.

It did not entirely assuage her, but I did not think that it would. Alas, when grief becomes bound up in guilt, it is almost impossible to assuage the guilt, and Mrs. Carson had, however innocently, been the agent of her daughter's death. She knew it and so did I, and she knew that I was fully sensible of that fact. To pretend otherwise would not have helped her. But she had been trying her best to help her daughter in this most terrible of circumstances, so that is what I reminded her of several times. There was nothing else to do.

The worst part, however, was that I did have to ask a question or two that I fervently did not want to ask her. As her sobs finally subsided and she pulled away from me, I held my breath.

"I apologize for that ghastly display," she said finally, wiping her face with a lovely linen handkerchief. "What you must think of me."

"I do not think ill of you in the least," I said softly. I took a deep breath. "However, I hope I have no reason to think so of your husband, but I am afraid there are rumors in the pueblo that his behavior has been less than salutary."

Mrs. Carson sniffed as she dabbed at her eyes. "He can be rather dreadful, can't he? But then you know about his gluttony and his tendency to abuse his employees."

"I'm afraid I've also been told that he will take liberties with a woman if she is in the shop by herself, even to the point of chasing her."

Mrs. Carson actually laughed. "Yes, he does think that is great fun. But nothing ever comes of it."

"That you know of."

She gasped. "What? What have you heard?"

"Nothing definitive." I looked down at my hands. "I hate asking, but there is a reason I do need to know. Have you had any signs of syphilis?"

"Oh, no." Mrs. Carson rolled her eyes. "I specifically requested that if he was going to satiate himself with ladies of ill-repute, that he at least go to Mrs. Medina's house. It's the cleanest in the pueblo. Everyone knows that."

I did my best not to gape. "You know that he visits there?"

"Well, of course." She sniffed. "I know that it doesn't do to say so. But to be honest, I have no interest in his passions. I am past my child-bearing years. Why should I put up with his efforts that way? Not to mention sparing myself the potential for that miserable disease."

"But does your husband have it?"

"Not that I know of. It would be rather easy for him to hide it as we do not share a bedroom. However, he shows no signs of madness or other discomforts, and knowing him, he would have at least something to say about it if he did pick it up."

"And what about his regard for your daughter?"

Mrs. Carson shrugged. "It was well enough, I suppose. To be honest, he mostly ignored her. He favors our boys, and even then, has not paid a great deal of attention to them, and as such was utterly shocked when our oldest decided to leave Los Angeles and make his fortune in New York." She leaned forward. "Our boy is doing remarkably well. Deals in stock or wool or some such nonsense. Even his father has had to sit up and take notice."

"That's very nice," I said.

Mrs. Carson took a deep breath and nodded. "If only our daughter…"

"I am so sorry, Mrs. Carson, and I hate to ask, but did she tell you who her tormentor was? Give you the least hint?"

"No. Not a word." Mrs. Carson stared straight ahead.

"I am told this villain has quite the hold on his victims. He promised not only to ruin them, but their friends, too."

"That is what she said."

"Then may I offer some other intelligence that I hope will be of some comfort to you. Even though your daughter was too afraid to name the cur, she made a point of warning other young ladies in the pueblo about him. She told them to be wary and not go behind blocks or alleys if invited. She probably saved a young woman or two."

Mrs. Carson smiled sadly. "That was my Julia. A kinder heart there never was." She wept silently for a moment. "Thank you, Mrs. Wilcox. You have been exceedingly kind."

"You're very welcome, Mrs. Carson." I got up. "I am afraid, however, that I must take my leave."

Her hand whipped out and held my arm in a steely grip. "Find him, will you?" Her voice grew low and hard. "And make him pay."

"I will do my best, Mrs. Carson. Good day."

I left her feeling deeply frustrated, and as I walked, I realized that it was not solely trying to find the monster, and possibly two other killers. It was the injustice of it all. Poor Lavina, her inheritance stolen away from her, and then her very life. Miss Carson blamed by her own mother when she had most likely been utterly innocent. All the young women too terrified of losing their reputation to name the villain preying upon them. That there was good reason for them to be so terrified was utterly infuriating.

If I had any independence, it was only because of my widowhood, and even then, should the wrong man file a lawsuit against me, I would be utterly ruined, not even able to testify on my own behalf. We women had so little control over our lives. There had to be something I could do to change things for the young women in the pueblo. And yet, I felt so completely overwhelmed at that moment, I was hard pressed to think of what.

As I made my way to the street, I pushed aside my melancholy thoughts, then realized that I was decidedly low on the salve Dr. Wang had made. My friend was alone in his shop when I entered.

"Maddie!" he exclaimed with a smile. "I was going to visit you later today. I have news for you."

"About what?"

Dr. Wang shuddered. "About that man in the pueblo you asked me about, the one forcing himself on young girls. I do not know who he is. He would not tell me his name. But I believe he may have come in here. He wanted herbs to cure syphilis. He had many sores all over his person."

I sighed. "That could have been many men."

"Yes, I know." Dr. Wang chuckled. "But this man, I tell him to avoid his wife, and he said that he did not bother with her. That he liked them younger."

"Oh, dear. That is suggestive."

"He was no taller than us, with black hair, and he smelled like fruit. Do you know someone like that?"

I sighed. "Unfortunately, several men. Well, not smelling of fruit, specifically." I thought it over. "However, this is more helpful than anything else I have learned. Thank you, Fu. Oh, and I need more salve for the measles."

I finished my business with Dr. Wang with my mind awhirl. Of all the persons I thought might be responsible, several of them fit his description of this strange man, but none of them smelled like fruit. I thought, perhaps, that Dr. Wang's nose had detected something mine hadn't. His sense of smell was especially acute.

But then, I eventually realized that of all the men I had been considering as possibly being the monster, there was no one who could be expected to carry that particular aroma. However, there was one man in the pueblo who was also small with dark hair and most certainly did have the aura of fruit about his person, as well as the habit of taking liberties with the women of the pueblo.

Why I had not considered him, I do not know. Still, I made my way as quickly as I could to Mr. Mahoney's saloon and the kitchen in the back.

"Annie!" I exclaimed as she opened the door to me. "I must know. Is there a grocer you find difficult or even repugnant?"

"Yes." She swallowed. "Mr. Larson. Alice and I do not dare go into that store alone. He has taken all manner of liberties with us, even then. But he has never accosted us."

"Probably because he doesn't want to try to force himself on two of you at once." I looked away, thinking. "Did Miss Carson go there?"

"All sorts of people go there," Annie said. "He stocks a great many specialties from Europe that you can't get anywhere else in the pueblo."

"And I don't doubt many women send their daughters there to pick up occasional items because their mothers are too busy." I frowned. "He can't be attacking all of the young ladies."

"No. But then most of us don't go there alone."

I sighed. "I shall have to speak to him, and best done sooner rather than later." I looked at her. "Please keep this conference to yourself. I must arrange some help."

I hurried from the saloon and went straight to the funeral parlor. Alas, Angelina was at one of the two funerals she had prepared for the previous day. I returned to the Calle Primavera feeling quite anxious and nonplussed, which may be why I turned in the direction of the courthouse and there found Mr. Navarro. I was not sure if I wanted that young police officer specifically to accompany me, but if Mr. Larson was, indeed, the killer I sought, then having Mr. Navarro there would be exactly what I would need.

I, however, did not explain what my plan was, partially because I had no idea what it would be and partially because I wished Mr. Navarro's unbiased opinion.

The grocery store was fairly busy, however, Mr. Larson was not in immediate evidence. Mrs. Larson, who looked remarkably like her spouse, was there, however and looked at me warily.

"I need to speak to you," I said.

She sighed. "As do I." She looked over at Mr. Navarro. "However, I do not wish to speak in front of him."

"We can go in the back if you prefer."

She nodded and went to the curtained doorway, calling for her eldest son, a stout lad of sixteen. Mr. Navarro shook his head but let me go with Mrs. Larson. A minute later, the two of us were in the small back room of the store, standing amid the rows of shelves containing all manner of goods and tins.

"I think I have syphilis," Mrs. Larson said, then went on to describe her symptoms.

I checked one of her sores, and it was that miserable contagion.

"Have you been with anyone besides your husband?" I asked, sighing.

"No. Of course not. He's with me little enough as it is." She flushed, then sighed. "At least he's home at night. That's more than I can say for many men in the pueblo."

"That is true." I sighed and began digging through my bag for the bark cure I'd tried with my other syphilis patients. "Do you remember the night of the dispensary fire?"

"Who doesn't?"

I looked at her. "What were you doing that day?"

"Our family was together," she said simply. "At least until the hue and cry went up over Miss Gaines having disappeared."

"Including your husband?"

"Oh, yes." She smiled. "As I said, he is at home with us when he isn't here."

"That's odd. Because if you are being truthful about not being with any other man than your husband, can you explain how he got the disease?"

Her bottom lip quivered. "He... He..." She began sobbing. "He is with us in the evenings, but he does go out during the day."

"I have also had reports that he makes himself quite free with the young ladies of the pueblo."

"Oh, everyone does that. He means no harm."

"Including forcing himself on them?"

Mrs. Larson cried loudly, and a loud roar of anger shook the back room.

"I do no such thing!" Mr. Larson burst through the curtained doorway, with Mr. Navarro on his heels. "They seduce me, flashing their eyes at me and smiling sweetly!"

"See?" Mrs. Larson cried. "My husband is being falsely accused!"

"Then why is it that no young woman wishes to come into this store alone?" I demanded.

"Edith. Leave." Mr. Larson glared at me as he pointed out the back door toward what was presumably the family's home.

Mrs. Larson left, still sobbing. Mr. Larson rushed up very close to me and tried to push his face into mine.

"Why are you persecuting me?"

"I am acting in the interests of the young women of this pueblo," I said, so furious that I found myself pushing forward into him. "No one has seduced you. You have merely decided that you can take what you like and are blaming innocent young ladies for your indiscretion. How dare you act out your baser instincts on these poor young women. Do you realize that one of them has died thanks to your actions? A perfectly lovely young woman that you despoiled."

"I cannot be held to account for such trollops' behavior." He moved away and turned. "They come to me, taunting me with their beauty and their freshness. It's not my fault!"

"It most certainly is." I went after him. "You are a mature man, fully cognizant and, one would think, in control of his passions. How is it that you insist that they tempt you and that you cannot resist? Are you truly that weak a worm?"

"I am not!" he screamed. He sank against a shelf. "No man could resist what I face."

"That is rubbish," I said softly. "The vast majority of men do not choose to force themselves on women. They may tease and take liberties, but they do not go any further. And it is bad enough when they take liberties."

"You can't prove that I did anything," Mr. Larson said. "It's my word against theirs, and no one will believe them. No one will accuse me."

Mr. Navarro grabbed the front of Mr. Larson's shirt. "I accuse you. I have heard everything you have said, and I stand here in testament to that." And he punctuated that by shaking the grocer hard.

"Leave him be, Mr. Navarro," I said, my voice cold and hard.

"What?" Mr. Navarro looked at me but did not let go of Mr. Larson. "We must rid the pueblo of this vile creature."

"And send him off to prey on some other young women?" I shook my head. "I think not. I suppose we could send him to trial, but that would tarnish the names of several young women who do not deserve it. That does not mean he will not face just repercussions for his depravity." I smiled coldly. "You and I, Mr. Navarro, will see to it that he does. We will spread the rumors. We will whisper in the back alleys. We will let the whole pueblo know what a monster Mr. Larson is. Even if the men want to believe that he is being unfairly persecuted, no young woman will come near him, and their mothers will stop buying their groceries here." I walked over to Mr. Larson. "Unless you stay in this back room at all times. The only places you will go are here and your own home. Let your sons and your wife run the business. I would not see them ruined when they are innocent. But you will remain mewed up, and trust me, Mr. Larson, I will find out if you go anywhere near another woman again."

Mr. Navarro let out an angry chuckle. "And, Mr. Larson, I will know, too, and I will hold you down as she performs surgery on you. Without benefit of ether."

We left the man cowering in his back room, then made our way through the store to the street. I was still trembling, as was Mr. Navarro.

"Mrs. Wilcox," he said softly. "Maddie, I owe you an apology. You were right about my teasing and how frightening it must be to an innocent young thing." He blinked back tears. "I had no idea. I mean, all the other fellows do it, and the ladies laugh. But sometimes, I do not think they find it all that amusing."

"Some do," I conceded. "But I think that most do not."

He shook his head. "I do love Miss Alvarez. I do not worry so much that she can hurt me if she is angry, or that you can. I truly do not want to hurt her."

"That is most commendable, Mr. Navarro." I sighed. "And I suppose that in Christian charity, I must forgive you. But you are still a rogue."

He laughed. "I wouldn't be so charming if I weren't."

He sauntered off, although I do believe he was hiding his deeper, more tender feelings in his easy stride and smile. It had been a terrifying and horrible encounter.

As I made my way home, however, I realized that it meant something else still more upsetting.

Chapter Twenty

The moment I arrived at the rancho, I sent messages to both Regina and Angelina, but then received another for myself, and hurried to Mrs. Mason's house.

Mr. Samples was there, in the front parlor waiting for me, alongside Mrs. Mason. We got ourselves settled and I took a deep breath.

"Mr. Samples, I have been told that you were occupied at the time Judge Gresham was most likely killed," I said. "Can you tell me where and how?"

He glanced at Mrs. Mason, then nodded. "I was at the Zanjero's office with Mr. Lomax. My zanja was blocked again."

"That is as I was told," I replied. "Thank you. I hated to ask, but I needed to be sure that what I was told was the truth."

"Mrs. Mason said that you had questions about something I saw."

I nodded. "The night that Miss Gaines was murdered. You told me you saw a mule and a man out by Mama Jane's hut for long enough that you wondered what he was doing."

"I got to be careful. Folks who hang around are usually up to no good."

"I'm sure that is true. Can you tell me anything about the man you saw, maybe what he looked like?"

Mr. Samples shrugged, then thought. "Looked like just another fellow in the pueblo, excepting us colored folk. Hair was dark, I think, and he seemed like he might be kind of short, but I can't rightly say for sure."

"He had something white hanging from his saddle."

"He didn't come with it, but it was on the saddle when he rode away. Some sort of flag, only it was in two parts, like arms."

I closed my eyes, suddenly knowing what it was that he had seen.

"Or nether limbs," I said quietly. "Thank you, Mr. Samples." I took a deep breath. "I should be able to use this to find the guilty party without requiring your testimony."

Mr. Samples shook his head. "They aren't going to let me testify, anyway."

"As I know all too well." I sighed, then looked at Mrs. Mason. "Thank you, ma'am, for arranging this meeting. I do hope, Mr. Samples, that you will be able to return to your farm."

He nodded. "I'm staying away until it's safe to go back to it."

I left soon after and returned to my rancho only to be chided quite severely for missing my lunch again. Olivia was only slightly mollified by the news that the man forcing himself on young women had been found and dealt with. Maria was ecstatic.

"I hated Mr. Larson, but I do like his groceries," she said.

"It will be such a relief to buy things without worrying about being chased or tickled."

I managed to stay at the rancho through supper, but then I had to go back to the pueblo to Regina's house for our conference. Angelina had already arrived, and Regina paced in her bedroom, still unable to don outerclothes.

"It's not even been a week," I told her. "Have patience. A few more days, then I can remove your sutures and you should be able to wear whatever you like."

"Hmph!" Regina snorted.

"I know how she feels," Angelina said, her eyes glinting with mischief. She opened up her little wooden desk and pulled two sheets of paper and a pen and ink from it. "I do have some news, but I'm afraid it's not very good."

"Regarding Mr. Lomax and Mr. Navarro?" I asked, settling into one of the other chairs.

"Yes." Angelina sighed. "They do not keep very good records at that jail. The one policeman I spoke with believes that Mr. Lomax was, indeed, doing guard duty the night of the dispensary fire as he generally serves that way on Sunday nights. But the officer isn't sure because Mr. Lomax sometimes doesn't."

"I have news, as well," I said. "And it is not happy news, either, though in some ways, it is. I have found the monster preying on the young women. However, he quite probably did not kill either Mama Jane or Lavina, let alone Judge Gresham."

"Who?" Regina asked.

"Mr. Larson, the grocer. Mr. Navarro and I confronted him over his ill deeds this morning." I told them about the entire encounter, including my conversation with Mrs. Larson.

"Are you sure he will do as you say?" Regina asked, one eyebrow cocked.

"As sure as I can be." I sighed and looked disconsolately at the decanter of angelica on Regina's bedside table.

Regina immediately poured glasses for all three of us.

Angelina took her glass. "Why are you so certain that Mr. Larson didn't kill Lavina or Mama Jane?"

"Because Mrs. Larson was quite clear that Mr. Larson had been home the afternoon of the dispensary fire, then out looking for Lavina." I sipped from my glass. "She also said that her husband is almost always at home in the evenings, which means he was probably not out killing Mama Jane."

"People do tell lies," Regina said.

"Which is why Mr. Larson could still be our killer," I said. "However, in the context in which I asked the question, Mrs. Larson had no reason to lie. We were talking about her health at the time." I paused. "She has syphilis, and I had to ask regarding her husband's habits and challenged her when she said he was at home most nights. She said he went out during the days."

"Oh, the poor thing," sighed Angelina. She looked at her list. "Maybe we should go through everyone we have been considering."

"We should," I said. "However, I also have intelligence that the person we are looking for is on the short side and probably has dark hair, a description, I might add, that also fits Mr. Larson. In addition, I do gravely fear that we are looking for more than one killer. There is no real reason to believe that the man who killed Judge Gresham is the same one who killed Mama Jane and Lavina."

"Oh, good Heavens!" Regina sank onto her bed with a most dramatic flourish and semblance of the vapors. "Why don't we assume that the person who shot me was aiming for me and is yet a third malefactor?"

I sighed. "I was just about to suggest that."

Even Angelina groaned. "The problem is, you're right. We cannot assume that all of the killings are related, except that you were speaking with the judge shortly before he was killed, and you were with Regina when she got shot. It could be they are related."

"But why would someone who murdered two women by strangling them suddenly pick up a shotgun to finish off his next two victims?" Regina asked.

"That is why I believe we are dealing with two killers," I said. "But as we cannot be certain, let us consider everyone on Angelina's list. Who do we start with, Angelina?"

She looked at the list, then dipped her pen. "Mr. Carson."

"Too large and his hair is too white to have been the person Mr. Samples saw," I said.

"And he was in his store when the judge was shot," Angelina said. "The most he could have done is shot at Regina."

"I can't imagine why he would," Regina said. "Were he the one who had been shot, he would have good reason to suspect me of the deed. He is constantly..." She stopped and looked at us. "Well, you both know already that he is a regular guest here, and not a favored one, I assure you. He is constantly asking me to reduce the fees, as if my girls were up for bid."

I sighed. "Which, I am afraid, comes as no surprise to me."

"But no, regarding Mama Jane and Lavina. No for Judge Gresham," Angelina muttered as she wrote. "Yes, for Regina." She looked up. "What about Mr. Samples?"

"He was in the Zanjero's office with Mr. Lomax when the judge was most likely shot," I said. "And he had no reason to hurt Mama Jane, let alone Lavina. Or to hurt Regina, either. He also seems to prefer a rifle to a shotgun."

"No on all counts," Angelina said. "Father Gallar."

I considered. "In regards to size, he could be the person that Mr. Samples saw. It also makes sense that he was riding a mule. He had known antipathy toward Mama Jane and would likely have similar antipathy toward Regina. But there is no discernable reason for him to have killed either Lavina or Judge Gresham."

"Oh, dagnabbit," Regina grumbled. "I was so hoping it was him."

I winced at Regina's language, even being as habituated to it as I was.

"What about Mr. Wiley?" Angelina asked.

"He is small enough, but fair-haired," I said. "However, it could look dark enough after twilight. The strange thing is that he has little to no reason to have harmed Lavina, unless he held her responsible for Julia Carson's death. The same could be said for Mama Jane. If he had some dispute in connection with the judge, I have no knowledge of it."

"Yes for Lavina and Mama Jane, no for the judge." Angelina looked up. "What about Regina?"

"I have not had the least indication that he had any complaints about me," Regina said.

"No for Regina." Angelina sighed. "Then there is this Mr. Lyons."

I nodded. "He certainly had a reason to be angry with Lavina. Mr. Smith even said that, when Lavina first went missing, Mr. Lyons was the first person he went after, fearing that Mr. Lyons had harmed her. It does not entirely explain Mama Jane's death, however. Mr. Lyons was definitely in the pueblo when Lavina was killed and could have been when Mama Jane was. Unfortunately, there is no connection to the judge that I know of."

"Nor do I know who he is," Regina said.

Angelina scribbled away, shaking her head. "Mr. Lawrence could not have killed the judge, as I saw him during the appropriate time. But could he have killed Mama Jane and Lavina?"

Regina snorted. "I know I have questioned his purity, but, alas, I had no reason to and there is every indication that he is as upright and true as he appears."

"I am of the same mind," I said. "What about Mr. Alverno? He has considerable antipathy toward the judge, although none to my knowledge regarding Regina. In addition, he has been trying most earnestly to find Lavina's killer. Why would he do that if he had killed her?"

"You can say the same regarding Mr. Smith," Regina said. "And yet, he probably had the best opportunity of all to kill her."

"But he had no reason to kill the judge," Angelina pointed out. "And he could have been aiming at Maddie if he thought she was coming too close to a conclusion regarding him."

"Then we must consider Mr. Lomax regarding Lavina's death," Regina said.

I frowned. "He's too tall, although Mr. Samples did say that he couldn't be certain that the fellow he saw was short. Nonetheless, he had no reason that I can see to kill anyone. He has been suffering the greatest of pangs over giving up his second wife and their children. Why would he have sought after a third wife, then killed her when she spurned him?"

"I'm inclined to agree," Angelina said. "And even though Mr. Navarro could be considered short enough, he has even fewer reasons to kill Mama Jane, Lavina, or even the judge." She looked again at her paper. "Can we safely consider Mr. Alverno for killing the judge?"

I groaned and shook my head. "Alas, no. He couldn't have. Mr. Mahoney told me that Mr. Alverno was in the saloon having his lunch with the rest of the clerks that day. Well, sitting apart from them, perhaps, but still there, which means he was away from the courthouse at the time the judge was shot." I sighed. "Is there anyone else to consider?"

Angelina's eyebrows rose. "What about the bit of lace? Mr. Smith said that it hadn't been in his pocket earlier in the morning."

I shook my head. "Anyone could have put it there, though, and not just Mr. Lomax. Mr. Alverno, Mr. Navarro, and Mr. Wiley were all at the funeral. Mr. Lyons could have been, as well, and I simply did not see him, or he could have passed by Mr. Smith before the funeral and placed the lace in his pocket at that time."

"Or Mr. Smith could have had it with him the whole time," said Regina. "And Mr. Alverno took note of it because why would a man be carrying a piece of lace, especially a bit off of a mourning dress such as Miss Lavina was wearing?"

Angelina shook her head in frustration. "Well, one thing is obvious. Someone is clearly not telling us the truth about all he knows."

"Which makes this no different from any other time that we've had to search for a killer," Regina said with a sigh. "I propose that we give up on deliberations and, instead, empty this lovely decanter of angelica."

I did send one of Regina's errand boys back to the rancho to ask Sebastiano to bring Daisy and the buggy to Regina's. It took just long enough for Sebastiano to arrive to ensure a headache for both Angelina and me the next morning.

Juanita was amused but brought me spicy tripe soup to ease my pain, and along with some herbs I had at the ready from Dr. Wang, I was soon feeling somewhat better. I had finished dressing when I could not help but look at Juanita as she bent to her morning tasks with a soft smile on her face.

"Are you thinking about Mr. Navarro, perchance?" I asked.

Juanita laughed. "And why are you so determined to think that he has not reformed himself?"

"I am not determined to think so." I sighed. "However, if I am to be honest, I would rather that he were not reformed."

"What?" Juanita stopped what she was doing and looked at me, puzzled. "Why would you want that?"

"Because I do not want to see you married," I said helplessly. "Once you are, you will be off taking care of your husband and you will not be here taking care of me." I sat on the side of the bed. "It is humiliating to think that I am being so unutterably selfish, but indeed, I am."

Juanita sat on the bed next to me. "You are not being entirely selfish, Maddie. I do not wish to stop taking care of you." She blinked her eyes. "It has been quite a struggle for me. When I first came to work for you when I was seventeen, I did not know I would find such a good friend in you. It was work, and I needed to help my family. But I came to love working for you and to love you, and in some ways, I want this to be my life, working at keeping your clothes clean and mended, bringing you soup, listening to your adventures and sometimes having something to add to them." She sighed. "The problem is, I also want to get married and have children. Perhaps not as much as I love being here, but as the years passed, I did not think I would attract a man. After all, being here all the time, how would I meet one? Besides, my family, we are workers and laborers and servants. I never thought I would capture the heart of someone who comes from a good family, with land and other property. So now, not only do I have a charming rogue of a swain, he is reasonably wealthy, too." She chuckled. "And I do truly love him. He is so sweet and kind."

"He can most certainly be that," I said.

"And we will still be friends, Maddie. I do hope so, and that you can come and tell me your adventures and I can sometimes have something to add to them."

"I will make a point of it." But I groaned. "However, please do not make any promises to Mr. Navarro until I have made it certain that he did not kill Mama Jane or Miss Lavina."

Juanita's face grew pale. "Oh, no. Could he have?"

"It's not likely, but still possible, I suppose." I looked at her. "Did he have any reason to be angry with Mrs. Medina?"

"Yes." Juanita swallowed and looked away. "He never said what, but she does have knowledge of something that he does not want his family or the rest of the pueblo to know."

"That's right," I groaned. "I should have remembered that." Juanita looked at me curiously, but I shook my head. "I do not know what it is, only that he can become enraged." I frowned. "That would explain Mama Jane's death, and Lavina's, but not the judge's. But then, it is entirely likely someone else, we do not know who, killed the judge."

"But Mr. Navarro!" Juanita's eyes filled as the sound of pounding horse hooves grew louder as they approached the adobe.

I got up, feeling most annoyed. "We do not know that he did anything."

"Mrs. Wilcox!" someone shouted.

I reflected that it was a good thing that I had decided to put on my brown riding habit that morning, even with a planned rest in the afternoon - it was again Saturday.

"Mrs. Wilcox!"

As I left the bedroom, I could see Maria hurry to the front parlor of the adobe and open the front door. Mr. Smith all but fell inside.

"Mrs. Wilcox," he gasped. "We have to hurry. The Sheriff's men are heading out to the Lomax place to arrest him!"

"For which offense?" I asked, shocked to my core.

"Well, for starters, they want to arrest him for polygamy."

"He is not guilty of that!" I snapped.

Mr. Smith gasped and nodded. "I don't know that he is, either, but he does have a second wife in Mrs. Sabrina. You said so."

"Did you tell anyone else?"

"Not a word, ma'am." He gasped again. "But that's only the beginning. They really think that he killed Miss Gaines."

Chapter Twenty-One

There was little time to spare. I had Rodolfo saddle Daisy as quickly as he could, while I convinced Sebastiano and Enrique to go to the courthouse and find out what they could there.

"Mr. Navarro is at the Lomax place now," Mr. Smith said. "And I'll be there, so Mrs. Wilcox will be as safe as can be."

"She'd better be," grumbled Sebastiano, giving Mr. Smith an angry glare.

Mr. Smith had borrowed a horse, he didn't say from whom, and to be truthful, I didn't bother with asking. We galloped toward the small farm by the most direct route we knew. I do not know how we got there before the Sheriff's men did, but I was profoundly grateful.

Mr. Navarro admitted Mr. Smith and me into the adobe, shaking his head. Mrs. Ruth and Mrs. Sabrina were busy packing, tears streaming down both of their faces. The children huddled nearby, and Mr. Lomax held the youngest, whispering that all would be well and that he would protect them.

"They'll be here at any minute," Mr. Smith said. "Mr. Lomax, do you give me your solemn oath of honor that you did not kill Miss Gaines?"

Mr. Lomax straightened and stood looking at Mr. Smith. "I solemnly swear that I did not kill Miss Lavina Gaines, nor did I kill Mama Jane. But that doesn't mean that you didn't, Mr. Smith."

A faint roar of angry voices grew outside.

"What?" I snapped. "There is no reason nor time to waste bandying about these kinds of accusations!"

"Never mind." Mr. Smith fixed his eyes on Mr. Lomax. "I, too, swear on my life that I did not kill Miss Gaines, nor anyone else. Now, which of your wives do you want to keep?"

Mr. Lomax turned pale. "I…"

"Lomax!" called a voice from outside. It was the same fellow as had tried to arrest Mr. Samples some days before. "It's Deputy Frawley. I want you to come out here with your hands up."

"Which of your wives, Lomax," Mr. Smith said. "We don't have time."

"Get the polygamist!" someone else screamed.

"Ruth," Mr. Lomax whispered. "I want Ruth."

Mr. Smith waved Mr. Lomax back, opened the cabin door slowly, then tossed his six-shooter onto the ground in front of the cabin.

"I'm coming out!" he called. "And I am unarmed."

I slid to the front window and looked out. There was a crowd of about ten men, led by Deputy Frawley. The deputy waved the men back and glared at Mr. Smith.

"That's not Lomax," someone else called.

"Why are you here, son?" Frawley asked, glancing back at the adobe.

"As I understand it, you are here to arrest Mr. Lomax on charges of polygamy," Mr. Smith said. "Now, I can vouch that he is not a polygamist and that his sister-in-law only waited to remarry to find the right man, and that man is me."

Both Ruth and Sabrina yelped as Mr. Lomax sank onto the lone bed in the place, his head in his hands. Fortunately, the rumbling of the men outside covered the sound of the women's tears.

"What about Miss Gaines?" Frawley yelled.

"Mrs. Wilcox is here," Mr. Smith said. "She can tell you that Mr. Lomax did not do the deed."

I looked over at Mr. Lomax and knew that he had not sworn falsely. But how to reassure the men outside that he hadn't when I did not, in fact, know who the killer was, and indeed, knew that one man who could have was also still in the cabin.

Mr. Navarro looked at me, placed his six-shooter on the sill of the window, then nodded at me.

I slid out the door. "What Mr. Smith says is true. I have come to believe that Mr. Lomax did not kill Lavina Gaines or Mama Jane."

"What about Judge Gresham?" Frawley demanded.

"None of them," I said. "I confess I do not know who did yet, but it was not Mr. Lomax. Of that, I am certain."

Several of the men slid back to the road. The deputy hemmed and hawed for a minute, then turned and left, himself. What men were left followed him.

I took a deep breath and closed my eyes against the

dizziness I felt. The last thing I wanted or needed was an attack of the vapors. A moment later, I opened my eyes. The yard had emptied and Mr. Smith was picking up his gun.

The tension inside the cabin had not abated by much, however. Mr. Lomax got to his feet as Mr. Smith entered.

"I can't say I'm not grateful," Mr. Lomax said, glaring at Mr. Smith. "But who are you to decide that you're going to take one of my wives?"

"I would've asked you first, but those deputies didn't give me the time." Mr. Smith swallowed. "Mr. Lomax, I'm from Utah, too. I know how it works there. And you're an honorable man."

"Which is why I do not want to simply hand Sabrina over."

"What other option do you have?" Mr. Smith said. "You've got a problem here, sir. On the other hand, I need and want a wife, and a farmer's wife would suit me a lot better than a town girl."

"You do not know Sabrina. How do you know that she will suit you?" Anger flashed in Mr. Lomax's eyes. "And how do I know that you will suit her and take care of her?"

"You'll know because I'll be living right next to you," Mr. Smith said. "Just yesterday, I put a bid in on that piece of property next to yours and as there aren't any others, nor are there likely to be, I expect to win that bid. As for Sabrina, you're right. I don't know if she or Ruth would suit me. But sometimes you just have to take a chance." He sighed. "Look, Mr. Lomax. I know you love your wives and love your children. I respect that. I really do. That's why I figure I'm the best shot you've got at finding a husband for one of these ladies."

"Then I should be the one to go with him," Mrs. Ruth said.

"No." Mr. Lomax looked at Mrs. Sabrina. "You know that I love you. I have sworn that I would for time and all eternity, and I will. But I have to give one of you up. I cannot have two wives, and frankly, I don't want two. But I do still love you, and your children are still my children, and if this..." He glared at Mr. Smith. "This man does not live up to his promise to care for you and for them, then I will kill him. Do you mind going with him?"

Mrs. Sabrina smiled softly at him. "I want more babies, Walter. If you cannot be a husband to me, then I want a man who will be."

I cleared my throat. "Perhaps before any more promises are made, we should wait and see if Mr. Smith does suit Mrs. Sabrina. After all, Mr. Smith, it has not been all that long since you lost the woman you professed to love beyond all others." I couldn't help glaring at him as yet another ugly thought crossed my mind. "In fact, I find it rather odd that you find it so easy to turn your affections toward Mrs. Sabrina after such a loss."

Mr. Smith went pale. "But I swore on my life that I did not kill Lavina! And besides, I have been trying to find her killer."

"You could have been mis-directing m—" I stopped. "Mr. Alverno."

"I thought he might be behind killing the judge," Mr. Lomax said.

"Except that he was having his lunch in Mr. Mahoney's saloon at the only time a shotgun blast would not have been heard, let alone remarked upon." I began pacing.

"But he was late to his luncheon," Mr. Smith said. "I

remember it quite clearly, as the clocktower struck the half hour just after he got there."

"Nor do I know where he was when Mama Jane and Miss Lavina were killed." I frowned. "But he loved Lavina. Why would he kill her?"

"If she spurned him," said Mr. Navarro.

I turned my gaze on him. "Didn't you tell me that Mama Jane had sold another love charm that she did not expect to work to someone with a black heart?"

"I did." Mr. Navarro frowned. "She needed the money."

"That it didn't work could have also induced a rage." I went back to pacing. "It is one of the few things that fits. But not entirely. Someone shot at me and Mrs. Medina a week ago. Why would someone who kills with his hands while in a rage suddenly start using a shotgun?"

Mr. Lomax shrugged. "If he wasn't in a rage but needed to kill somebody who knew too much."

"And I had just spoken to Judge Gresham about a piece of lace that had probably come from Lavina's dress, not to mention the fact that..." I flushed. "Miss Gaines' nether garment was missing when she was found. It was one of the reasons we believed that the monster forcing himself on the young women of the pueblo was responsible."

"So, what do we do now?" Mr. Navarro asked.

"The first thing I need to do is talk to Mr. Alverno," I said. I looked at Mr. Smith and Mr. Lomax. "You two may as well stay here. Hopefully, the men won't be back, and you have a great deal to discuss and arrange."

"I'll go with her," Mr. Navarro said.

His horse had been tethered next to Daisy, and the two of us trotted back into the pueblo proper and the courthouse. Enrique had gone back to the rancho, but Sebastiano was still nearby.

"The men came back," he said. "They said that Mr. Lomax did not kill Miss Gaines."

"And I have arrived at an idea of who did," I said, looking grimly upstairs. "You wouldn't happen to know if Mr. Alverno is in the clerks' room, would you?"

Sebastiano shook his head. "I have been out here all morning. I haven't seen him."

"Then let us assume that he is there," I said, glancing up at the clock. "We have a little over an hour until lunchtime. I think we should also assume that he has his shotgun close at hand. Clearly, he did this past Tuesday. Mr. Navarro, Sebastiano, we need some way for you two to be witnesses, and yet not scare him. If you both accompany me, then it is all too possible that he will see it as threatening and start shooting. On the other hand, Mr. Navarro, if you go in first, you can ascertain that he is there, then signal me from a window. That should not arouse comment, don't you think?"

"I'm there all the time," said Mr. Navarro.

"Sebastiano, you can wait in the corridor, where Mr. Alverno cannot see you. That way, I can question him, and if he starts to get angry, I can get out of the way and hide while you and Mr. Navarro capture him."

Sebastiano did not think much of the plan but was forced to agree that there seemed to be little better alternative. Mr. Navarro went ahead, and, after some minutes, I saw him open the window of the front courtroom and wave. Sebastiano followed me up the stairs to the clerks' room, but as requested, stayed in the corridor.

Mr. Alverno and two clerks worked busily as I approached the counter between them and the door. I was somewhat surprised that Mr. Alverno saw me and looked up from his desk.

"Good day, Mrs. Wilcox," he said with a smile. "How can I help you today?"

The other two clerks looked at him curiously, then each other, then went back to their work.

"You can tell me where you were the afternoon before the dispensary fire," I said.

He swallowed. "I— I was at home. I generally am on Sunday afternoons."

"What about the Monday prior to that day?"

"I was here, of course. You saw me."

I smiled. "I did, but I did not see you later that evening."

"I was at home, of course."

"And your landlord can verify that?"

He shook his head suddenly. "My landlord is of no concern to you. I pay my rent. I can go about as I please."

"I am not here to suggest that you can't. However, I do wonder why you continued your pursuit of Miss Gaines when she routinely spurned you." I smiled again. "She was kind enough about it, but it was clear on that Monday that she was not interested in you."

"She had just lost her case. Of course, she wasn't."

"Is that what Mama Jane had to say?"

He pulled himself up straight. "I don't know what you're talking about."

"You went to see Mama Jane that night, after Miss Gaines had been robbed of her inheritance. You told her that the charm she'd made for you hadn't worked."

He swallowed and began breathing heavily. "It didn't. I mean, it wouldn't. It was a charm. Such things are for children."

"Perhaps, but you were desperate. As for Miss Gaines, is it possible that the judge asked you about a bit of lace? It would be difficult for him to ask about Miss Gaines' missing nether garment."

I should have been watching his hands. Unfortunately, they had slid under his desk, and the next thing I knew, his hands reappeared holding a shotgun.

I screamed and ducked behind the counter that separated me from the clerks. The gun roared and a huge hole in the counter's front opened up next to me. I scrambled through the door to the corridor taking care to stay down.

"That Indian witch laughed at me!" Alverno cried. "And Miss Gaines, she said she didn't want me, and she pitied me."

The shotgun roared again as the clerks yelled and, presumably, hid.

"I will not be pitied!"

A third blast seemed directed at the door to the corridor, and I heard glass shattering with it. Terrified, I saw the courtroom door open several yards away and decided to run for it. I had almost made it to the end of the corridor when the shotgun roared, a hole burst into the door ahead of me and

I felt the burning stings of buckshot lacing my shoulders and nether limbs. I fell on my face as Mr. Navarro appeared and fired three times.

The shotgun had been stilled. Mr. Alverno would not annoy anyone again.

"Maddie!" Sebastiano ran up. "Are you all right?"

"Well enough," I gasped through my pain. "I do believe Mrs. Medina is going to find my condition quite amusing."

Sebastiano sighed loudly. He and Mr. Navarro got me home, where Elena was making ready to go to the hospital for that evening's usual mayhem. Instead, we had to send to Dr. Richardson that I would not be available and to ask him to wait at the hospital for casualties instead of me. I do not know if he did or not.

Regina had somehow gotten dressed earlier that day, which was how she was able to arrive at my adobe in good time to smirk as Elena prepared to remove the shot from my back. I, however, happily accepted a full dose of morphine and slid into slumber even before Elena could begin and did not awake again until the next morning.

Mr. Navarro had stayed to supper and regaled the rest of my household with the day's events. I had to tell the story again the next afternoon when Angelina and Regina came by to visit. Mr. Navarro had found Lavina's pantaloons in Mr. Alverno's desk, along with a love letter that had been returned. Angelina had already prepared Mr. Alverno's body, although she expected that there would not be much of a funeral.

"That poor little man," I observed as she and Regina sat next to my bed. "He had been routinely abused by the three judges and chose to respond by being as difficult as he could be with everyone else, only to fall into a rage and kill Mama Jane, let alone the one woman who was kind to him."

"It is no surprise then that he fell in love with Miss Gaines," Angelina said. "She always treated him far more kindly than he deserved."

I could not help the tears that sprang to my eyes. "Lavina was always far kinder to everyone than they deserved. She would not say a word against her father, even when she despaired of the men that he asked to be her suitors. It was the same with Mrs. Gaines, and her brother. I wonder at that, but there is nothing to be done."

And, indeed, there wasn't. Mr. and Mrs. Gaines had quite a companionable marriage, as it turned out, but they did not learn a thing from the events that had ensued and remained miserly and unkind. While I could not entirely condone Mr. Smith's duplicity when it came to the piece of land that he'd told Mr. Gaines was too far from the Zanja Madre, I must admit I was quite happy to hear that Mr. Gaines was quite put out when Mr. Smith finalized the purchase. Mr. Smith chose to open his own land agency in addition to farming and later told me that he'd opened his own office because he did not want to work with so miserly a man as Mr. Gaines.

Mr. Smith did take Mrs. Sabrina as his wife and by the end of the summer, I am happy to relate that both she and Mrs. Ruth Lomax were expecting. Mr. Lomax was no less laconic, but I could tell that he was ecstatic.

Sadly, Mrs. Larson languished and died by the end of July and Mr. Larson shortly after her from an apoplexy. Their sons sold the store and left the pueblo. The man who took over was much better behaved, but still prone to taking the occasional liberty. In fact, Maria went so far as to declare that he must have liked being slapped as he would not stop doing the very things that got him slapped.

Mr. Samples and his family were able to return to his farm, fortunately. I was a little concerned that Mr. Smith would not look kindly upon his neighbors, but he was even kinder to the family than Mr. Lomax was.

Mr. Wiley and Mr. Lyons prospered as partners, and when Mr. Lyons married the following spring, it was as a wealthy man. Mr. Wiley, however, chose not to endanger any more young women by falling in love with them.

Mrs. Carson never fully regained her usual bluster. Given how much she had feared for her daughter's reputation, I would have thought that she would have been less prone to gossip, but sadly, no. Indeed, her chatter took on a nastier tone to it to the point where even Mrs. Glassell began to avoid her.

Regarding Juanita and Mr. Navarro, they were married in early September. However, Juanita had no end of difficulty finding just the right ladies' maid for me. I, in fact, was quite open to each of the young women that came to request the position. It was Juanita who rejected girl after girl. Marisol Velasquez, however, did manage to pass muster, although she wore a hole in my brown riding habit trying to get out a blood stain the first week she was there. She felt terrible about it, but I assured her the habit sorely needed replacing, anyway.

As for me, I did find a new friend in Mrs. Gresham, and I did not begrudge it of her when the probate on her husband's will, which truly left her everything, went through with nary a problem. Nonetheless, I spent the weeks after the incident feeling decidedly melancholy, until it occurred to me that there was something I could do to fight the injustices we women faced.

It was late July, one early morning, that I clipped some roses from the bushes planted around my rancho and brought them up to the cemetery. As I laid the blooms on Lavina's grave, I wept not only for the loss of her, but for all the other women I'd known who'd suffered as she had.

"Lavina, my dearest," I said softly as I gazed at the simple tombstone. "I gravely fear that you will not be the last woman I will know who will be denied her rights and even her life by the men around her. So, it will be in your memory, and in the memory of Julia Carson and Mama Jane, that I will fight. I will fight to give young women a chance to go to college. I will fight for more opportunities for women to have real careers. I will fight to see that no woman is robbed of an inheritance simply because she is a woman." I choked. "And I will begin my fight with achieving votes for women. In your honor and in your memory."

And I have done so. Indeed, it was Lavina's face before me a few years ago when I was first able to cast a ballot in a presidential election. Yes, Lavina's kindness left its mark upon me, and even as I feel her loss, I am happy to have called her my friend.

The Next Book in the Old Los Angeles Series

It's the holiday season of 1872 in the pueblo, and the days will be filled with gifts, balls, masquerade parties, and a murder. The victim is poor, drunk Mr. Hewitt, and Maddie finds herself up to her neck in the usual ills that come with winter and her most puzzling case ever.

DEATH OF A TOWN DRUNK will hopefully arrive on bookshelves in time for Christmas of 2023.

Other Books by Anne Louise Bannon

I'm so glad you liked this book! Check out my other novels, available in print or ebook at your favorite retailer:

Freddie and Kathy Series:

Fascinating Rhythm

Bring Into Bondage

The Last Witnesses

Blood Red

Operation Quickline Series

That Old Cloak and Dagger Routine

Stopleak

Deceptive Appearances

Fugue in a Minor Key

Sad Lisa

These Hallowed Halls

My Sweet Lisa

Old Los Angeles

Death of the Zanjero

Death of the City Marshal

Death of the Chinese Field Hands

Death of an Heiress

Daria Barnes

Rage Issues

Mrs. Sperling

A Nose for a Niedeman

Brenda Finnegan

Tyger, Tyger

Romantic Fiction

White House Rhapsody, Book One and Two

Fantasy and Science Fiction

A Ring for a Second Chance

But World Enough and Time

And I would be honored if you left a review for this and any of my books on GoodReads or any other retail site. It really helps.

Connect with Anne Louise Bannon

Thank you for sticking it out this long! Please join my newsletter. It's the best way to stay up-to-date on my upcoming projects, blog posts and even games and giveaways.

Sign up here: http://eepurl.com/zH0Ab

Or connect with me on your favorite social media platforms:

Visit my website: http://annelouisebannon.com

Friend me on Facebook: http://facebook.com/RobinGoodfellowEnt

Follow me on Twitter: http://twitter.com/ALBannon

Favorite my Smashwords author page: https://www.smashwords.com/profile/view/MsBriscow

Connect on LinkedIn: http://www.linkedin.com/in/annelouisebannon

Follow me on Pinterest: http://pinterest.com/msbriscow

About Anne Louise Bannon

Anne Louise Bannon is an author and journalist who wrote her first novel at age 15. Her journalistic work has appeared in Ladies' Home Journal, the Los Angeles Times, Wines and Vines, and in newspapers across the country. She was a TV critic for over 10 years, founded the YourFamilyViewer blog, and created the OddBallGrape.com wine education blog with her husband, Michael Holland. She is the co-author of Howdunit: Book of Poisons, with Serita Stevens, as well as author of the Freddie and Kathy mystery series, set in the 1920s, the Old Los Angeles series, set in 1870, and the Operation Quickline series, plus several stand alones. She and her husband live in Southern California with an assortment of critters.

CPSIA information can be obtained
at www.ICGtesting.com
Printed in the USA
LVHW080732240622
722031LV00008B/445